Andrea Boeshaar never fails to deliver a story rich with spiritual truths and filled with God's healing for broken relationships. In *Threads of Hope*, she truly gets to the heart of God's healing grace in a way readers can carry into their own lives.

—LOUISE M. GOUGE
AWARD-WINNING AUTHOR OF *THE GENTLEMAN TAKES A BRIDE*

Andrea Boeshaar plucks the home strings with her newest historical romance. Not only does she tell a ripping good tale about émigrés from Norway in early settlement times, she also draws from her own family history. As a Wisconsin historian, I am well pleased with her efforts to make life at the dawn of our state authentic. A worthy addition to Ms. Boeshaar's delightful body of work.

—LISA LICKEL
AWARD-WINNING AUTHOR OF *A SUMMER IN OAKVILLE*

Andrea Boeshaar's story pulled me back into the middle 1800s. Her knowledge of the history of the times and her strong, three-dimensional characters kept me in the story. The feuding reminded me of Romeo and Juliet, but with an ending I liked much better. Human frailties were dealt with head-on with wisdom winning in the end. An excellent read that I didn't want to put down until the last page.

—LENA NELSON DOOLEY
AUTHOR OF *MAGGIE'S JOURNEY*, BOOK ONE OF THE MCKENNA'S
DAUGHTERS SERIES, AND THE WILL ROGERS MEDALLION AWARD–
WINNING *LOVE FINDS YOU IN GOLDEN, NEW MEXICO*

Threads of Hope is a beautifully tender story of the way God works in the lives of His own to teach lessons of forgiveness and love. Andrea's talent at weaving genuine characters, vivid descriptions, and a compelling story line together drew me into the story from the first page, and I felt Kristin's and Sam's heartaches and joy. It touched my heart, and I highly recommend this book.

—SALLY LAITY
AUTHOR OF *REMNANT OF FORGIVENESS*
AND COAUTHOR OF *ROSE'S PLEDGE*

Author Andrea Boeshaar weaves timeless themes of honor, equality, and mercy in this tender love story. Heroine Kristin Eikaas is sweet yet resourceful as she faces difficult situations in a new land. *Threads of Hope* is a wonderful addition to historical inspirational fiction bookshelves.

—KACY BARNETT-GRAMCKOW
AUTHOR OF *THE GENESIS TRILOGY*

THREADS of HOPE

BOOK ONE

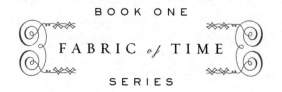

FABRIC *of* TIME

SERIES

ANDREA BOESHAAR

REALMS

Most CHARISMA HOUSE BOOK GROUP products are available at special quantity discounts for bulk purchase for sales promotions, premiums, fund-raising, and educational needs. For details, write Charisma House Book Group, 600 Rinehart Road, Lake Mary, Florida 32746, or telephone (407) 333-0600.

THREADS OF HOPE by Andrea Kuhn Boeshaar
Published by Realms
Charisma Media/Charisma House Book Group
600 Rinehart Road, Lake Mary, Florida 32746
www.charismahouse.com

All Scripture quotations are from the King James Version of the Bible.

The characters in this book are fictitious unless they are historical figures explicitly named. Otherwise, any resemblance to actual people, whether living or dead, is coincidental.

Cover design by Gearbox Studio
Design Director: Bill Johnson

Visit the author's website at www.andreaboeshaar.com.

Library of Congress Cataloging-in-Publication Data:
Boeshaar, Andrea.
  Threads of hope / Andrea Boeshaar. -- 1st ed.
    p. cm. -- (Fabric of time ; bk. 1)
  ISBN 978-1-61638-497-5 (trade pbk.) -- ISBN 978-1-61638-637-5
(e-book) 1. Women immigrants--Fiction. 2. Norwegian Americans--Wisconsin--Fiction. I. Title.
  PS3552.O4257T48 2012
  813'.54--dc23
                                    2011036583
First edition
12 13 14 15 16 — 9 8 7 6 5 4 3 2 1
Printed in the United States of America

DEDICATION

This novel is dedicated to the memory of my great-grandparents, Andreas Johannessen Fluge (renamed Johnson here in the United States) and Louisa Hansdatter Eikaas. They came to America in the late 1890s to begin new lives, escaping the oppression in Norway at the time. Because of their courage, I enjoy the freedoms this great country has to offer!

A big THANK YOU to my grandfather's first cousin, Harvin Abrahamson, his wife, Mary Ann, and to their friend Kristin Wisely for sharing their extensive knowledge of Norway and checking over my use of the Norwegian language.

Also special thanks to everyone at the Brown County Historical Society, the Hazelwood Museum, and the Wisconsin Historical Society.

Additional "thank yous" go to Anne McDonald Editorial Services and Teresa Morgan for all the helpful insights and critiques.

Be of good courage, and he shall strengthen
your heart, all ye that hope in the LORD.
—PSALM 31:24

CHAPTER 1

September 1848

*I*T LOOKS LIKE *Norway.*

The thought flittered across nineteen-year-old Kristin Eikaas's mind as Uncle Lars's wagon bumped along the dirt road. The docks of Green Bay, Wisconsin, were behind them, and now they rode through a wooded area that looked just as enchanting as the forests she'd left in Norway. Tall pine trees and giant firs caused the sunshine to dapple on the road. Kristin breathed in the sweet, fresh air. How refreshing it felt in her lungs after being at sea for nearly three months and breathing in only salty sea air or the stale air in her dark, crowded cabin.

A clearing suddenly came into view, and a minute or so later, Kristin eyed the farm fields stretched before her. The sight caused an ache of homesickness. Her poppa had farmed…

"Your trip to America was good, *ja?*" Uncle Lars asked in Norwegian, giving Kristin a sideways glance.

He resembled her father so much that her heart twisted

painfully with renewed grief. Except she'd heard about *Onkel*—about his temper—how he had to leave Norway when he was barely of age, because, Poppa had said, trouble followed him.

But surely he'd grown past all of that. His letters held words of promise, and there was little doubt that her uncle had made a new life for himself here in America.

Just as she would.

Visions of a storefront scampered across her mind's eye—a shop in which she could sell her finely crocheted and knitted items. A shop in which she could work the spinning wheel, just as *Mor* had…

Uncle Lars arched a brow. "You are tired, *liten niese*?"

"*Ja*. It was a long journey." Kristin sent him a sideways glance. "I am grateful I did not come alone. The Olstads made good traveling companions."

Her uncle cleared his throat and lowered his voice. "But you have brought my inheritance, *ja*?" He arched a brow.

"*Ja*." Kristin thought of the priceless possession she'd brought from Norway.

"And you would not hold out on your *onkel*, would you?"

Prickles of unease caused Kristin to shift in her seat. She resisted the urge to touch the tiny gold and silver cross pendent suspended from a dainty chain that hung around her neck. Her dress concealed it. She couldn't give it up, even though it wasn't legal for a woman to inherit anything in Norway. But the necklace had been her last gift from *Mor*. A gift from one's mother wasn't an inheritance…was it? "No, *Onkel*."

She turned and peered down from her perch into the back of the wooden wagon bed. Peder Olstad smiled at her, and Kristin relaxed some. Just a year older, he was the brother of Kristin's very best friend who had remained in Norway with their mother. She and Peder had grown up together, and while he could be annoying and bad tempered at times, he was the closest thing to a brother that she had. And Sylvia—Sylvia was closer than a sister ever could be. It wouldn't be long, and she and Mrs. Olstad would come to America too. That would be a happy day!

"You were right," John Olstad called to Uncle Lars in their native tongue. "Lots of fertile land in this part of the country. I hope to purchase some acres soon."

"And after you are a landowner for five years, you can be a citizen of America and you can vote." The Olstad men smiled broadly and replied in unison. "Oh, *ja, ja*…"

Uncle Lars grinned, causing dozens of wrinkles to appear around his blue eyes. His face was tanned from farming beneath the hot sun, and his tattered leather hat barely concealed the abundance of platinum curls growing out of his large head. "Oh, *ja*, this is very good land. I am glad I persuaded Esther to leave the Muskego settlement and move northeast. But, as you will soon see, we are still getting settled."

"*Ja*, how's that, Lars?"

Kristin heard the note of curiosity in Mr. Olstad's voice.

"I purchased the land and built a barn and a cabin." He paused and gave a derisive snort. "Well, a fine home takes time and money."

"Oh, *ja*, that way." Mr. Olstad seemed to understand.

And Kristin did too. One couldn't expect enormous comforts out in the Wisconsin wilderness.

Just then they passed a stately home situated on the Fox River. Two quaint dormers peered from the angled roof, which appeared to be supported by a pair of white pillars.

"That is Mr. Morgan Martin's home. He is a lawyer in town." Uncle Lars delivered the rest of his explanation with a sneer. "And an Indian agent."

"Indians?" Kristin's hand flew to her throat.

"Do not fret. The soldiers across the river at Fort Howard protect the area."

Kristin forced her taut muscles to relax.

"Out here the deer are plentiful and fishing is good. Fine lumber up here too. But the Norwegian population is small. Nevertheless, we have our own church, and the reverend speaks our language."

"A good thing," Mr. Olstad remarked.

"I cannot wait for the day when *Far* owns land," Peder said, glancing at Mr. Olstad. "Lots of land." The warm wind blew his auburn hair outward from his narrow face, and his hazel eyes sparked with enthusiasm, giving the young man a somewhat wild appearance. "But no farming for me. I want to be rich someday."

"As do we all!" exclaimed Mr. Olstad, whose appearance was an older, worn-out version of his son's.

Kristin's mind had parked on land ownership. "And once you are settled, Sylvia will come to America. I cannot wait. I miss her so much."

She grappled with a fresh onset of tears. Not only was Sylvia her best friend, but she and the entire Olstad clan had also become like family to her ever since a smallpox epidemic ravaged their little village two years ago, claiming the lives of Kristin's parents and two younger brothers. When Uncle Lars had learned of the tragic news, he offered her a place to stay in his home if she came to America. *Onkel* wrote that she should be with her family, so Kristin had agreed to make the voyage. Her plans to leave Norway had encouraged the Olstads to do the same. But raising the funds to travel took time and much hard work. While the Olstads scrimped and saved up their crop earnings, Kristin did spinning, weaving, knitting, and sewing for those with money to spare. By God's grace, they were finally here.

Uncle Lars steered the wagon around a sharp bend in the rutty road. He drove to the top of a small hill, and Kristin could see the blue Lake Michigan to her left and farm fields to her right.

Then a lovely white wood-framed house came into view. It didn't look all that different from the home they'd just past, with dormers, a covered front porch, and stately pillars bearing the load of a wide overhang. She marveled at the homestead's large, well-maintained barn and several outbuildings. American homes looked like this? Then no wonder Mr. Olstad couldn't wait to own his own farm!

Up ahead Kristin spied a lone figure of a man. She could just barely make out his faded blue cambric shirt, tan trousers, and the hoe in his hands as he worked the edge of the field. Closer still, she saw his light brown hair springing out from beneath his hat. As the wagon rolled past him, the man ceased his labor and turned their way. Although she couldn't see his eyes as he squinted into the sunshine, Kristin did catch sight of his tanned face. She guessed his age to be not too much more than hers and decided he was really quite handsome.

"Do not even acknowledge the likes of him," Uncle Lars spat derisively. "Good Christians do not associate with Sam Sundberg or any members of his family."

Oh, dear, too late! Kristin had already given him a little smile out of sheer politeness. She had assumed he was a friend or neighbor. But at her uncle's warning she quickly lowered her gaze.

Kristin's ever-inquiring nature got the best of her. "What is so bad about that family?"

"They are evil—like the Martins. Even worse, Karl Sundberg

is married to a heathen Indian woman who casts spells on the good people of this community."

"Spells?" Peder's eyes widened.

"*Ja*, spells. Why else would some folks' crops fail while Karl's flourish? He gets richer and richer with his farming in the summer, his logging camps in the winter, and his fur trading with heathens, while good folks like me fall on hard times."

"Hard times?" Peder echoed the words.

"*Ja*, same seed. Same fertile ground. Same golden opportunity." Uncle Lars swiveled to face the Olstads. "I will tell you why that happens. The Sundbergs have hexed good Christians like me." He wagged his head. "Oh, they are an evil lot, those Sundbergs and Martins. Same as the Indians."

Indians? Curiosity got the better of her, and Kristin swung around in the wagon to get one last glimpse of Sam Sundberg. She could hardly believe he was as awful as her uncle described. Why, he even removed his hat just now and gave her a cordial nod.

"Turn around, *niese*, and mind your manners!" Uncle Lars's large hand gripped her upper arm and he gave her a mild shake.

"I...I am sorry, *Onkel*," Kristin stammered. "But I have never seen an Indian."

"Sam Sundberg is not an Indian. It is his father's second wife and their children. Oneida half-breeds is what we call them."

"Half-breed, eh?"

Kristin glanced over her shoulder and saw Peder stroke his chin.

"Interesting," he added.

"How *very* interesting." Kristin couldn't deny her interest was piqued. "Are there many Indians living in the Wisconsin Territory?"

"*Ja*, they trespass on my land, but I show my gun and they

leave without incident. Sundberg brings his Indian wife to church." He wagged his head. "Such a disgrace."

"And the Territory officials do nothing?" Mr. Olstad asked.

Uncle Lars puffed out his chest. "As of three months ago, we are the State of Wisconsin—no longer a territory." Uncle Lars stated the latter with as much enthusiasm as a stern school-master. "Now the government will get rid of those savages once and for all." He sent Kristin a scowl. "And you, my *liten niese*, will do well to stay away from Indians. *All* of them, including our neighbors, the Sundbergs. You hear, lest you get yourself scalped."

"*Ja, Onkel.*"

With a measure of alarm, Kristin touched her braided hair and chanced a look at Peder and Mr. Olstad. Both pairs of wide eyes seemed to warn her to heed Uncle Lars's instructions. She would, of course. But somehow she couldn't imagine the man they'd just passed doing her any harm. Would he?

~❦~

Sam Sundberg wiped the beads of perspiration off his brow before dropping his hat back on his head. Who was the little blonde riding next to Lars Eikaas? Sam hadn't seen her before. And the men in the wagon bed...he'd never seen them either.

After a moment's deliberation he concluded they were the expected arrivals from the "Old Country." Months ago Sam recalled hearing talk in town about Lars's orphaned niece sailing to America with friends of the family, so he assumed the two red-haired men and the young lady were the topics of that particular conversation. But wouldn't it just serve Mr. Eikaas right if that blonde angel turned his household upside down—or, maybe, right-side up?

He smirked at the very idea. Sam didn't have to meet that

young lady to guess Mr. Eikaas would likely have his hands full. Her second backward glance said all Sam needed to know. The word *plucky* sprang into his mind. He chuckled. Plucky she seemed, indeed.

But was she wise enough not to believe everything her uncle said?

Sam thought it a real shame. Years ago Pa and Lars Eikaas had been friends. But then Pa's silver went missing, insults were traded, and the Eikaases' prejudice against Ma, Jackson, and Mary kept the feud alive.

The Eikaas wagon rolled out of sight, leaving brown clouds of dust in its wake. A grin threatened as Sam thought again of that plucky blonde's curious expression. Maybe she did have a mind of her own. Now wouldn't that be something? Sam thanked God that not everyone around here was as intolerant of Wisconsin Natives as the Eikaas family. There were those who actually befriended the Indians and stood up to government officials in their stead. Like Pa, for instance. Like Sam himself.

The blistering sun beat down on him. Removing his hat once more, he wiped the sweat from his forehead. He started pondering the latest government proposal to remove the Indians from their land. First the Oneida tribe had been forced out, and soon the Menominee band would be "removed" and "civilized." As bad as that was, it irked Sam more to think about how the government figured it knew best for the Indians. Government plans hadn't succeeded in the past, so why would they now? Something else had to be done. Relocating the Menominee would cause those people nothing but misery. They'd stated as much themselves. Furthermore, the Indians, led by Chief Oshkosh, were determined not to give up their last tract of land. Sam predicted this current government proposal would only serve to stir up more violence between Indians and whites.

But not if he and Pa could help it.

In the distance he heard the clang of the dinner bell. Ma didn't like him to tarry when food was on the table. Across the beet field, Sam saw his younger brother run on ahead of him. He wagged his head at the twelve-year-old and his voracious appetite.

With one calloused hand gripping the hoe and the other holding the bushel basket, Sam trudged toward their white clapboard home. Its two dormers protruded proudly from the second floor.

Entering the mudroom, he fetched cold water from the inside well, peeled off his hat, and quickly washed up. Next he donned a fresh shirt. Ma insisted upon cleanliness at the supper table. Finally presentable, he made his way into the basement where the summer kitchen and a small eating area were located. The cool air met his sun-stoked skin and Sam sighed, appreciating the noonday respite.

Next he noticed a cake in the middle of the table.

"That looks good enough to eat," he teased, resisting the urge to steal a finger-full of white frosting.

Ma gave him a smile, and her nut-brown eyes darkened as she set the wooden tureen of turkey and wild rice onto the table. "Since it's Rachel's last day with us, I thought I would prepare an extra special dessert."

Sam glanced across the table at the glowing bride-to-be. In less than twenty-four hours Rachel Decker would become Mrs. Luke Smith. But for the remainder of today she'd fulfill her duties as Ma's hired house girl who helped with the cooking, cleaning, sewing, washing, and ironing whenever Ma came down with one of her episodes, which were sometimes so intensely painful that Ma couldn't get out of bed without help. Rachel had been both a comfort and an efficient assistant to Ma.

"I helped bake the cake, Sam."

He grinned at his ten-year-old sister, Mary. "Good job."

They all sat down, Mary taking her seat beside Rachel. Sam helped his mother into her place at the head of the table then lowered himself into his chair next to Jackson, who'd been named after Major General Andrew Jackson, the seventh president of this great country.

"Sam, since your father is away," Ma began, "will you please ask God's blessing on our food?"

"Be glad to." He bowed his head. "Dearest Lord, we thank Thee for Thy provisions. Strengthen and nourish us with this meal so we may glorify Thee with our labors. In Jesus's name, amen."

Action ensued all around the table. The women served themselves and then between Sam and Jack, they scraped the bowl clean.

"Good thing Pa's not home from his meetings in town," Jack muttered with a crooked grin.

"If your father were home," Ma retorted, "I would have made more food."

"Should have made more anyhow." Jack gave her a teasing grin. "No seconds." He clanged the bowl and spoon together as if to prove his point.

"You have seconds on your plate already," Ma said. "Why, I have never seen anyone consume as much food as you do, Jackson."

His smile broadened. "I'm growing. Soon I'll be taller than Sam."

"Brotherly competition." Sam had to chuckle. But in the next moment, he wondered if his family behaved oddly. Didn't all families enjoy meals together? Tease and laugh together? Tell stories once the sun went down? According to Rachel, they didn't. The ebony-haired, dark-eyed young woman had grown up without a mother and had a drunkard for a father...until Ma got wind of the situation and took her in. She invited Rachel to stay in the small room adjacent to the kitchen and offered her a job. Rachel had accepted. And now, years later, Rachel would soon marry a fine man, Luke Smith, a friend of Sam's.

Taking a bite of his meal, he chewed and looked across the table at Mary. Both she and Jack resembled their mother, dark brown hair, dark brown eyes, and graceful, willowy frames, while Sam took after his father, blue eyes and stocky build, measuring just under six feet. Yet, in spite of the outward dissimilarities, the five Sundbergs were a closely knit family, and Sam felt grateful that he'd known nothing but happiness throughout his childhood. He had no recollection whatsoever of his biological mother who had taken ill and died during the voyage from Norway to America.

Sam had been but a toddler when she went home to be with the Lord, and soon after disembarking in New York, his father met another Norwegian couple. They helped care for Sam and eventually persuaded Pa to take his young son and move with them to Wisconsin, known back then as part of the "Michigan Territory." Pa seized the opportunity, believing the promises that westward expansion touted, and he was not disappointed. He learned to plant, trap, and trade with the Indians, and he became a successful businessman. In time, he saved enough funds to make his dreams of owning land and farming a reality.

Then, when Sam was a boy of eight years, his father met and married Mariah, an Oneida. Like her, many Oneida were Christians and fairly well educated due to the missionaries who had lived among them. In time Sam took to his new mother, and she to him. Through the years Ma cherished and admonished him as though he were her own son. She learned the Norwegian language and could speak it fluently. As far as Sam was concerned, he was her own son—and Mariah, his own mother.

They were a family.

"Was that the Eikaas wagon driving by not long ago?" Mary asked.

Sam snapped from his musing. "Sure was. It appears they have relatives in town."

"Mr. Eikaas didn't stop and visit, did he?" Mary's eyes were as round as gingersnaps.

Sam chuckled. "No, of course not. I can't recall the last time Lars Eikaas spoke to me…or any of the Sundbergs, for that matter."

"Erik is nice to me at school." Mary took a bite of her meal.

"Glad to hear it."

"I can't wait to begin school next week."

Sam grinned at his sister's enthusiasm. He'd felt the same way as a boy.

"Sam, what made you assume Mr. Eikaas transported relatives in his wagon today?"

He glanced at Ma. "A while back I'd heard that Lars's niece was coming to America, accompanied by friends, and since I didn't recognize the three passengers in the wagon this morning, I drew my own conclusions."

"Is she pretty?" Jackson's cheeks bulged with food.

"Is who pretty?"

"Mr. Eikaas's niece…is she pretty?"

Sam recalled the plucky blonde whose large, cornflower-blue eyes looked back at him with interest from beneath her bonnet.

And pretty? As much as Sam hated to admit it, she was about the prettiest young lady he'd ever set eyes on.

Jackson elbowed him. "Hey, I asked you a question."

Sam gave his younger brother an annoyed look. "Yeah, I s'pose she's pretty. But don't go getting any big ideas about me courting her. She's an Eikaas."

"You're awful old to not be married yet." Jack rolled his dark eyes.

"What do you know about it? I'm only twenty-one." Sam grinned. "Hush up and eat." It's what the boy did best. "So... did everyone have a pleasant morning?" He forked another bite of food into his mouth, wondering why he tried so hard to shift the subject off of Lars Eikaas's niece.

Kristin looked around the one-room shanty with its unhewn walls and narrow, bowed loft. Cotton squares of material covered the windows, making the heat inside nearly unbearable.

Disappointment riddled her being like buckshot. Although she knew she should feel grateful for journeying safely this far, and now to have a roof over her head, she couldn't seem to shake her displeasure at seeing her relatives' living quarters. It looked nothing like her uncle had described in his letters nor the homes she'd glimpsed on the way.

"Here is your trunk of belongings," Uncle Lars said, carrying the wooden chest in on one of his broad shoulders. With a grunt, he set it down in the far corner of the cabin. "Where is my inheritance? Let me have a look at it."

"Right now, *Onkel*?"

"*Ja, ja...*" Impatience filled his tone.

Pulling open the drawstring of her leather purse, she reached inside and extracted the key. She unlocked the trunk and opened its curved lid. Getting onto her knees, Kristin moved aside her clothes and extra shoes until she found what she searched for. Poppa's gold watch. She held the black velvet-covered box reverently in her hands for one last, long moment before she stood and presented it to her uncle.

"This belonged to my poppa."

"Ah..." Uncle Lars's face lit up with delight as he opened the box. Looking to Aunt Esther, he nodded. "This will bring a fair price, do you think?"

Disbelief poured over her. "But...you would not sell Poppa's watch, would you?"

"None of your business!"

Kristin jumped back at the biting reply. Her opinion of her uncle dropped like a rock into a cavern.

"Anything more?" Her uncle bent over the wooden chest and quickly rummaged through it, spilling clothes onto the unswept floor.

"*Onkel*, please, stop. My garments..."

"Does not seem to be anything else." Uncle Lars narrowed his gaze. "Is there?"

"No." The necklace *Mor* had given her burned against her already perspiring skin. Still, Kristin refused to part with the gift. "Nothing more. As you know, Poppa was a farmer. He supplemented his income by working at the post office, but no money was ever saved. After my parents died, I sold everything to help pay for a portion of my passage to America. I earned the rest myself."

"Any money left?"

Kristin shook her head as she picked up the last of her belongings, careful not to meet her uncle's stare. A little money remained in the special pocket she'd sewn into her petticoat. For safety, she'd kept her funds on her person throughout the entire voyage. The last of her coinage would purchase much-needed undergarments. She'd managed to save it throughout the journey for the specific purpose of buying new foundations when she reached America. It wasn't inherited. She'd worked hard for it.

With a grunt Uncle Lars turned and sauntered out of the cabin.

"You will sleep in the loft with your cousins." Aunt Esther's tone left no room for questions or argument. Wearing a plain, brown dress with a tan apron pinned to its front, and with her dark brown hair tightly pinned into a bun, the older woman looked as drab as her surroundings. "Your uncle and I sleep on a pallet by the hearth."

"Yes, *Tante*. I am sure I will be very comfortable." Another lie.

"Come, let us eat." Aunt Esther walked toward the hearth where a heavy black kettle sat on top of a low-burning fire. "There is venison stew for our meal."

"It sounds delicious." Kristin's stomach growled in anticipation. She'd eaten very little on the ship this morning. Excitement plus the waves on Lake Michigan made eating impossible. But after disembarking in Green Bay, her stomach began to settle, and now she was famished.

Aunt Esther called everyone to the table, which occupied an entire corner of the cabin. Her three children, two girls and one boy, ranging in ages from seven to sixteen, came in from outside, as did the Olstads. After a wooden bowl filled with stew was set before each person, the family clasped hands and recited a standard Norwegian prayer...

I Jesu navn gar vi til bords,—We sit down in the name of Jesus,
Spise drikke pa ditt ord,—To eat and drink according to Your Word,

Deg Gud til are, oss til gavn,—To Your honor, Oh Lord, and for our benefit,

Sa far vi mat i Jesu navn.—We receive food in the name of Jesus.

Amen.

Having said grace, hands were released, and everyone picked up a spoon and began to eat. Kristin noticed her cousins, Inga and Anna, eyeing her with interest. They resembled their father, blonde curls and blue eyes.

"What do you like to do on sunny afternoons such as this one?" she asked cheerfully, hoping to start conversation. After all, Inga's age was close to hers. Perhaps her cousin would help her meet friends.

"We do not talk at the table," Aunt Esther informed her. "We eat, not talk."

"Yes, *Tante.*" Kristin glanced at Peder and Mr. Olstad who replied with noncommittal shrugs and kept eating.

Silently, Kristin did the same. The Olstads always had lively discussions around their table.

When the meal ended, the girls cleared the table and the men took young Erik and ambled outside.

"May I help with cleaning up?" Kristin asked her aunt.

"No. You rest today and regain your strength. Tomorrow we are invited to a wedding, the day after is the Sabbath. Then beginning on Monday, you will labor from sunup to sunset like everyone else in this place."

"Except for one," Inga quipped. No one but Kristin heard.

"Who?" Her lips moved, although she didn't utter a sound.

"*Far,* that is who." Disrespect seeped from Inga's tone, which was loud and clear.

Hadn't Aunt Esther overheard it?

Tante suddenly whirled around and glared at Kristin. "Do something with yourself. We are working here."

With a frown, Kristin backed away. Her aunt's brusque manner caused her to feel weary and more homesick than ever. She missed her parents and her little brothers. Why did God take them, leaving her to live life without them? And Sylvia...how she longed for her best friend!

Kristin knelt by the trunk and carefully lifted out a soft, knitted shawl that had once belonged to her mother, Lydia Eikaas. *Mor* had been an excellent seamstress, expert in spinning wool into yarn and thread, as well as in weaving and sewing garments. She'd taught Kristin everything she knew about the craft. Surely Kristin could now put her skills to good use in this new country, this land of opportunity.

She sighed and glanced over to where her aunt and two cousins continued straightening up after the meal. Inga and Anna barely smiled, and her aunt's expression seemed permanently frozen into a frown. Is that what this country really afforded...misery?

Allowing her gaze to wander around the dismal cabin once more, Kristin began to wish she had not come to America.

CHAPTER 2

*T*HE FOLLOWING MORNING Kristin's eyes popped open at
a woman's shouts to arise. At first she thought she was
at still at sea. But then she realized she'd heard her aunt's voice.

"Up, up, up, with your lazy bones!"

Kristin sat upright but didn't move until Inga and Anna had
climbed over her for fear they'd all go sailing over the edge
of the loft. There hadn't been room on the bowed plank for
Erik last night, thank the Lord, so he had slept in a pallet near
Kristin's trunk. As it was, Kristin had feared their beds would
go crashing down at any minute.

"You had best hurry," Inga said, "if you want something to
eat."

Kristin's stomach rumbled as if in reply, and once her cousins
had descended, she climbed from the loft. Aunt Esther stoked
the fire in the stone hearth. Her braided hair hung down as far
as her hips.

"Good morning," Kristin ventured. Back in Norway, morn-
ings were always cheerful. Poppa would read from the Bible and
Mor would serve fried eggs or fish, and perhaps there would
even be enough rye flour left for a loaf of bread.

Aunt Esther didn't even turn from the hearth. "*God morgen.*"

"Did we oversleep?" Kristin couldn't fathom what had ignited all the hostility crackling in the air.

Finally her aunt faced her and inclined her head toward the door. "Go and wash up now, or lose your chance in the *toalett.*"

Kristin didn't want that to happen. She strode to her trunk. Erik yawned and stretched from his place beside it on the floor. He smiled at her, and she found his happy face a bright spot in this sorry home.

"*God morgen*, Erik."

"Morning."

Locating her cotton robe, she pulled it over her high-necked ivory nightgown.

"Oh, and Kristin?" Inga walked to her and whispered in her ear. "Your job from now on will be to fetch the water. I am telling you this so Momma will not yell at you."

"I am grateful."

Her cousin pushed a wooden bucket at Kristin. Fetching water wasn't a big deal. Taking hold of the pail, she stepped from the cabin. The cool morning breeze greeted her like a welcome friend. Between the heat inside the shanty and worrying the loft would crash down, Kristin hadn't slept well last night. She wondered if maybe tonight she should offer to sleep beneath the stars instead. But, of course, that came with its own set of troubles. She'd heard there were Indians lurking about, waiting to scalp innocent women and children. She'd read about giant bears traipsing around that could eat a man in a single bite.

No, Kristin would rather suffer in the hot cabin tonight. But perhaps it would cool off by then.

She reached the open well and grabbed hold of the rope. Tying it to the bucket, she lowered it into the water. Peder called to her from the barn and waved. She returned the gesture with her free hand, adding a smile, before returning to the task at hand. She struggled to pull the bucket back up. Had it caught on something?

A movement beside her gave Kristin a start, and she lost her hold on the rope. She clutched her nightgown and robe together while the bucket sailed down the well and landed with a splash.

When she saw it was Peder, she relaxed. "You scared me."

"What a frightened little girl you are." Peder now stood beside her, wearing a smirk.

"I should have known it was just you." Annoyance at both the pail and Peder filled her. "The bucket got snagged in the well."

"Or maybe a troll is down there, vexing you."

Kristin sent a glance skyward. She never believed in the fabled creatures and didn't think Peder did either, but it didn't stop him from teasing her.

"How did you sleep last night up in that sorry excuse for a loft?"

"Horrible."

"Hmm… well, I hope you are not hungry." All humor drained from his freckled countenance. "The scrawny chickens have not laid an egg in weeks, and the cow looks so sickly I am surprised she gives any milk at all."

"But *Tante* lit a fire in the hearth just now."

"For coffee, perhaps, and bread if she has flour."

"But the stew yesterday evening?"

"A gift from the minister and his wife. There is no repast."

Kristin felt somewhat alarmed. "Maybe there is food here that you do not know about."

"None that *Far* and I could see. But the trouble might change to good. *Far* managed to find an old piece of string and a long stick. He is fishing in the nearby stream. Guess where your uncle is?"

"Where?" Kristin couldn't conceal a wince.

"Dozing in the hay."

"He is exhausted from working."

Peder shook his head. "Kristin, take a look around you. Little effort goes into this place. Living here is worse than what we had in Norway."

"You do not know that yet." Kristin's gaze spanned the area surrounding her. Maybe the house had been nice at one time.

No, she realized, it hadn't.

"I do not understand. My uncle's letters stated—"

"Your uncle lied. He tricked you into coming and bringing any inheritance."

"How can that be?"

"Did your uncle pay for your trip? No? So what did he lose if you traveled all this way? Nothing. But he gained a gold pocket watch—and free laborers, which would be *us*."

"Stop it, Peder." Kristin didn't want to hear any more. This was her family. They had wanted her to come because *Mor*, *Poppa*, and the boys were dead.

Except she didn't feel very wanted.

In the next moment Kristin remembered the farm they'd passed yesterday. It seemed oddly familiar to her—

And that's when she realized it looked just like the one Uncle Lars had described in his posts.

"My uncle needs some help with building and repairs." She tried to see the brighter side. "Then the farm will look every bit as good as we imagined."

"Kristin, your uncle expects *Far* and me to work hard. For that we should live in a smelly barn with no wages? How do we get ahead?"

"I cannot say." She hadn't expected her uncle's place to be in such a sorry state.

Peder folded his arms. "And my mother and sister should travel all the way from Norway for this?" His gazed quickly roved about the property before settling back on her.

Kristin's heart sank. She wanted Sylvia to come soon.

"*Far* says I will have to find work in town or hire on as farmhand to someone able to pay me. But I think *you* should be the one to have to find work. You brought us here."

Kristin lifted her chin. "I would be willing."

Peder snorted.

Suddenly weary, the fight went out of her. "At least the traveling is over. No more sleeping on a ship, tossed by the ocean's waves. No more rocking train rides that left my low back sore and my muscles stiff."

"And the Great Lakes steamship, which took us to the port of Green Bay?" Peder arched an auburn brow.

"I suppose that last leg of the journey was not so bad." Kristin smiled. She had, for the most part, enjoyed sailing across Lake Michigan and into the bay. However, even the roll of the lake's waves proved enough to make her a bit seasick.

Peder's mood seemed to lighten. He took the rope from her hand and lifted the bucket easily up from the well. Its contents sloshed over the side and the ice-cold water covered Kristin's feet.

"Ah!" Laughing, she jumped back when the water hit her feet.

Peder chuckled.

"Kristin!" Inga stood at the cabin's entryway.

The water. Of course. They are waiting. "Coming!" She struggled to carry the heavy bucket, irritated that Peder stood by, making fun of her efforts.

Before long she reentered the house and poured some water into the basin.

"Fetching the water is Inga's job." Aunt Esther scowled. "I have other chores in mind for you."

"Oh…" Confused, Kristin swung her gaze to Inga. Her cousin pointed and giggled, reminding Kristin of Peder. Some prank that was!

"So wash up, already. There is work to do, and the wedding begins in just a few hours. As you know, Norwegian weddings are an all-day affair."

"*Ja*, I know." Kristin smiled, thinking about all the fun she and Sylvia had at weddings past.

Removing her robe, Kristin rolled up her sleeves. She splashed water on her face and arms and told herself to enjoy the feel of the cold water against her skin, for it promised to be another hot day.

Her cousins went out to do their chores. Kristin finished washing then approached her aunt. "What tasks would you like me to do?"

"I already told you. You rest today and tomorrow. Your chores start on Monday."

Kristin thought she should feel relieved, even privileged, but instead she felt chastened. Her self-confidence teetered.

Walking to her trunk, she found her *bunad*. A traditional outfit, the dress consisted of a vestlike bodice and full skirt. She slipped behind the curtained-off area in which her aunt and uncle slept and where everyone could dress, one at a time, in some semblance of privacy. With her undergarments in place, she pulled on the special chemise that her mother had given to her. Next came a white linen blouse with puffy sleeves. Amazingly, it had fared well on the journey and didn't appear all that wrinkled. Kristin pulled on her black stockings, followed by a dark green wool dress, which was gathered at the waist. Her *bunad*. The deep green color of the fabric symbolized the area of Norway from which she'd haled: Nordre Bergenhus amt, and particularly Jølster. And the embroidery…

Kristin fingered the red and pink roses that *Mor* had painstakingly sewn into the bodice and along the hem of her skirt that closed in the front. *Mor* had modeled the flowers after the climbing *rød* and *rosa* blooms that had climbed up along the back of their small cottage. Kristin tied on the white apron, which covered the skirt's front hooks. More embroidered roses, along with ribbons of green, made for exquisite edging around the circumference of the garment.

Smiling, Kristin recalled how she hadn't any idea that *Mor* worked so diligently on her *bunad*, until the day of her confirmation when she'd received the outfit as a very special gift.

And speaking of…

Kristin made sure *Mor's* necklace remained concealed beneath her blouse, just in case.

Then, hairbrush in hand, Kristin stepped around the partitioned-off area and walked into the kitchen and dining area. "Will you help me with my hair, *Tante*?"

Aunt Esther glanced up from the empty flour canister she held in her hand. "Brush your own hair. I am busy." She gave Kristin a once-over glance.

Kristin sensed her aunt's disapproval. "No one else wears a *bunad*?"

"Some do." Her aunt shrugged.

"And you?"

"I had one, but…times got tough. I had to cut it up so your uncle had warm socks for the winter."

Kristin tried not to let her surprise show. To cut up her *bunad* must have meant her aunt and uncle fell on hard, lean times here in America. Kristin wondered if she would meet that same fate.

"Would it be best if I changed clothes, *Tante*?"

"No, no…wear your pretty outfit. Your uncle still has his *bunad*, his embroidered vest."

"And the Olstads will most likely wear theirs too."

"Then, see? You will not stick out like a sore thumb."

The remark stung and Kristin's cheeks grew hot. She left the stuffy structure for the sanctity of the outdoors. She walked a ways from the house and closed her eyes. Familiar and comforting sounds wafted to her. The lowing of cows in the distance, the rustling of leafy tree branches, and the whisper of the wind passing through a tall evergreen. She missed her home in Norway. Was Peder right? Had she been tricked into coming to America?

⌁◦⊕◦⌁

Sam shifted his weight and smiled at Luke Smith's nervous expression. Together they stood near the altar as the small church filled with guests. Pa and Jack sat only a few feet away on the Sundberg family's usual front pew. The Smith family had filed into the polished wooden bench on the other side of the aisle, where the Eikaases normally sat each Sunday. Sam anticipated Lars Eikaas's irritation with the temporary seating arrangement. But Luke's family members were guests in Emmanuel Christian Church. The Smiths haled from the neighboring county, so God's little brick house would be packed today with visitors as well as regular attendees. Mr. Eikaas would have to understand.

Glancing around the mostly familiar faces, Sam's gaze suddenly fell on Lars Eikaas's niece as she and her family entered the church. Her dancing blue eyes were a stark contrast to her aunt's stern squint and her cousins' downcast looks. And, as he expected, Lars appeared none-too-pleased when he glimpsed the Smiths' seating arrangements. Sam fought back his urge to grin, and then his gaze shifted back to Lars's niece. She looked stunning in her forest-green *bunad*, and Sam rather liked the pretty blush on her peachy complexion.

"What? What is it?" Luke ran his calloused fingers through his dark-blond hair.

Sam replied with a curious glance at his friend.

"You're wearing an odd sort of grin. Do you see Rachel? Is the wedding about to start?"

"Relax. It's nothing." Sam shook himself. "Ma, Mary, and Mrs. Wollums are tending to Rachel and…" He inclined his head toward the side entrance, which led to the parsonage. "Look behind you, Luke. The reverend has just arrived."

"Thank God." The groom-to-be let out a relieved sigh. "I thought maybe he changed his mind about performing the ceremony for Rachel and me."

"Nonsense." He clapped Luke on the shoulder.

Once the reverend took his place next to Luke and began conversing with him, Sam stepped back and seated himself between Pa and Jack. Luke's brother would stand in as the best man.

Jack leaned his shoulder up against Sam's. "She sure is pretty."

"Who would that be?" In spite of his reply, Sam knew to whom his little brother referred. Lars Eikaas's niece. Even now as he faced the altar, he sensed her presence one row back and across the aisle. He suddenly overheard her aunt introduce her in Norwegian. "This is our niece, Kristin Eikaas, from the Old Country."

Kristin. A lovely name. At least he'd learned that much about her.

"I think I just heard that her name is Kristin," Jack whispered a little too loudly.

Sam sent a gaze upward. "I heard the same thing, wise guy."

"So you're listening, eh?"

"Mind your own business." Sam shifted.

The boy chuckled. "Well, all right." He leaned closer. "But

Miss Kristin Eikaas is awful pretty. A man can't help notice. Why, Big Artie Svensen's got his eye on—"

"Enough, already."

Pa leaned over. "Quiet down, you two."

Jack sat up a little straighter.

Sam grinned. "Everything's fine, Pa."

"Hmph." Karl Sundberg jutted out his chin and folded his thick forearms. "I hope you two aren't discussing that Eikaas girl."

Sam felt his face flush.

"Oh, no, Pa," Jack said. "Not discussin'."

Sam turned to find Pa's gaze boring into him.

"No son of mine is going to court an Eikaas. Understand me?"

"Perfectly."

Sam rolled his shoulders, adjusting his dress coat. He knew of Lars Eikaas's past. The man had earned a bad reputation by brawling in Muskego. Finally the authorities had asked him to leave. Since moving to Green Bay, Eikaas had gotten himself in occasional trouble, but nothing to get him thrown in jail—or to prove he'd stolen Pa's silver spoons.

And as far as Kristin Eikaas was concerned...

Sam looked straight ahead at the altar and rubbed the side of his clean-shaven jaw. Pa needn't worry. Sam had no business even thinking of courtship. His father wanted him to begin a career in politics so he could fight social injustices. Sam thought he'd be good at mediation and agreed to give it a try.

Redirecting his thoughts, Sam gazed at the polished oak cross, which hung above the matching altar, before he looked around the whitewashed plaster walls. When the church had first been built, both the men and women of their congregation participated in decorating the sanctuary. However, Pa paid most of the costs of building the church, along with its small parsonage. The pastor's wife, Agnes Wollums, had been overjoyed when she first stepped into her new home. And the church and sanctuary itself were unique in the area. Pa had the bricks shipped up from Manitowoc. Typically only the wealthiest in Wisconsin could afford a brick dwelling. Pa figured no other family but this here body of believers was the richer, and they deserved a church home befitting of their heavenly Father's glory.

But Lars Eikaas had taken issue with building a fine church and parsonage. He maintained the rickety wooden structure served the same purpose as a new one. He was also adamant about the fact that the reverend and his wife ought not to live in a home better than his. The Wollumses were "servants of the Lord," after all.

Pa, however, had disagreed. As agents of the King of kings, the Wollumses should have everything this community could offer.

So with the support of his family, Pa stepped out and offered to pay for the new church. Several other men in the Green Bay community rolled up their sleeves and helped with its construction. All around, some sacrifice had been involved, but Sam and the rest of the Sundbergs were only glad to do it—and how glad and grateful they were to worship inside a solid building whose walls were stronger than last winter's north wind. Mrs. Wollums said her daughters were healthier, and each time she spoke about her new brick home, tears of joy filled her eyes.

Yes, it had been worth it.

However, Lars Eikaas saw it, not as beauty or blessing, but as some sort of outward gloating on the Sundbergs' part. The tension between the two families only seemed to escalate, in spite of the reverend's efforts.

Sam couldn't help sneaking a look over his shoulder. His gaze happened to catch Kristin Eikaas's sky-blue eyes. She sent him a timid grin before quickly turning away. In that moment a powerful sense of hope, wonder, and possessiveness all rolled into one coursed through him.

"Don't even think it, son."

The growled warning brought Sam up short. He gazed into his father's weathered face. "Think what, Pa?"

"You know *what*." He gave his brown dress coat an indignant tug. "Like I said, no son of mine will ever court an Eikaas."

⚜

"I never saw such a beautiful wedding ceremony." Kristin smiled as she watched the bride and groom make their way down the church's aisle. Lively music from the piano and an accordion followed them. The couple paused here and there to greet guests as they passed by.

Kristin took note of the bride's headpiece. Quite plain, as far as Norwegian customs were concerned. Kristin was accustomed to seeing brides wearing an extraordinary silver crown with spoon-shaped sterling-silver bangles dangling down their backs. Each time brides moved their heads, the spoons struck one another and the bangles made a metallic-sounding music, which, many believed, kept evil spirits away. But perhaps there were no evil spirits in America. Perhaps they stayed in the Old Country.

The smiling couple paused a ways down to quickly acknowledge another family, and Kristin admired the bride's lovely lace collar that she wore around a white blouse. The young woman's white skirt had been embroidered with silver thread. Kristin appreciated the needlework. It was what she did best, working with a needle and thread. She could spin too. *Mor* had always admired Kristin's efficiency on the spinning wheel.

"*Ja*, lovely wedding," Inga replied to her earlier remark. Her quiet voice sounded rather wistful.

Kristin glanced at her cousin just in time to see her exchange glances with a stocky man with hair the color of a maple leaf in the peak of autumn. "Who is he?"

Inga appeared startled, but then the features on her round face relaxed. "You won't tell *Far*, will you?"

Kristin shook her head. "No. Of course not." The less she had to say to her ornery uncle, the better.

A timid smile curled her cousin's full, pink lips. "He is Oskar Frantzen, the blacksmith's apprentice in town." Her features fell. "But he does not know I exist."

"He just looked your way. I saw him."

"*Ja*, but only because I was staring."

Kristin peeked over at Mr. Frantzen. He spoke to a man standing nearby, and his gaze didn't stray to Inga again.

Peder tugged on Kristin's arm. "Time for the wedding dinner and celebration in the churchyard."

Kristin followed him out of the pew and into the aisle where they trailed a throng of people out of the church.

Sandwiched between Peder and her cousin, Kristin leaned close to Inga and whispered, "Perhaps Mr. Frantzen will notice you this afternoon and evening."

A hopeful spark entered the younger girl's blue eyes. "Yes, perhaps."

Outside, Peder politely assisted Kristin down the steps and onto a dirt pathway, which led to the lot where the horses and wagons stood.

"I will go help bring the food." Peder dropped her arm and headed for the wagon.

Kristin stood there a moment, deliberating whether she should wait for him or catch up to her cousins who had headed for the grassy yard on the side of the sturdy brick church. The latter won out. Whirling around, Kristin took a blind step forward then suddenly slammed into something hard and muscled. She bounced backward.

"Oh! Oh!" One hand flew to her bonnet as she fought to regain her balance. She felt herself sailing downward, destined to land on her backside.

But then someone reached out and grabbed hold of her arm just in time, bringing her upright.

Kristin stared into the sea-blue eyes of Sam Sundberg.

"Excuse me, but I thought you were walking toward the wagons."

She only understood the English word *wagon.* "Beg your pardon." The stammer in English came breathlessly. She knew that much of the new language from traveling on the ship, the train, and the steamship. But then she reverted to her native tongue. "I changed my mind at the last minute."

His eyes twinkled. "My mother says it is a woman's prerogative to change her mind," he stated in perfect Norwegian. A slow grin stretched across his mouth. "So long as she does not get herself run over doing it."

Kristin's breath returned, and she appreciated the way the man joked about the accident rather than be angry with her.

"Are you all right?"

She nodded.

He gave a polite nod and released her arm. "I, um, do not believe we have been formally introduced." He took a step back. "I am Sam Sundberg."

"*Ja*, I know." She felt her cheeks grow warm. "I am Kristin Louisa Danielsdatter Eikaas. My American name is Eikaas—from the farm on which my father was a cotter, same as my Uncle Lars." She pressed her lips together to forestall her babbling.

Sam's grin never left his face. "A pleasure to make your acquaintance, Miss Eikaas."

A low male voice interrupted them. "Sam!"

He turned toward the speaker.

Kristin watched as an older man hailed him from several yards away. A frown clouded the man's face as he spoke abruptly in English.

"That is my father, Karl Sundberg. If you'll excuse me, Miss Eikaas, he needs my assistance."

"*Ja*...of course. And thank you."

Sam dipped his head and strode toward his father, who seemed to give him a good tongue-lashing. And it was then that Kristin recalled her uncle's warning not to associate with the Sundbergs. Perhaps the same was true with them—they were not allowed to converse with an Eikaas.

Kristin gazed up at the church and deemed the practice quite un-Christian. She wondered why the reverend—or God Himself—didn't intervene.

Gathering her skirts, she turned to make her way to the churchyard and the wedding celebration. She could hear strains from a fiddle and accordion, playing a festive melody.

Uncle Lars stepped in front of her. His features bowed like tree limbs beneath heavy snow. Had he seen her speaking with Sam Sundberg?

He folded his thick forearms across his chest, and Kristin guessed that he had.

"It was an accident, *Onkel*."

"I should horsewhip you!"

Her eyes grew. "But...but—" Horror gripped her.

"For all I know, that Sundberg boy could have cast a spell on you." Uncle Lars's arms fell to his side. "He touched you. I saw him!"

"Spell?" Sam came forward. "My family does not cast spells on anyone or anything. With all due respect, sir, any spells are the product of one's imagination."

"I'll give you my imagination, boy." Uncle Lars shook his fist at him.

"*Onkel*, please...try to understand. Mr. Sundberg only kept me from falling and injuring myself."

"You are in enough trouble, *niese*."

Sam's father stepped forward, eyed Kristin, then regarded Uncle Lars. "You would horsewhip a girl? Really? Now why am I not surprised? You are a monster!"

Kristin backed away from the two angry men. A small gathering looked on nearby.

Uncle Lars puffed out his chest. "If I am a monster, you are the devil himself!"

"Watch your tongue, Eikaas!"

Uncle Lars balled his meaty fist again.

A collective gasp emanated from the crowd.

The reverend quickly approached the men and set his hand on Uncle Lars's shoulder. His gaze lingered on Mr. Sundberg. "Gentlemen, there are ladies present. This is a day of celebration, and I do not have to remind you that Sheriff Brunette is in attendance." His eyes swung to Uncle Lars. "Come. Drink some berry punch and relax in the shade. The midday heat is vexing."

The reverend, still garbed in his purple robe with its blue yoke, managed to dissuade Uncle Lars and Mr. Sundberg for the time being. They accompanied him to the table on which a large silver punch bowl sat.

Sam shook his head, and Kristin noticed the light-brown sprigs curling at his neck in the heat. He glanced at Kristin. She looked back, unsure of what to say or even think. Poppa never solved problems with violence, but her uncle's anger frightened her. Would he really have horsewhipped her for a mere collision with Sam Sundberg?

The onlookers dispersed, and Peder approached. Reaching her, he set his arm around Kristin's shoulders.

"What do you think you are doing?" He whispered the question close to her ear. "You are to stay away from the Sundbergs."

"It was an accident, Peder." She shook inside, afraid of her uncle's bad temper. "A simple misstep on my part." She glanced around for Sam, but it seemed he'd disappeared.

CHAPTER 3

*A*s Sam carried a host of items from the wagon, he spied the man with carrot-colored hair walking Kristin toward the table that Mrs. Eikaas had set for her family. Was that her betrothed? Clearly he comforted her now.

Sam's biceps flexed, not from the load in his arms, but from sheer disappointment. And yet, hadn't he heard his father's warning loud and clear? Kristin was Lars Eikaas's niece. Even if she wasn't already promised to another, Sam couldn't think of courting her. Look what had happened between the two men after he and Kristin innocently bumped into each other!

What a shame, and what a sin that Pa and Mr. Eikaas behaved like two boys about to brawl in the schoolyard. They needed to settle their differences once and for all. He wondered what it would take. Pa served as an important liaison between the government and the Indians, and yet he couldn't get along with Lars Eikaas. Pitiful. Sam was dismayed with Pa for his display of temper. But on the other hand, he was grateful too that Pa called Mr. Eikaas on the horsewhipping threat. Sam hoped it carried no weight.

Reaching the table, he set down the contents in his arms on

the grass. Thankfully, Ma had a respite from her chronic pain. She came over and pulled out the patchwork quilt and covered the rough-hewn plank. Men from the church, including Sam, had hammered these tables and benches together last spring. The wood had been donated from various construction sites in Green Bay. When not needed, the tables could be stacked and stored away until another churchwide event called for their use. They came in quite handy.

Sam watched his little sister lift the pot containing Ma's wild rice from the crate. He rushed to help her so she wouldn't drop it. Sam couldn't help feeling strains of protectiveness toward her. After all, she was only ten years old.

"I can carry it, Sam."

"Are you sure?"

Mary bobbed her head, and strands of her nut-brown hair fell onto her forehead.

"All right, then." Sam didn't think the kettle was all that heavy.

He watched as she carried it to the front table where everyone had donated a meal. The idea was that everyone would sample each other's food. The result was a delicious feast.

Luke Smith, the flock's newest husband, motioned for the group to be silent. "Thank you all for coming. Reverend Wollums will say grace, and then Rachel and I will share our first meal as husband and wife with our closest friends and family members."

Applause, cheers, and laughter filled the evergreen-lined churchyard. When the merriment wound down, the reverend prayed over their food, and then a queue formed near the food table.

Sam hung back so he could observe Kristin Eikaas. How had she captured his curiosity—and why couldn't he shake it off? Seconds later, her robin's-egg blue eyes met his before she quickly looked away. Happenstance or purposeful?

She peeked at him again, and Sam's heart swelled in the most peculiar way. He stifled a grin. It would seem that Kristin Eikaas was capable of casting a few spells of her own.

⁓°❦°⁓

With each passing hour, Kristin felt her spirit lighten as the wedding celebration escalated around her. Uncle Lars was jovial, and she rather preferred him that way than angry and hollering.

By evening a cooler breeze blew off Lake Michigan, and everyone seemed to catch their own second wind. Tables had been moved to the edge of the churchyard to make room for dancing. In addition to the piano accordion player, a gifted fiddler turned out one lively melody after another, accompanied by an interesting variety of homemade bells and flutes. Lanterns were lit and dancing continued. Kristin smiled and clapped her hands to the music.

Suddenly the newlyweds strode into the midst of their guests.

"May I have your attention," Luke Smith, the groom, called. "Attention, everyone!"

The instruments fell silent.

"This is the moment that all the bachelors have been waiting for." He chuckled. "It's time for the curtain dance!"

Whoops and cheers rang from the men while female squeals of delight filled the churchyard. Kristin watched in awe as several agile men strung up a long, mismatched drape, extending from one tree to another. Kristin laughed to herself as the grinning young men and giggling ladies parted like the Red Sea.

"Come with me, cousin." Inga grabbed hold of Kristin's arm. "*Far* said we can play."

"Play what?" Kristin didn't know about this strange custom.

"Let us get in line, and I will explain." Inga led her to the one side of the linen panel where ladies removed the shoes and stockings from their right legs.

"The boys will walk down the line and select a dancing partner by examining, not her face, but her feet!" Inga's broad smile hiked up her round cheeks. "Perhaps tonight Oskar Frantzen will choose me to dance with him."

"*Lykke til*—good luck." Kristin turned to go back to her seat and watch.

"Where are you going?"

"I am not playing, Inga."

"But you must!" She snatched a hold of Kristin's elbow. "*Far* said that I can only participate if you come with me."

Kristin glanced over to where her uncle laughed with friends. "He is right there. He can watch you from the sidelines."

"*Ja*, except in the past there has been trickery behind the curtain."

Kristin frowned. "What sort of trickery?"

"Sundberg trickery." Inga squared her shoulders. "But at least now Rachel Decker has married Mr. Smith, so she'll not be dancing with my Oskar again like she did last year."

Folding her arms, Kristin tilted her head. "It is a game of chance, Inga."

"No. Mrs. Sundberg hexed Oskar; otherwise he would not have chosen Rachel." Inga leaned closer. "She has a deformed foot from a childhood accident." Inga nodded as if the fact proved her superstition.

But Kristin found the likelihood of such magic difficult to believe.

"Now off with your shoe and stocking!" Inga pouted. "Or I shall tell *Far* you are consorting with the Sundbergs again."

Kristin enlarged her gaze. "You would not!"

"Just try me and see."

Blinking once, twice, Kristin couldn't believe the nerve of her cousin. Her impulse was to call Inga's bluff. However, her uncle's threat of a horsewhipping still sounded in her memory.

Her jaw set against her actions, Kristin kicked off her right slipper. Then she rolled down one black stocking. Following her cousin and the other young ladies, she placed her foot just outside the curtain. With any luck she'd get passed by altogether.

The music began to play and the men whooped and laughed and clapped their hands. Kristin inched her foot back, but then suddenly a large, dusty brown boot gently landed across the tops of her toes. Disappointment, dread, and a tinge of anxiousness flooded Kristin's being. But what was this compared to the journey she'd just endured? Squaring her shoulders, she determined one dance wouldn't be so bad.

Soon all the girls were spoken for, and as Kristin gazed down the row she noted the different shades of boot leather, wide and narrow, covering each feminine foot.

The curtain was yanked open, revealing dance partners. Kristin stood in shock as she stared at the man across from her.

"Mr. Sam Sundberg."

He gave her a tiny bow, looking a bit taken aback himself.

"We cannot dance together," she said.

"If you say so."

Kristin couldn't discern his expression beneath the light of the lamp and the moon above. He had removed his overcoat and rolled the sleeves of his white shirt to his elbows.

"It is not I, but my uncle…and your father."

"I chose you by accident, not out of spite or disobedience to either man."

Before Kristin could reply, a well-dressed man appeared beside Sam, giving him a friendly slap on the shoulders. He said something in English that Kristin didn't understand, although she recognized the use of her last name, Eikaas. Then, she noted the hint of a grin that pulled at one side of Sam's mouth before he nodded. Next he gave Kristin a hooded glance. Were they poking fun at her and her family?

Sam seemed to sense her discomfort and explained in Norwegian. "That is Judge Jensen, the territorial judge here in Wisconsin. He is a friend of our family and is familiar with the strife between the Sundbergs and the Eikaases. He, um, finds it amusing that I chose you for my curtain dance partner. He said there is no getting out of it. Rules of the game state one cannot refuse the dance partner once the choosing has taken place." Sam took her hands. "Looks like we have, at least, the law on our side."

"I am not sure about this."

"You are afraid of your uncle?"

Kristin gave a timid nod.

Sam's expression grew serious beneath the moon's glow. "More than just my father and I heard your uncle's threat earlier today. If he lays a hand on you, the sheriff will get involved, and your uncle will go to jail." Sam glanced over his shoulder. "But for now, it looks like Judge Jensen has him and my father occupied."

Kristin arched a brow. "Oh, to be a fly on the food table now."

Sam's features lit up, and he slipped one arm about her waist. He pulled her close enough to him that she could feel the heat of the evening's celebration radiating from his moist skin. He smelled manly, yet she detected the subtle scent of pine emanating from his linen shirt. As the music played and they stepped out together, his warm breath touched her cheek.

Kristin worked to follow his lead in the unfamiliar pattern of steps. Her parents had seen to her education back in Norway, which included music and dancing, but she'd never experienced anything like this before. It seemed a cross between a waltz and Norway's traditional *gangar* dance. She guarded her bare foot so it wouldn't get trampled on by Sam's heavy boots. It felt odd to dance with only one shoe on.

Finally able to take her eyes off her footwork, she glanced up at Sam. He gave her a broad smile. She returned the gesture before noticing several hard stares from onlookers.

"People will have something to say about our dancing together."

"I am sure of that." Sam drew his chin back and regarded her. "Are you afraid of what people say?"

"I am new to America..." She left it at that.

"And what are your plans, now that you are here?"

"Oh, I have my plans." Kristin wondered if he mocked her.

"Such as?" His tone sounded more interested than amused.

"I am gifted with a needle and thread. Perhaps I will someday work in a store."

Sam pushed out his bottom lip and gave a single, sideways nod as though such a thing were possible. "So you are an ambitious girl?"

"Hardly a girl."

He chuckled lightly. "Hmm...well, if you hope to enter into the business world, you will need to learn English." Beneath the lantern light Kristin thought his eyes darkened. "And you will have to grow accustomed to hearing people speak their minds. Norwegians make up only a small portion of Brown County. The French, English, and Germans have settled here too. All opinionated people, I assure you."

Kristin found the information quite interesting. "I do not think people are so very different from each other. On the train in New York, I met people from all different ethnic backgrounds.

When the car became too hot, we all perspired. At lunchtime, we all felt hungry."

After a moment's pause, Sam replied, "You're a wise young lady, Miss Eikaas."

Had she impressed him? Kristin couldn't help a little smile.

The music stopped and everyone applauded. Laughter flitted around the churchyard. Kristin stared up into Sam's face. Starlight hallowed his head. As his gaze sank into hers, she wondered what it would it be like if he gathered her in his arms and... *kissed her.*

Surprise and shame speared her being. How could such a thought enter her head?

A hard clap on Kristin's shoulder shattered the remainder of her romantic delusions.

"The curtain dance is over." Uncle Lars's voice boomed close to Kristin's right ear. "Get away from this evil Sundberg man!"

She felt herself being yanked backwards.

"Hey, Eikaas, do not speak to my son that way!" Mr. Sundberg immediately stepped in beside Sam.

The wedding party quieted until Kristin could only hear the crickets' night song.

"Tell your boy to stay away from my niece!"

Kristin cast an *I told you so* glance at Sam.

He grimaced an apology.

"Tell your niece to stay away from my boy!"

The reverend stepped between the two angry men. "Enough!"

"I apologize, Mr. Eikaas," Sam said. "The judge thought it would be all right just this once."

Uncle Lars couldn't seem to find a way to argue. "Out of my way!" he finally bellowed. He elbowed his way around Sam and glared at Kristin. "How dare you drag my daughter into the curtain dance when she is not old enough!"

Kristin gaped. "But I thought…Inga said—"

"Do not talk back to me, *niese*! Respect your elders!"

"She did not know the rules." Sam inched toward Uncle Lars.

"Rules! Rules!" Uncle Lars's glare swung to Karl Sundberg. "Your family should talk about rules? You and that Indian woman—you cast spells on the good folks in Brown County. Where are the rules for that?"

"You are a madman, Eikaas, otherwise I would send you reeling with my fist."

"Go ahead. I will give you the first punch."

"Don't tempt me!"

Uncle Lars sneered. "*Ja*, and you're a coward too, Sundberg."

Sam put his hands on his father's shoulders. "Enough of this, already!"

Kristin had slowly backed away until she stood behind Sam. Somehow she felt a measure of safety there.

Cool fingers touched her hand, and when Kristin looked to see who they belonged to, she found herself staring into the dark eyes of Sam Sundberg's stepmother. All day she'd only seen the woman from afar.

Swallowing hard, Kristin realized she'd never seen an Indian up close, although she'd heard about native people during her travels. Some said the Indians had strange, bewitching powers. Certainly Uncle Lars believed that. Was there any truth to the rumors?

Except—Kristin tilted her head—Mrs. Sundberg looked like any other woman, dressed in her dark green, slightly flared skirt and ivory pin-tucked blouse.

"Do not be afraid." Her Norwegian was very good. Then she lifted her gaze, and Kristin followed her line of vision to the star-filled sky. The woman held onto Kristin's hand, closed her eyes, then murmured words Kristin didn't understand.

Uncle Lars caught a glimpse of them and exploded in a rage. "Get away from my niece! Get away from her, you heathen spell-caster!"

He charged them and Kristin screamed. It took three men, Mr. Olstad included, to hold Uncle Lars back.

And that's when Kristin decided not to wait and see if he broke free.

Giving no thought to her one bare foot, Kristin sprinted from the lantern-lit churchyard and ventured into the night. The tender sole of her foot let her know at once when she'd left the grass and came upon the gravelly road. From somewhere behind her, she heard Peder's voice calling to her, but her hammering heart propelled her onward, past the horses hitched to buggies and wagons.

Darkness enfolded her, her only light came from the clear sky above, and soon Kristin realized she'd left the road. She was accustomed to going barefoot in Norway, but not like this—not in the woods with unfamiliar and uneven terrain. Now the tender flesh on her bare foot felt scraped and raw.

Suddenly, she stepped on something that made her cry out into the night. Angry-sounding insects immediately buzzed around her. Kristin swatted at them as she hobbled in search of safety.

Picking her way over several large rocks, she pushed leafy tree limbs out of her path. The sound of rushing water grew louder, and soon she happened on a narrow river. Moonlight glimmered off the shallow water and its rocky bed. Lifting her hems, she dipped her injured foot into the water, expecting it to be icy like the streams and rivers in the Old Country. Instead, she discovered the water felt cool, refreshing.

She lowered herself onto a flat-topped boulder. Her foot

throbbed from the insect bite, although the temperate water had a soothing effect on it.

Allowing herself a moment's solace, she recalled her dance with Sam and decided she'd enjoyed it very much. But why had Inga set her up as the recipient of Uncle Lars's wrath? Any trickery tonight had come from Inga!

And Sam's mother...she didn't appear to be any kind of spell-caster. But what had she done after she'd taken Kristin's hand and stared into the sky? Had it been a mystical chant of some sort?

Or a prayer?

The crunching of dried leaves and twigs alerted Kristin of someone's approach.

"Kristin?"

She recognized Peder's voice. He'd followed her. "Here I am. By the river."

He located her within seconds.

"I hurt my foot. I stepped on some sort of insect."

"*Ja*, well, it serves you right for running off like that." Peder handed over her stocking and kid slipper. "I figured you might need these."

"*Takk.*"

Peder sat down beside her on the immense rock. "You should not have danced with that Sundberg man."

"Inga deceived me into playing, and then I could not help who chose me."

"When you saw it was a Sundberg, you should have refused."

"In truth, we both considered it. But an important-looking man insisted. Rules of the game. So I complied." Kristin didn't add that she couldn't have asked for a better dance partner. Sam had held her and guided her steps in all gentleness and respect.

"What if the Sundbergs have hexed you, Kristin?"

"Hexed me? That is ridiculous. The Sundbergs are ordinary people." She shifted. "You do not believe in such superstitions, do you, Peder?"

"I believe in myself."

"You should believe in God."

"Sure—and the trolls under the bridges in Norway who disguise themselves as humans by day. Should I believe in them too?"

"There are no such things as trolls."

"*Ja*? Then talk to Hans Alsaker."

"Poppa said Mr. Alsaker drank too much of his homemade cider."

Peder snorted. "That is my point. Mr. Alsaker was a deacon in our church! If there is a God, He has little power here on earth."

"Do not speak like that!" Such talk rattled her. Of course there was a God.

"Look what happens among these so-called Christians. Tavern brawls in the churchyard."

"Sin finds its way into the church too, Peder."

He didn't reply. "We had better get back to the celebration. I will go on ahead so you may put on your stocking and shoe."

"*Takk.*"

Once Peder left, Kristin did her best to dry off her foot. It felt bruised and continued to throb. Still, she managed to put her stocking and slipper over it before standing. But after two steps up the riverbank, Kristin knew she wouldn't be able to walk unassisted.

"Peder? Peder, come back. I need your help!"

❦

Sam had seen Kristin running from the churchyard, and it was all he could do to keep from following her. But then he saw the red-haired man go after her and realized that he'd never found out whether she was betrothed. Maybe he had no right to insist she dance with him, although she'd willingly participated in the event, which signaled she had no commitment to any man.

"You Sundbergs stay away from my family!" Mr. Eikaas behaved like a snorting, raging bull.

Sam and Luke Smith held Pa back while the reverend, Judge Jensen, and John Olstad hung onto Mr. Eikaas as he bucked and sputtered.

Sheriff Brunette stood between them, shaking his head. "Time to go home, Lars," the lawman said. "Gather your family and go." He looked at Pa. "You too, Karl."

Pa squared his shoulders and shook off the hands that held him. "Sam, find your brother and sister." He spoke from out of the side of his mouth, indicating his anger. "Your mother and I will meet you at the wagon."

Sam inclined his head.

He turned and discovered Ma and Mary stood hand-in-hand about six feet away.

"Mariah," Pa called to Ma, "fetch our belongings."

She stepped away quietly to do his bidding. Mary trailed along to help her.

Sam motioned to his brother, and they headed for the wagon.

"You Sundbergs are a lot of trouble," Eikaas hollered.

Several other men concurred. A boy standing nearby gave Jackson a shove. Sam quickly intervened before his brother reacted with his fist.

"Problems can't be solved with violence."

"Pa thinks they can—and so do I." Jackson's voice sounded tight, constrained.

"Pa doesn't usually behave this way, and you know it."

Jack didn't reply.

"We've got too much to lose. Fighting will only fuel our enemies' contempt."

"I heard Pa say we got a right to defend ourselves."

"From attack, not a girly little push."

Jack's tone lightened. "Guess you're right." He turned out a short laugh. "I'll save myself for the real fight."

"You do that."

Sam checked the horses' harnesses while Jack opened the back of the wagon bed.

"At least you got your dance with that pretty Eikaas girl. What's her name...*Kristin*?"

Sam just gave a curt nod in reply. He knew his little brother meant to goad him good. In fact, he anticipated getting teased for a full week at least.

"Did she smell as pretty as she looks?"

Sam didn't answer, although he had noticed the hint of honeysuckle in her hair as he twirled her in his arms.

Yes, he enjoyed dancing with Kristin Eikaas. Maybe more than he cared to admit.

"Huh, Sam? Answer me."

"If you paid as much attention to your books as you do to prospective wives for me, you'd be a straight-A student."

"I'm already smarter than anyone in my class. But you, Sam...you're gettin' old. Don't you want to get married?"

Sam drew in a deep breath and rounded the wagon until he stood close to his half-brother. "Jack, I suppose twenty-one years does seem elderly to a boy of twelve." He smiled. "But the truth is, when it's God's time for me to get married, He will be bring just the right woman into my life."

"Maybe it's Kristin Eikaas."

Sam glimpsed the smirk on Jack's face while at the same time he spotted Mr. Eikaas stomp toward his wagon. "I rather doubt she's the one, *Little Fox*," Sam replied, using his brother's Oneida name. "For now I'll heed Pa's warning and stay clear of her. We've got enough threats coming from the Menominee to worry about. We don't need more coming from our Christian brothers."

"The Menominee will not attack a white settlement, no matter how angry they are."

"I don't know. Anger is a peculiar thing. It makes people do things they never dreamed possible. Like our Pa." Sam wagged his head. "Look what happened tonight because he let his anger get the best of him."

Jackson grew quiet, and Sam could tell he thought over their conversation.

Several more long minutes ticked by. Finally, Ma and Mary came walking from the churchyard. Pa tagged along, carrying the crate of their belongings. Sam helped the ladies up into the wagon and Pa slid the wooden box into the wagon. Next he jumped in and sat down. Sam took a seat beside Mary. The wagon jerked forward.

"Sam, you and I are going to have a man-to-man talk when we get home."

"All right, Pa." Sam didn't fear his father—not in the sense that he was afraid of any abuse. Pa was a gentleman and, usually, quite reasonable.

They rolled down the rutty road and Sam glanced over his shoulder. He spotted Kristin and her carrot-top friend walking alongside the road. Moonbeams haloed Kristin's bright-blonde head, but what Sam noticed is the way the man's arm encircled her waist and how she clung to him.

Sam stiffened as Pa slowed the wagon. No one said a word as they passed by. Under different circumstances Pa would have stopped to offer a ride, even if the traveler was an Eikaas.

Leaning forward, Jackson gave Sam a rap on the arm. "Looks like you've got more than Pa's disapproval to worry about."

Sam's good nature turned sour. "Hush up, Jack." He whispered the command through gritted teeth. "What did we just talk about?"

"We-ell," the boy replied thoughtfully, "we still don't know for sure that God *didn't* bring Miss Eikaas to town for you to marry."

Sam decided to change the subject. "When we talk later, Pa, you'll have to bring me up to date on what transpired in town yesterday."

"The debate over Indian relocation wasn't half as lively as the one with Lars Eikaas," Pa grumbled. "But we will talk more about that later, when there aren't ladies present."

"Good." Sam squared his shoulders, anticipating the future discussion with his father. He'd even welcome the good talking-to Pa promised.

Anything to shift his thoughts—and Jack's imagination—from Kristin Eikaas.

CHAPTER 4

*A*s the wagon bumped along the jutted road, Kristin couldn't decide which proved more painful, her sore, throbbing foot, listening to Inga whine because Oskar Frantzen didn't dance with her tonight, or Uncle Lars's rants about the Sundberg family.

"The Sundbergs are evil." Inga's statement only emboldened her father.

"*Ja, ja,* they are!"

"And I will not be surprised to find they have put spells on Kristin."

"Oh, stop, Inga." Kristin grew weary of her cousin's ill-intended pranks.

"No more talking!" Aunt Esther twisted around in her seat beside Uncle Lars. "We will have quiet the rest of the ride home."

No singing? Kristin found it peculiar. Years ago, before the fever took the lives of her family, they would sing on the way home from church or social events, like tonight's wedding celebration. But it was just as well that the conversation ceased. How different her uncle and aunt were to Poppa and *Mor.*

Kristin closed her eyes and saw her parents in her mind's

eye. The cherished memory made her forget how much her foot throbbed. And if she tried hard enough, she could hear them as they sat at the supper table, talking, laughing. Poppa and *Mor* were outspoken and frequently discussed the issues of the day as well. However, that did not include malicious gossip.

Oh, how Kristin missed her parents and siblings. She wondered once again why God had spared her life and not theirs.

The wagon suddenly pulled to a halt, and Kristin realized she'd daydreamed away the rest of the ride to *Onkel's* shanty.

Everyone piled out of the wagon, and Uncle Lars began to unhitch the team. Mr. Olstad helped him.

"Peder!" Kristin motioned to her foot, and he reluctantly assisted her to the ground. But when her toes first touched the ground, the world began to swim.

"I cannot walk."

"What do you want me to do? Carry you?"

Kristin couldn't think straight.

"How just like a female."

In the next moment Kristin felt herself falling over Peder's shoulder. "I am not a sack of potatoes, you know."

"True. You are much heavier."

She ducked her head to avoid the top of the doorway.

"What is this?" Aunt Esther's stern expression said she didn't approve of such chivalry.

"Kristin injured her foot tonight." Peder set her into a chair near the table then hunkered down to examine the inflamed limb.

"Momma, look how swollen it is." Anna bent to have a closer look.

"A curse!" Inga snapped her fingers.

Kristin sent her cousin a cold stare. "I stepped on a buzzing insect. I did not have a shoe or stocking on because of the curtain dance—a game *you* tricked me into playing."

"How dare you blame your disobedience on my Inga!"

Kristin gazed at her aunt. "But it's true."

A dark scowl wafted across the older woman's suntanned face. "Change your clothes, go to bed."

"But...my foot."

"Maybe it will be better in the morning."

No offer of medicine or even a cold compress? Confused, Kristin glanced at Peder. He shrugged and left the cabin.

Aunt Esther closed the uneven door behind him. Without so much as a word to each other, the girls began peeling off their garments. Kristin did the same, managing to sit down most of the while. Then, hopping to her trunk, she carefully replaced her *bunad* and threadbare undergarments. She found her cotton nightgown and pulled it over her head.

However, climbing the ladder to the loft proved difficult. Inga gave her intermittent shoves.

Once in the loft, Kristin situated herself on her pallet. Inga climbed up behind her.

She giggled. "What did Sam Sundberg say to you as you danced?"

"Not too much." She didn't dare confide in her cousin. "Polite chitchat."

"He did not tell you how pretty you look or comment on how well you dance?"

"No."

Inga sat on her pallet and unbraided her hair. "That proves he has no manners." She jutted out her chin. "Joel Rouland danced with me. He must have commented on my beauty at least three times."

"He is smitten with you perhaps." Kristin unknotted her own hair then gave her flaxen tresses a good brushing.

"Every man in Brown County is smitten with me."

"Hmm…except for one, it seems." Kristin arched a brow. "Oskar Frantzen."

"Oh, you would have to bring him up!"

Anna climbed into the loft and quietly slipped into her pallet.

Inga's voice became a whisper. "It is your fault Oskar didn't choose me tonight. If you would not have gotten yourself hexed by a Sundberg…"

"What nonsense!" Kristin retied her hair into one fat braid before stretching out on her pallet. "Only an ignorant mind would believe such a thing."

Her cousin replied with a prissy-sounding, "Hmph!"

"Stop that talking up there!"

Kristin cringed at her aunt's command, but she didn't say another word. Erik and Uncle Lars came in from tending to the horses. Aunt Esther shooed young Erik to his corner pallet.

And all the while Kristin's foot throbbed with every beat of her heart. Another night without much sleep seemed imminent.

"You could have endangered that girl's life, Sam. Did you ever think of that? Why, there's no telling what that crazy man, Lars Eikaas, might do out of spite."

"You acted pretty crazy yourself, Pa."

A second's pause. "That man irks me to no end!"

"No excuse—that's what you've taught me all my life. Self-control."

Pa grumbled.

Sam watched him pace the dusty floor of his office in the

corner of the barn. Pa moved his political life out here so he could keep Ma's house free from the clutter and still oversee the animals. The horses, oxen, and cows were in stalls on the ground level, unless outside in the grassy fields and hills beyond, while the pigs and sheep had pens of their own on opposite sides of the barn, and they too grazed outside much of the time. Hay and feed were stored in the upper level of the barn along with the chicken coop—and now Pa's office.

"Judge Jensen insisted I dance with Miss Eikaas, so I did—and I'll take full responsibility for her well-being. If her uncle lays one hand on her, I'll—"

"You'll what?" Pa ceased his pacing and narrowed his eyes, making his bushy brows look like dark slashes across his tanned face, a stark contrast to his wheat-blond hair.

"I'll report him to the authorities, of course. I gave her my word."

"Hmm…I think I told you that I forbid you to court an Eikaas."

"Who's talking about courtship?" Sam stood from the wooden chair in which he'd been sitting. "It was a dance, Pa. That's all. Besides…" He tried to ignore the jab of disappointment. "She's obviously spoken for."

"*Ja*, so it appeared when we saw her strolling back to church with that young man tonight." Pa lifted his stubbly chin. "And for your sake, as well as hers, I hope she is betrothed." He moved his stocky frame toward his desk. "You have more pressing issues to occupy your time."

"Such as?" Sam stepped forward. He'd been hoping to discuss the outcome of yesterday's meeting with Pa long before now. "Does it concern what happened in town yesterday?"

"*Ja*, it does." Pa expelled an exasperated-sounding sigh. "As you know, the Menominee are refusing to cede the remaining western half of their land."

Sam gave a nod.

"Do you recall our brief meeting with Chief Oshkosh?"

"Of course." The round-faced brave had been a protégé of the war chief Tomah and was now the Menominee leader.

Pa sat on the edge of the scuffed table, which served as a desk. "Oshkosh reminded government officials that a little more than fifteen years ago, the Menominee protected white settlers in Green Bay against the threat of attack from the Sauk Indians."

Sam could just barely recall the fear that had spread like wildfire. He and his family had been forced to leave their farm and take refuge with friends in town until the threat from the warring tribe abated. Sam recalled how at night he and Pa would keep up with the news by reading the local newspaper, the *Green Bay Intelligencer.*

It had whet Sam's appetite for politics, specifically United States Indian affairs.

"Chief Oshkosh feels whites should be grateful for the protection. I assured him that we are, but..." Pa folded his arms across his barrel-shaped chest. "Oshkosh wants me to prove it by helping to pass a petition in hopes of amending the treaty. As you know, the Menominee were not properly represented at the committee meetings."

"So you agreed?"

"I did. Already Oshkosh and other Menominee braves have signed it."

"I'm of age. I'll sign it too."

"I knew I could count on you, son." The corners of Pa's blue eyes lifted. "But I'm going to need more than just your signature. I need your help in collecting signatures. You can begin tomorrow after church."

Sam set his hands on his hips. "Of course." He arched a brow. "But I won't count on Lars Eikaas signing your petition."

Pa snorted then his shook his head. "The Sundbergs have lived here for more than a decade. The Eikaases only half that time. Even so, Lars has had more impact on our community with his hatred and bigotry than I have trying to spread a message of unity and camaraderie with the natives of Wisconsin. But, no, Eikaas has divided our congregation and turned men who I thought were friends against me."

Sam had heard this discourse before. "Our true friends stick by us, Pa. And don't forget, they make up the majority of the business community."

"That's right." Pa's lips pressed together, and he exhaled through his nose.

"You could try to reason with Mr. Eikaas. There was a day, long ago, when you two were friends."

"The man is unreasonable, Sam. Mark my words, it won't be long and that pretty niece of his will turn her nose up at the Sundberg family. Lars will poison her mind against us—and all our friends too." He shook his head. "Spells…bah! Neither your stepmother nor any other Indians hold that kind of power. Lars probably believes that trolls live under the bridges in Norway too. What nonsense!"

"I don't know, Pa." Sam returned to his seat and stretched his legs out in front of him. "Kristin seems smarter than to believe her superstitious uncle." He grinned, recalling the determined glint in her eyes when she spoke about her future in America.

"I think you're smitten, son. But I'm warning you—"

"If we're done talking…" Sam stood. "I've got chores in the morning and then church, so I'd best get my sleep."

Pa folded his arms but said nothing.

Spinning on his heel, Sam left the barn and set off for the house.

⚜

The next morning Sam glanced over his shoulder in time to see the Eikaas family and John Olstad enter the back of the church. Lars removed his hat while his wife and daughters kept their bonnets securely tied under their chins. Where were Kristin and her carrot-topped beau?

Looking straight ahead, Sam told himself he didn't care. He shouldn't.

But then Mary elbowed him. Looking at her, he noticed his sister's troubled expression. Sam followed her gaze and he saw what most folks did—Kristin Eikaas limping into church on the arm of the man in question. Her white ruffled bonnet shielded most of her face, although Sam thought he saw her wince before she slipped into the pew.

That ogre beat her like he'd threatened yesterday after the wedding! Tension spread across his shoulders.

Suddenly Ma's hand came to rest on the sleeve of his wool dress coat. Sam's eyes met her cool brown gaze. Though he knew Kristin was none of his concern and that she was already spoken for, he felt the need to do something. "I plan to speak with Sheriff Brunette after the service."

Ma slowly lifted her hand, but Sam saw a glimmer of approval in her eyes.

Reverend Wollums began the service with a hymn, and Mrs. Hansen made her way up the outer aisle and sat at the square grand piano. Sam couldn't help a small grin as he recalled how their little church acquired the ornate instrument. Made of Brazilian rosewood, the piano had been shipped from Chickering & Sons in Boston to Jakob Adams, one of Green

Bay's most prominent citizens. When the piano arrived, there was notable damage to one side, although it still played and sounded wonderfully. Since it was to be a gift for his talented son, Mr. Adams donated this piano to his friend, Reverend Wollums, and promptly purchased another one for young Lawrence.

The congregation stood, and Sam thought he heard a gasp coming from somewhere behind him. Had it been Kristin? Collectively they sang a hymn based on Psalm 62:8.

"Trust in him at all times, ye people, pour out your heart before him, God is a refuge for us. Selah and selah."

Reverend Wollums motioned everyone to sit down, and he opened his Bible. After a word of prayer, he began his sermon.

Sam tried to concentrate. He never treated the Word of God with flippancy. Nevertheless, while the reverend spoke, Sam couldn't help but think of Kristin. At one point he even went so far as to cast a glance at her from over his shoulder. He saw her dab her eyes with her hankie. Was the pain so bad from her uncle's thrashing that she now struggled just to keep her composure?

The service finally ended, and Sam stood to find Sheriff Brunette. The man and his family usually sat three rows behind the Sundbergs. Locating his man, Sam leaned over to shake his hand.

"Well, good morning, Sam." The sheriff gave him a jovial smile.

"Could I have a word with you?"

"Of course." The sheriff stepped out of the pew and met Sam in the far aisle. He smoothed down his light-brown beard. "What's on your mind, son?"

Sam relayed his concerns.

"Well…" Sheriff Brunette puffed out his chest, and his steely gray eyes shifted toward Lars Eikaas. "I'll investigate and let you know. Thank you for calling the matter to my attention."

With an incline of his head, Sam watched the sheriff return to his family and exit the pew in the center aisle. Would the man look into the issue soon? Right away? Kristin's very existence might depend on it!

⁓⸙⁓

"Everyone has almost left the church, Kristin. I think we can go now."

"But—"

"You needn't be embarrassed, Kristin. You hurt your foot and you have me to lean on as we make our way from the sanctuary."

She glanced at Peder, grateful that he was so willing to help her, and then at the lingering few, chatting between the pews. Sam Sundberg was among them, and try as she might to keep her eyes off the man, she couldn't help sneaking a glance at him from time to time. Dressed in a brown wool suit that accentuated his strong shoulders, he looked quite handsome. And his necktie looked interesting. Slung around the collar of his ivory linen shirt, it appeared to be a strip of leather with beaded work on the ends. It clipped together so it dangled down in front.

"I do not know how long your uncle will wait for us."

Kristin forced her attention back to Peder. "You think *Onkel* will go home without us?" A sense of horror rippled through her very core. "I cannot walk out of this church, let alone all the way back to my uncle's farm."

"You want me to go outside and make sure he waits, don't you?"

"Yes. And I am sorry for the inconvenience. I would do it for you."

Peder tossed a glance at the ceiling then stood.

Kristin turned her knees to the side to allow Peder to exit the pew. She watched him leave the church, feeling like a burden. Her aunt and uncle told her at breakfast this morning that they would not accept any excuses from her tomorrow, the first day she was to begin doing her chores on the farm. They gave her a place to sleep, they fed her—just barely—and she would be expected to work like everyone else. Except how? She'd scarcely got her foot into her leather ankle boot this morning and could not pull the laces tight. The sole of her foot burned while a painful throb traveled from her toes to her heel and up her leg.

Kristin lowered her head, wondering how she'd manage.

A man cleared his throat close by. She looked up to see a bearded man standing just a few feet away.

"Miss Eikaas?"

"Yes?" She noted that Sam stood behind the man along with Mrs. Wollums, the reverend's wife.

"I would like to inquire over your injuries." He spoke in Norwegian.

"Injuries?"

"Yes." Mrs. Wollums leaned forward. "We saw you limp when you came into church, and you have not walked out yet. Are you able to?"

"I do not think so." Kristin lowered her chin.

Sam came around and hunkered next to the pew. "Did your uncle make good on his threat because I danced with you last night?"

"No!" She looked up in surprise. "Not my uncle. I did this to myself. I stepped on something with my bare foot. Buzzing insects rose up like smoke. And now my foot is hopelessly swollen."

The sheriff's features relaxed, although a slight look of

concern lingered. "I hope your foot is better soon, Miss Eikaas. A poultice might help."

"As do I." But where would she get the ingredients for that at *Onkel* and *Tante's* house?

The sheriff gave her a quick half bow before donning his hat. "Sorry to have troubled you."

"No trouble."

The man took his leave, passing Peder on his way out of the church.

"Kristin," Peder called from the doorway, "your uncle said he will wait only a few more minutes." He stopped short and narrowed his gaze at Sam.

Mrs. Wollums spoke up. "Mr. Olstad, I believe." She smiled cordially.

"Yes, ma'am." Peder gave the minister's wife a smile and a courteous bow. They had been introduced at yesterday's wedding celebration.

"Since you are new to Brown County, I would like you, your father, and Kristin to be my guests for our noon dinner. My husband will drive you all home this afternoon."

Hope like she hadn't felt since arriving filled Kristin.

Mrs. Wollums's smile widened. "Please go tell Mr. Eikaas that he does not have to wait."

"Well…"

Peder glanced at Kristin, who decided getting acquainted with the Wollumses appealed to her more than returning to her uncle's farm. She nodded.

"*Ja*, all right," Peder said at last. "Thank you for the invitation."

"You are very welcome."

Once Peder had left to do her bidding, Mrs. Wollums gave Sam instructions. "Help Miss Eikaas out through the altar door and into my house. I will find your mother. She'll know what to do for such a sore foot."

"As you wish."

Kristin's heart felt like an anvil, dropping through her insides. If Uncle Lars discovered her alone with Sam Sundberg...

"Not to worry." He seemed to have read her thoughts. Then he took her hand and helped her to stand on her one good foot. "If we hurry, no one will be the wiser."

Kristin tested her foot and winced. "Forgive me, but I do not think I can walk."

"Nothing to forgive. The problem is easily solved." Wearing a slight grin, Sam leaned in and, moments later, scooped Kristin into his arms. "I will carry you."

She clung to his thick neck and tucked her chin. "I am heavy."

"Like a feather." He chuckled.

The compliment momentarily won over her concern. "But what if someone sees us and my uncle learns of it? He might follow through with his threat to horsewhip me."

"Dear Lord, command Your angels to guard the doorway," Sam prayed aloud as he took the few steps leading up to the altar. "And keep any busybodies away from the Wollumses' home until I can get Kristin settled."

"Amen!" Fear allowed her to only eke out the response. But, under different circumstances, she might have enjoyed her close proximity to Sam. He smelled quite appealing, like strong soap and sweet hay.

They came to a side door and Sam bent at the knees. Instinctively Kristin turned the knob, and Sam carried her into a breezeway that led to the square, brick parsonage. Another door. Sam hunkered. Kristin opened it.

Inside, the kitchen area looked neat and clean with its simple furnishings. Two towheaded little girls stood by the table and stared, wide-eyed.

"Miss Eikaas, please meet Belinda and Margaret Wollums." He explained why he carried her.

The girls stared at her foot.

Sam walked into the sitting room and stopped in front of a blue upholstered settle. Kristin let her arms fall away from his shoulders and noticed he didn't huff or grunt when he set her down into its horsehair cushion. He paused before straightening and sank his sea-blue gaze into her. Kristin held her breath, unsure if he meant to say something. Was he tongue-tied—or did he have other intentions?

Like stealing a kiss?

She hoped so—

The thought startled her.

Kristin looked away, uncomfortable with the rush of emotions warming her insides. Was she wicked to have such thoughts about Sam?

"Hold still." He touched her bonnet, and when he pulled his hand away, she saw he held a fat black bug between his thumb and forefinger. Had that been the object of his scrutiny all along?

"Beetles…annoying things. This one got himself stuck in the ruffle of your bonnet." Sam looked from it back to Kristin and grinned. "You are not afraid of bugs, are you?"

Was he teasing or mocking her? "No, but I do not like them much."

A smile tugged at the corners of his mouth. "To tell you the truth, I dislike them too." He strode to the front door, walked outside, and disposed of the insect.

The littlest girl strolled in and pulled out her bottom lip. "Wook."

Kristin smiled at the space between the girl's small white teeth.

"Did you lose a tooth, Margaret?" Sam asked.

"*Ja.*" The girl bobbed her head.

"That means you are becoming a big girl now." Kristin's smile grew.

Margaret grinned broadly.

With the door still open, Sam leaned against the frame and folded his arms. His gaze was fixed off in the distance. "Your aunt and uncle are leaving with Mr. Olstad. I can see their wagon turning onto the road."

"Do not let them see you since they know I am here."

"They cannot see me. They would have to look hard through the evergreens." Sam swung himself from the entryway. "Besides, your *forloveden* is on his way to the house. He'll be here in a moment."

"My...*forloveden*?" Kristin wasn't sure she understood. Had Sam misused the Norwegian word? He must have meant to say the English word *friend*. "Are you referring to Peder?"

Sam replied with a curt nod. Margaret put her hand over her lips and giggled.

"I had best take my leave." His pleasant tone turned brusque, and a muscle worked in his jaw as he stepped out the door.

"*Takk*—thank you," she called after him.

"Glad I could help," Sam muttered.

Why did he look miffed? Kristin opened her mouth to ask, but it was too late. Sam had gone.

CHAPTER 5

*K*RISTIN BIT HER lower lip as Peder unlaced her boot. "If you take it off," she warned, "we might never get it back on."

"Mrs. Wollums will be back soon with medicine to put on your foot. Your boot and stocking must come off in order for her to apply it."

Peder gave the boot a tug, and Kristin cried out in pain. A moment's dizziness caused her to recline on the settee. "You might take some care with my injured foot."

"I wanted to remove it quickly instead of agonizing and slowly."

"You hurt me, Peder."

"Your shoe had to come off."

Kristin felt unusually warm. She untied her bonnet and swept it off her head.

"It is done now. I will leave and join the men outside so you can remove your stocking."

Kristin nodded.

"But I will have you know that I am not happy about staying for dinner. The Sundbergs are here also."

"Oh?" Kristin wondered if that meant Sam would dine with them too. Then she wished the man didn't occupy so much of her mind lately.

"I only stayed to keep an eye on you."

"An eye on me?" Kristin gave a curt laugh of disbelief. "I am not a child."

"But you showed poor judgment last night." Peder's voice was low, almost menacing.

Kristin didn't know how to respond. What he said was true. It seemed she did possess poor judgment where Sam Sundberg was concerned.

Standing to his feet, Peder left the sitting room just as Belinda, the Wollumses' oldest daughter, walked in balancing a large tin bowl in her arms.

"This is for your foot."

"*Takk.*"

The girl set it down and water sloshed over its rim. Margaret appeared then with fresh linens, and Kristin took a small towel from her to quickly wipe up the spill.

Then, taking care, she lifted her swollen extremity into the bowl. The water felt so cold against her inflamed foot that it made Kristin shiver, and she had to immerse it in gradual stages.

Strains of women's voices reached her ears, and within moments Mrs. Wollums, Mrs. Sundberg, and Sam's sister, Mary, entered the sitting room.

"I am sorry we took so long." Mrs. Wollums removed her blue bonnet. "It took some time to locate the plantain."

Kristin eyed the leafy-green stems in the Indian woman's graceful hand. Kristin presumed Sam's mother would put them in the soak.

Instead, Mrs. Sundberg hunkered down, inspecting Kristin's foot. Her touch was cool, gentle, and expert. She spoke in

English to Mrs. Wollums, who gave a nod in reply, whirled around, and left the sitting room.

"*Tehalutawe ésta.*" Mrs. Sundberg lifted her brown eyes and met Kristin's gaze. "It is what my people call the black and yellow insects that make their nest in hollow logs or under wooded brush." She spoke Norwegian quite well, and Kristin understood her without difficulty. "They will sting if the nest is disturbed."

"Looks like I found that out the hard way. I must have stepped on the nest with my bare foot."

Mrs. Sundberg lifted her delicate brows and nodded. "A poultice will help." She held up the leaves, still in her hand. "But first I must remove any remaining stingers."

The reverend's wife returned with a long blade, and Kristin felt her eyes grow wide. "I held it in the fire a few moments, as you told me."

"Thank you, Agnes." Mrs. Sundberg took the knife by the handle.

Kristin drew in a startled breath.

"Do not be afraid." Mary gave her a comforting smile. "This will not hurt." Gathering the folds of her brown and green checked skirt, she sat down on the settle beside Kristin.

At that moment a realization fell over Kristin. She sat between two Indians. She had never been so close to such a people before. She'd only read stories in the Old Country and heard about Indians on her journey, how fierce they were, and how they scalped innocent women and children. But Sam's stepmother and sister resembled nothing of those wild-eyed savages. Just the opposite. Here they were, trying to help Kristin, not hurt her. Besides, what she'd said to Sam last night was what she believed—people were not so different.

Mary took her hand as Mrs. Sundberg lifted Kristin's foot

out of the cold water. She laid the blade against Kristin's heel then slowly ran it upward, toward her toes.

"There, that was not so bad, was it?"

"No." Kristin turned to Mary, noting how the smile on the girl's lips made its way to her dark, shining eyes. "Not a bit."

"And look…" Mrs. Sundberg held the knife to her. "Look closely. See the two fine hairs on the blade? They are actually stingers. Little wonder your foot hurt so badly."

Kristin squinted and saw the fine particles on the sharpened edge and thought how remarkable it was that such tiny things could be so harmful.

A movement by the door caught Kristin's eye. She looked over and saw Peder, standing at the entryway, watching. Quickly, she tried to cover her exposed legs with her skirts. *How dare he spy on me when I am in such a state of undress!*

Mrs. Wollums spotted him too and shooed him off. Peder stepped back and then turned and walked away. Kristin felt embarrassed for him and his less than chivalrous behavior.

None of the women or girls said a word about the incident but returned to their task of helping Kristin with her sore foot.

Mrs. Sundberg handed Mary a few of the leaves. Using a small wooden bowl that Mrs. Wollums provided, they placed the plantain inside and spat on it. Next Mrs. Sundberg crushed the leaves with a wooden spoon.

Kristin sat by in stunned wonder.

Once a sort of paste had been made, Mrs. Sundberg carefully placed it on the bottom of Kristin's foot. Next she wrapped one of the linens around it like a bandage. Mrs. Wollums took away the bowl of water, and Mary carried the wooden bowl and utensils into the kitchen.

"We will leave it on for about a half hour."

"May I inquire…I mean, I am just curious…why did you

not wet the leaves with the water in the bowl? Instead you used spittle."

"Spittle contains healing powers that mix with the plantain and make it work." Mrs. Sundberg got up from where she'd been kneeling on the floor. She must have glimpsed the doubt in Kristin's eyes, for she added, "It will work. You will see."

Mrs. Wollums reentered the room. "I should get our dinner on the table." She turned to her daughters. "Belinda, Margaret, come and help Mary and me."

The reverend's wife led the way out of the parlor, leaving Kristin alone with Mrs. Sundberg, who had rapidly won her respect.

Kristin smiled to herself. Just wait until she wrote to Sylvia and told her about this adventure in America!

Sam balanced his white ironstone dinner plate on his knees and watched Mary and the Wollums girls chase two kittens in the yard. A tree-dense area surrounded the clearing and provided welcomed shade. As he ate, Sam carefully kept his gaze away from Kristin, although Ma appeared to be enjoying her company. Even so, her *forloveden* looked nothing short of annoyed as he leaned against a distant maple with arms folded tightly across his chest.

"When Lars finds out his niece and that guest of his from Norway are eating Sunday dinner with us," Pa said, "there will be hell to pay. I just hope that girl won't suffer for it."

"She won't." Reverend Wollums smiled and nodded a thank-you to his wife as she handed him a cup of coffee from the tray she carried.

Sam accepted a cup too, as did Pa. Then Mrs. Wollums moved on to Ma and Kristin.

"When I drive her and Mr. Olstad back to the Eikaas farm,"

the reverend continued, "I'll explain the situation to Lars. His niece's foot required medical attention. Mariah Sundberg offered her services—*for free.*" Reverend Wollums grinned. "Putting it that way, I can usually reason with him."

Pa snorted.

Sam thought it pathetic, but Revered Wollums spoke the truth.

"Pa?" Jackson tilted his head and squinted into the sunshine. "Why do you and Mr. Eikaas hate each other?"

"I don't hate him. He hates me—and my family."

"But why?" Jack persisted.

"Oh..." Pa leaned back in his chair. "It's a long story and for another day."

"Is it cuz Ma, Mary, and me are Oneida?"

"That's part of it." Pa sipped his coffee. "Maybe even most of it. You see, son, many Norwegians are superstitious people. Not all, but some. When I grew up, I heard stories about trolls roaming the mountains and forests, and of dragons hiding in the depth of the lakes. Once my grandfather told me a tale about the witches living in the apple orchards and casting spells on little boys who ventured too close." Pa guffawed. "It was most likely his way of keeping me from eating the harvest."

Sam, Jack, and the reverend added their chuckles, and Kristin's head turned their way. When Sam met her gaze, a strange and foreign sensation coiled around his gut. In effort to quell it, he slid his gaze to Olstad, only to meet the other man's stone-cold stare.

"Miss Eikaas's foot seems to be better." Reverend Wollums observed as he swallowed more coffee. "Her shoe is back on, and earlier she walked around the yard." He sighed. "But Mr. Olstad seems to be the one with the problem right now. Perhaps I'll go speak with him."

"Hmph. Good luck," Pa quipped.

Reverend Wollums raised his brows.

"You know as well as I do," Pa explained. "Prejudice spreads and multiplies like those black beetles that infect our potatoes. It's hard to stop."

"But God's power is stronger than prejudice…and potato beetles." The reverend's smile broadened before he stood. "Excuse me, gentlemen."

Sam watched him go and sent up a prayer that their godly minister would find success in nipping any hatred in the bud.

"Sam!" Ma waved him over. "Come here and tell Kristin that funny story about when you and your friends went skiing last winter."

"Some other time." The last thing Sam wanted to do was fuel Olstad's jealousy—and fuel something else too.

"Please, Sam?" Mary came up alongside him, dark eyes beseeching him, and Sam felt himself caving like he always did when it came to his little sister's requests. "Please?"

He inhaled and fired a glance upward. "Oh, all right."

"Watch yourself, son." Pa flicked his gaze over his shoulder, indicating to Kristin. "Need I remind you that she's an Eikaas?"

"No, sir. I don't need reminding of that."

Lifting his chair with one arm, Sam carried it over to where the ladies sat. Mary plopped down on the lawn and the Wollums girls copied her. His gaze stumbled into Kristin's, and he noticed her blue eyes rivaled the sky above. Expectancy shone on her face like sunshine. He laughed to himself. Since when had he become so poetic?

And suddenly Sam felt a little worried too.

The wagon bumped along the dirt road. The tall pines and evergreens that lined it whispered in a gust of wind.

Kristin shivered.

"Wind shifted." Reins in hand, the reverend turned to her. "It is coming off the lake now, which means cooler weather on the way."

"That will be nice." Kristin hoped it wouldn't be so hot now up on the bowed loft she shared with Inga and Anna. Perhaps she'd actually sleep tonight. "*Takk*, Reverend, for the nice afternoon."

"You are welcome, Miss Eikaas."

"We should not have eaten our Sunday dinner with those Sundbergs."

Kristin glanced behind her into the wagon bed and noted that Peder's expression appeared stoic at best.

"Now, Mr. Olstad, there is nothing wrong with the Sundbergs. I have been their pastor for many years. They are good people."

Peder pressed his lips together as he stared out into the woods.

"God has said in the Book of Proverbs that love covers all sins. Saint Paul reiterated it by saying that the greatest gift from God is love." Reverend Wollums paused. "There is too much hatred in this community already. Please do not add to it, Mr. Olstad. You have been here only a couple of days."

Peder said nothing, and Kristin wished that he would heed the pastor's word. The Sundbergs did, indeed, seem like good people. Kristin had enjoyed chatting with Mrs. Sundberg, and she was grateful for the insect remedy. Her foot felt almost healed. And young Mary and Jackson were well behaved, and Sam...

She suddenly realized she'd never gotten a chance to straighten him out about her and Peder's relationship. But what did it matter anyway?

Kristin looked around her, taking in the scenery. They came upon a clearing, and drying cornfields spread out on either side of her. At this late stage of summer, the corn would most likely be ground into meal and the rest used for animal feed. But why hadn't Uncle Lars planted any corn this year? And why did he and Mr. Sundberg hate each other?

"Reverend, can you help me understand the relationship between my uncle and Mr. Sundberg?"

"I can try." He paused as if collecting his thoughts. "It started years ago—before I came to Brown County. No one will tell me the full story, but from what I understand, they were friends in the beginning. The Eikaas family had gone to the Sundbergs' for dinner one night. Later it was discovered some valuable coin silver was missing, and Karl accused Lars of taking it. Lars denied it."

Kristin wondered if her uncle was really guilty of the crime. She wouldn't doubt it.

"After that Lars spoke out against Mariah Sundberg, as she is Oneida—Jack and Mary too. But they are believers and have just as much right to be in church as the Eikaases. Well, Karl took umbrage. It has continued from there." The reverend expelled a ragged breath. "I do not mind saying that I am at my wit's end. And yet, I do not want to give up hope." He smiled. "There is always hope because there is a God."

Kristin overheard Peder's derisive snort and ignored it. "But I do not understand what Mrs. Sundberg and Jack and Mary have to do with the feud between my uncle and Mr. Sundberg."

"It's not them. It's their heritage and the color of their skin. And unfortunately, prejudice is a weapon fueled by the fact that this community is torn over the situation with the Menominee tribe. Half the folks in Brown County, including your uncle, say it would be a good thing if the Indians cede their land to the government and move out of Wisconsin. The other half, led by Karl and Sam, feel the Indians are entitled to stay, citing that they did not get proper representation before the treaty was signed."

"They were tricked?" Kristin was beginning to know how that felt.

"Some say so." The reverend glanced at her.

"It does seem a bit unfair for the Indians." Kristin recalled her father talking about how unfair the government was in Norway—how it taxed their food so high, including the crops they grew and the fish they caught—so that many people went hungry in spite of a healthy harvest. "It pains me to think that I traveled so far to escape oppression only to find it again here in America."

"Oh, now, Miss Eikaas, please do not feel that way." The reverend hiked his floppy hat higher onto his forehead. "The situation will be resolved with the Indians, and in the meantime, people like the Olstads can stake a claim and purchase the land and own their own farm in a matter of months. America is nothing like the Old Country. You will see."

"*Ja*, and that's what we are hoping for," Peder said. "A farm of our own."

"And then Sylvia will come." The thought of her best friend arriving in Green Bay made Kristin smile.

The wagon suddenly rolled by rows of apple trees, and Kristin glimpsed several ripe fruits bowing their limbs. How good an apple would taste. Did her uncle own this orchard?

Before she could ask, the reverend steered the horses to the right and up the narrow dirt road, leading to Uncle Lars and

Aunt Esther's cabin. They hit a rut, and Kristin clung to the seat's sidebar so she wouldn't tumble off the wagon.

"I might mention to Lars that he needs to repair those divots before someone gets hurt." The reverend straightened his hat, and moments later, the cabin came into view. A dreary cloud descended over Kristin's head. The place exuded gloom.

"We had a fine time years ago when the community held a barn-raising for your uncle. Mr. Hampton, from the brickyard, even offered to make the hearth in which your aunt bakes and cooks. It also heats the home."

"I should say it does, especially the last couple of days." Kristin only wished the volunteers had helped her uncle build a decent home too. "*Ja*, the barn is very nice." She couldn't seem to curb the wistfulness in her tone.

Reverend Wollums turned her way. "Our community assists your uncle whenever possible. It troubles me that he and his family live in that hovel. We have taken up collections at church and people have donated supplies and time to help with repairs. But things do not change. I hate to think of your aunt and the children going to bed hungry."

"Why do things not change?" Kristin turned slightly on the wagon bench.

"Good question."

"There is rotten lumber in back of the barn." Peder's tone held a note of disgust. "It is worthless—not even good enough for firewood anymore."

Kristin thought she glimpsed a wave of anger brush across the minister's brow.

He managed to shake it off. "I will speak to Lars about that— and explain about our additional guests this afternoon."

The Sundbergs. Kristin hadn't begun to think about the

ramifications of associating with them. She hadn't wanted to. Sunday dinner at the Wollumses' place had proved most pleasurable.

Reverend Wollums pulled the wagon to a halt. Peder jumped out then helped Kristin from the wagon. Uncle Lars sauntered from the barn.

"Welcome, Preacher." His gaze flitted over Peder and landed on Kristin. "Did you enjoy your meal with the Wollumses, *liten niese*?"

"*Ja, Onkel.*" Guilt twisted inside of her, and she sent a glance toward the reverend as he climbed from the wagon seat. Her cousins and aunt poured into the yard. They too greeted the minister.

"Lars, I would like a word with you if I may." Reverend Wollums straightened after tousling Erik's blond hair.

"Of course. Come into the barn where we can find privacy. Erik, water the reverend's horses."

"Yes, *Far.*"

Kristin smiled as the boy ran for the bucket.

"I would offer something—"

"No need, Mrs. Eikaas." With an understanding expression, the reverend waved his hand in the air. "Do not trouble yourself. I will not stay long."

Kristin thought Aunt Esther looked embarrassed as she turned for the cabin door. The hem of her mud-brown dress swirled at her ankles. Peder followed the men into the barn just as Inga came forward and hooked her arm around Kristin's elbow.

"I did not have a chance to speak with you after church. Did you see Oskar Frantzen this morning?" Inga whispered. "I believe he smiled at me."

Kristin hadn't even noticed the man. She'd been in too much pain.

They strolled toward the well, passing Erik, who struggled to carry a bucket of water toward the horses. Kristin opened her mouth to offer some assistance, but seeing his determined expression, she snapped it closed again. If he wanted help, he could say so.

"Tell me about your afternoon at the Wollumses'." Inga smiled. "Beatrice and Margaret are precious, eh?"

"*Ja*, they are." Kristin eyed her cousin warily. Why was she being so nice? Another prank?

"I watch the girls sometimes when Reverend and Mrs. Wollums are called away for an afternoon."

Kristin sat down on the grass in a shady patch of the yard.

"Your foot is better," Inga observed. She lowered herself down several feet away and arranged her skirt over her knees. Kristin admired how the coral color of the miniscule-checked fabric matched Inga's complexion.

"*Ja*, my foot is much better. I soaked it in cold water at the Wollumses' home."

"Oh, that's good." Inga picked at the blades of grass. "Maybe we can be friends."

"Maybe." Kristin was willing to start anew. She gazed up at the sky just as several white, puffy clouds blew by.

"I will admit that it is not easy living here."

Kristin turned her gaze back to her cousin.

"I am sure you have seen that *Far* is not the easiest man to live with."

Pressing her lips together, Kristin refused to comment. She still didn't trust her cousin.

"I do not mind working hard, but when Momma, Anna, and I break our backs in the field while *Far* putters around in the barn all day, accomplishing nothing…" She paused. "A neighbor man plowed our fields this spring, but then Momma got sick." Leaning closer to Kristin, she whispered, "She did not know she was going to have a baby until she got sick."

"She miscarried?"

"*Ja,* so she could not plant the seed. I had to take care of Momma, and Anna and Erik tried to plant with *Far* looking on and hollering at them that they were doing it all wrong." Inga gazed heavenward and shook her head. "Why he did not take over the job and plant the seed himself, I cannot understand."

"He has an impediment of some sort?"

"He is lazy," Inga spat. "I hate him, and I cannot wait to get married and leave this place!"

"Inga!" Kristin's eyes widened. "You must not disrespect your father."

"Some father. He thinks only of himself."

Kristin stared at the grass beneath her and knew in her heart Inga spoke the truth about *Onkel.* She had only been here two days, but her uncle's character had already revealed itself.

And no wonder *Tante* was so unhappy that she lashed out at others.

A sudden ruckus behind her made Kristin turn. She saw Uncle Lars storm from the barn. After sending an angry glare her way, he thundered off in the direction of the woods.

Kristin slowly stood to her feet. Prickles of unease fell over her as she watched the reverend take his leave.

Peder had followed *Onkel* out and strode toward her and Inga.

"What has happened?" Inga got up from the lawn. "Why is *Far* so…so angry?" Her gaze went from her father's retreating back to Kristin. Curiosity brightened her blue eyes.

"He says you are cursed, Kristin," Peder told her. "The Sundbergs cursed you with their remedy for your foot."

"That is absurd!"

"Your uncle said it is witchcraft of the heathens, meaning Mrs. Sundberg and her daughter."

"That is why your foot is better?" Inga carefully backed away.

"Mrs. Sundberg put a poultice on my foot. That is all."

"But I hid around the door and watched how she and her Indian daughter spat on the plant first, putting a spell on you."

"Peder!" Kristin's cheeks burned with incredulousness over both his actions and his words. "How could you spy on me?" She set her hands on her waist and tipped her head. "And how can you believe such nonsense?"

"It is not me, Kristin. It is your uncle."

Inga lifted her hems and ran for the cabin. "Momma! Momma! Wait until you hear!"

"And your cousins will believe too. And soon your aunt."

"They will hate me now."

"Your uncle said he will not allow you to sleep in the house or his barn for fear your spell will harm his family and the animals."

"Then where shall I sleep?" A deep sense of hurt spread through Kristin's being. She was truly an outcast here.

"He will put your pallet in the wagon bed and park the vehicle nearby."

"But…" Kristin felt like she might cry. "What about bears? What if it rains?" She paused in thought. "What did Reverend Wollums say about this—*arrangement*? Surely he could not have left knowing of it. He would try to change *Onkel's* mind."

"The reverend had been speaking with my father when your uncle muttered his decision."

"Well, that is just fine with me." Kristin hiked up her chin. "I will not mind sleeping in the wagon. It will be more comfortable there than in the loft in *Onkel's* hovel or on a mound of hay in his precious barn."

Peder's chest rose and fell with a deep sigh. "I knew we should not have dined with the Wollumses' once I learned the Sundbergs were guests too."

"But—"

Kristin clamped her mouth shut. It was no use trying to explain. In silence she watched as Peder strode back to the barn.

CHAPTER 6

*T*HE PINKS OF dawn crept over the horizon as Kristin climbed into the wagon. She wondered how much longer she could last with no one in the family speaking to her. For two solid days her aunt, uncle, and cousins spoke through the Olstads, and either Peder or his father relayed their messages. In that manner she learned which chores were now her responsibilities. From mucking stalls to weeding neglected vegetable gardens, the work had kept Kristin busy from sunup to sundown. But, thankfully, she slept peacefully at night in the back of the wagon, too exhausted to worry about bears and uncivilized Indians, and so far, God had kept away the rain.

"Tell that girl to hurry up," Uncle Lars suddenly barked. "We do not have all day!"

Halfway into the wagon, Kristin looked over her shoulder and caught Peder's gaze.

He shrugged. "You heard him." Setting his hands on Kristin's waist, he all but tossed her into the flatbed. Her pallet had been removed, and now she nearly fell into the basket of freshly picked green beans.

She narrowed her eyes at Peder. "You are a toad. A toad!"

"So now you cast spells on people too? Like the Sundbergs?" He laughed while inspecting his hand. His lingering grin mocked her. "But your magic did not seem to work on me."

"A pity!" She grit her teeth.

He chuckled again before swinging himself up into the wagon. Mr. Olstad sat on the bench beside Uncle Lars. Kristin's aunt and cousins would remain home this morning. However, *Tante* didn't want Kristin to stay with them and insisted she help the men at the street market in town this morning. That was fine with Kristin as she had purchases to make—secret purchases, since she'd never told her uncle about the extra money left from her journey.

Uncle Lars slapped the reins, and the wagon jerked forward, causing Kristin to fall hard onto her backside, which, of course, made Peder laugh all the more.

Smarting in more ways than one, Kristin seated herself and did her best to ignore him. Sometimes he was her friend—and sometimes not. She focused on the trip ahead of her. For the first time in days she felt hopeful and glad. She hadn't seen much of Green Bay, other than its docks and many warehouses, and she longed to explore the city and make her purchases— that is, if she could sneak away from her uncle long enough to do so.

Kristin eyed the many baskets beside her in the wagon bed. Her uncle's crop, while plentiful, looked puny in her estimation. If only Uncle Lars would take interest in his harvest and his home...

The wagon rolled along at a good clip, and Kristin only half paid attention to the men up front talking of their dreams. Uncle Lars didn't sound so angry when he talked about his goals of owning a large house and many more farm animals, other than his one cow and the team of horses. Kristin wasn't all that surprised to learn that they and the cow had been gifts from the community a while back.

Buildings came into view, signaling their arrival in town. Uncle Lars steered his team through the unpaved roads until they reached their destination in the city. Kristin noted the many wagons parked in neat rows all the way down the wide street. Already farmers were selling their milk, eggs, cheese, fruits, vegetables, flowers, and other homemade goods.

Uncle Lars cursed a blue streak. "Again I did not get my desired spot on the street, and I came even earlier than last week. Look how I will have to sit in the hot sun!"

"Oh, it is not so bad, Lars." Mr. Olstad jumped from the wagon. "You might get shade by early afternoon."

"By early afternoon I hope to be sold out. Today I want to beat Karl Sundberg at his own game. His wagon is always empty by noon." He barked at Kristin. "Help me get set up, and be sure to smile at the customers."

Kristin tossed a glance at Peder before she started unstacking the baskets of vegetables. Silently he began helping her.

Before long the street filled with people, women mostly, who walked from one wagon to another, bartering and sharing snippets of news and gossip.

"Watch the wagon, Peder. I should like to introduce your father to my friends," Uncle Lars said.

"*Ja.*" Peder agreed, but looked none too pleased about it.

Uncle Lars and Mr. Olstad sauntered down the street. When they disappeared in the crowd, Kristin decided to make a dash to find her necessities.

"I will return soon, Peder."

"And where might you be running off to?"

"Do you really want me to discuss a lady's practices with you?"

Peder looked away. "Go!"

Kristin lifted her hems and headed in the opposite direction of her uncle and Mr. Olstad. As she strode down the plank walkway, she passed shoppers as well as a group of uniformed men, whom she guessed to be soldiers. On the street side, farmers called out in loud voices, but Kristin couldn't understand a word they said. She could only assume they hailed customers.

An overwhelming feeling came over her like a fog. She felt suddenly lost. Everywhere she looked, in shop windows, on the tops of buildings, on street signs, there were words she could not read. She decided that Sam had been correct when he said she needed to learn English—and somehow she would!

With tentative steps she made her way farther down the busy walk, peering into windows, hoping to find a store that carried what she wanted. She came to an intersection. Turning left, she prepared to cross the road when she realized the man who occupied her thoughts more often than not stood just a few feet away. She decided not to acknowledge him. However, a lovely array of flowers fanned in a large jar drew her attention. She paused to inhale their heady fragrance. It was then she noticed bunches of brown leaves, hanging upside down from the side of the wagon. And inside the bed were baskets of shining red apples and flats of deep-red cherries, purple grapes, and pink raspberries. On the street, surrounding the wagon, were more baskets filled with sweet corn, beets, broccoli, carrots, onions, squash, and potatoes.

"*God morgen*, Miss Eikaas."

She glanced at Sam in time to see him politely remove his hat. "Good morning." The phrase was part of only a handful of English phrases she knew, mostly from her travels. She reverted back to Norwegian. "You have a fine harvest here."

"Thank you." He smiled and then a customer beckoned him. "Please excuse me."

"Of course."

As he took care of business, Kristin inspected the Sundbergs' healthy crop. She lifted a bunch of meaty carrots for closer inspection. Uncle Lars's vegetables could not compare to these.

Replacing the bunch, Kristin watched Sam finish with his customer. He appeared washed and clean-shaven, and the sleeves of his beige shirt had been rolled to his elbows. Attached to his brown trousers were suspenders that crisscrossed over his broad back.

Sam turned toward her then, and she quickly lowered her gaze. How could she stare at the man so openly? What if her uncle saw her? What if Sam noticed?

But he was so appealing…

"Can I interest you in anything today, Miss Eikaas?" The smile in his voice sounded somewhat patronizing, and her cheeks burned with embarrassment. He noticed, all right!

She changed the subject. "What are these?" She pointed to the curious dried brown leaves hanging off the wagon.

"Tobacco. It is a crop that is primarily grown on the western side of the state, but Pa wanted to try it out, and we have done surprisingly well with it."

"Hmm…" Kristin pressed her lips together in disapproval.

"Not to your liking?" Sam chuckled.

"I should say not!" She jerked her chin. Was he teasing her, or did women in America smoke tobacco like men?

Sam laughed again. "Perhaps some delicious raspberries will suit you better. Here…have a sampling." He plucked several berries from the wooden flat and held them out to her.

"No, thank you." Kristin shook her head. "I cannot accept."

Uncle Lars would be furious if he caught her tasting the Sundbergs' wares, let alone speaking with Sam. "I have errands to do."

"Oh?" He leaned one shoulder against the wagon and popped a deep pink berry into his mouth. "Where are you headed?"

"Well...I am looking for a..." How did she say it? "...a woman's shop."

His light brown brows drew inward, and he kneaded his jaw. "You can try Betsy Biddle's place first. If Miss Betsy cannot help you, she will, at least, send you along to someone who can."

Relief flooded Kristin's being. Now she had an idea of where to go.

"Cross the street and keep walking straight. Miss Betsy's is right down the road. The last shop on the block. You can't miss it. But if you do, you'll find yourself at the schoolhouse."

"*Takk.*"

"In English, please." Sam grinned and his blue eyes twinkled.

Kristin tucked a few strands of her hair beneath her white bonnet. "Th–thank you."

"You're welcome." He dipped his head politely before glancing down the row of wagons. "No traffic. It is safe." He waved her across the street.

She replied with a parting smile, lifted her hems, and picked her way to the other side of the mucky lane. As she headed toward Miss Betsy's, she felt grateful for Sam's assistance—and worried too. Her troubles would multiply if one of her aunt's or uncle's friends had seen her conversing with Sam and reported her.

As she neared the end of the plank walk, she heard children playing. No, wait—

Kristin brought herself up short and listened harder. Venomous, taunting tones reached her ears, along with a girl's cries to stop. Kristin knew that English word too. *Stop.*

She stepped out again and quickened her pace. A clearing

came into view, and her eyes widened when she spied a group of boys accosting one little girl. Strands of the girl's brown hair had worked loose or been pulled from their braids, and her pretty dress had been torn. Rage welled up inside of Kristin, doubling when she realized the girl was Mary Sundberg. Next young Jack came into view, his nose bloodied. He fought with two other boys.

Without a second thought, Kristin ran toward the group. "*Nok! Nok av dette*—enough of this!"

Her heart sank as reality set in. The boys hurting the Sundberg children didn't seem to hear her or couldn't understand her Norwegian—or they didn't care.

Spotting a large stick nearby, Kristin had a hunch they'd understand a good whack on the shoulders. She stooped and curled her gloved fingers around the switch. Lifting it from the dirt, she began striking the bullies hard, as if she were beating off a pack of mad dogs.

Her efforts worked. After several shouts, the *slem gutter*—nasty boys—ran away. Breathless, Kristin watched their retreating backs as they passed the schoolhouse. She turned her gaze to Jack first, then Mary, who covered her face. Her shoulders began to shake.

She seemed to need the most comfort, so with opened arms, Kristin stepped toward her. "There, there…do not cry." She looked back at Jackson, who struggled to stand.

"Are you hurt, Jackson?"

"Naw…" He brushed the dirt off the seat of his pants.

"Go fetch your older brother. He is just down the road."

After wiping his bloody nose with his sleeve, Jackson sent her a nod and took off down in the direction of the farmers' market.

Mary's head fell onto Kristin's shoulders. "Those horrible boys! I hate every last one of them!"

"You know them?"

"Some, not all." Mary drew in a ragged breath.

"Are you badly injured?" Kristin gently took Mary by the shoulders. She searched the younger girl's tear-streaked face.

"They called me a heathen half-breed and jumped on Jackson when he tried to help me."

"Those terrible boys will not get away with this."

"If you had not come along," Mary sobbed, "I do not know what they might have done to Jack and me."

Kristin hugged the ten-year-old close. "God works in mysterious ways. I was on my way to Miss Betsy's shop."

Mary clung to her.

"Shh...you are safe now."

Just then Kristin saw Sam sprinting toward them. When he reached them, he stopped so quickly that his boots slid on the gravel. With one hand on Mary's shoulder he stared down the road.

"The *slem gutter* are long gone," Kristin said of the boys, "but Mary knows of their identities."

"Yes, Jack told me who they are." The muscle in his jaw flexed before he glided his gaze to his sister. "Are you all right, Mary?"

She nodded and turned to her brother. Her eyelids were puffy from so many tears. Her hands flittered to the tear in her dress. A piece of the tiny floral-print fabric from her shoulder to her sleeve had been ripped in the assault. "Look what they did!"

"It can be repaired." Kristin fingered the fabric. "Quite easily too, I must say."

"But I will miss school today." More tears trickled down her tanned cheeks.

An idea came to Kristin. "Will Miss Betsy lend me a needle and thread? I can fix it for you. It will not take me long."

"If I know Miss Betsy," Sam said with a grin, "she will be happy to help out."

Kristin wondered if Miss Betsy held a special interest for Sam.

He honed his gaze in on his little sister. "Mary, go and introduce Kristin to Miss Betsy while I speak with the sheriff about those boys. I'll meet you right here in about…" He glanced at Kristin. "An hour?"

"*Ja*, that is all the time I need."

"Once your dress is sewn," Sam said, looking back at his sister, "I will see that you and Jack get to school without any more problems. Pa finished his business at the bank, so he can watch the wagon."

"Yes, Sam." Mary stepped back, taking hold of Kristin's elbow.

"And, Miss Eikaas?" Sam's tone softened.

She met his eyes and a warm feeling poured over her. She thought she'd like to bask in his gaze all day long.

"I cannot begin to thank you enough for helping my sister and brother. Not everyone in this town would. *Takk*."

She smiled, feeling a blush in her cheeks. She'd try out her English once again. "You well-comb."

Sam pursed his lips. "Not too bad." He grinned before turning and making quick strides down the boardwalk.

"Come with me." Mary tugged on her arm, causing the glow of that special moment to vanish. "You will like Miss Betsy."

They walked back to the shop and up a few steps to the door. Heavy ivory lace curtains hung inside the windows, making it difficult to peer into the establishment. Once they'd entered, Kristin realized why. Ladies' foundational garments and pinnings hung on racks. Filled with cotton drawers, chemises, corsets, camisoles, and starched petticoats, Miss Betsy's shop seemed to have everything a woman required.

A thin, older woman approached them. She greeted Mary in English and then eyed Kristin curiously. Her face resembled a dried apple and her wiry gray hair looked like it belonged on the end of a scrub brush. However, she had a warm, welcoming smile that somehow managed to soothe Kristin's still-jangled nerves.

Mary made the introductions. "Miss Betsy, please meet Miss Kristin Eikaas." She went on to explain the situation, both outside with the boys and how her dress got ripped, further stating that Kristin was a friend—unlike the rest of the Eikaases.

As she listened to the child, Kristin almost laughed aloud at herself for imagining that Sam would have a romantic interest in the older woman. For all intents and purposes, Miss Betsy could be his grandmother.

"I am happy to lend you a needle and thread. Come this way."

They followed Miss Betsy into the back of the shop. A few strides later, fingers of dread ran up Kristin's spine. If Green Bay resembled her village in Norway, then gossip spread like floodwater from the mountain top. Soon Uncle Lars would hear of Mary's mishap with the boys as well as Kristin's benevolence toward her—a Sundberg. What then?

Miss Betsy showed Kristin where to find everything she'd need to repair Mary's dress. Kristin threaded a needle while Mary slipped out of the torn garment.

"*Takk*, Kristin." The girl sat on a stool and watched.

"I do not mind."

"But you are frowning."

"Oh, it is nothing." But that wasn't the truth.

"Tell me."

"I am concerned that my uncle Lars will be angry with me if he learns I am mending your dress. I am already being punished for allowing your mother to help me with my sore foot—which, by the way, doesn't hurt me anymore." Kristin smiled. "I am ever so grateful."

"How are you being punished?" Miss Betsy's gray brows pulled together. "And for what?"

"My uncle thinks the Sundbergs put a spell on me. You see, Mrs. Sundberg and Mary treated my sore foot and it healed quite miraculously. So I sleep in the back of the wagon. I am not allowed in the house or barn. They also refuse to speak to me." Kristin glimpsed Mary's frown. "But, as I said, it is nothing." She hated to make the little girl feel worse than she already did.

"Oh, that ornery Lars Eikaas!" Miss Betsy folded her thin arms. "He is always blaming someone for something."

"*Ja*, so it would seem." Kristin blinked away the sudden moisture accumulating in her eyes and concentrated on her sewing. "My father, Daniel Eikaas, was nothing like *Onkel*."

"Oh?" Miss Betsy sounded interested, so Kristin went on.

"He was a good man, soft spoken, kind to everyone. And he loved *Mor* very much. But my family perished with the smallpox a couple of years back."

"I am sorry to hear it, dear."

Mary sat quietly by, her brown eyes looking wide and sorrowful.

Kristin decided to change the subject, lest she give in to her misery and upset Mary further. "Miss Betsy, your shop is quite unique."

"The only one like it around here." Miss Betsy's light green-eyed gaze swept over all the feminine items. "So much in life belongs to men. But I decided a woman needs to feel pretty, even out here in the rugged territory. And with all the ships sailing in and out of Green Bay, I can order all manner of dainty foundations, from New York—or even London, England, if I choose."

Kristin decided she liked Miss Betsy Biddle's spunk.

Several minutes ticked by, and Kristin began pondering her situation again.

"You are fretting, Miss Eikaas," Mary observed. "There is a little pucker in your brow, so I can tell."

Why deny it? "It is just that if Uncle Lars finds out I am here…and especially with you, Mary." Kristin groaned. "He is so unreasonable about curses and spells."

"I know!" Mary snapped her fingers. "You can tell him that your good deed today canceled the spell from last Sunday and then everything will be fine."

Kristin couldn't quell a bit of laughter. "Ridiculous as it sounds, the explanation might suffice."

Mary bobbed her head.

At last Kristin finished the repair, and Mary slipped her dress over her head.

"Now we shall fix your hair."

Removing the only remaining ribbon, Kristin retied Mary's hair, this time into one silky braid that came to rest between the girl's shoulder blades.

Mary primped in the looking glass, wearing an expression of pleasure. "Thank you."

Kristin smiled, deciding to try out her English once more. "You well-comb."

With a laugh, Mary skipped out of the store. Kristin followed her as far as the windows and couldn't help peeking through the lacy curtains. As she anticipated, Sam stood on the wooden walkway, waiting for his sister just as he promised. He glanced at the window, and Kristin pulled back so that she wouldn't get caught staring at Sam for the second time that morning.

"He is a handsome man, that Sam Sundberg."

Kristin pushed out a smile through her embarrassment.

"Is there anything else I can help you with today?"

"As a matter of fact…" Making her way to the rack where a variety of undergarments hung, Kristin pointed to them. "I am in need of some foundations."

"Then you have come to the right place!"

⚬⚬⚬

"It's none of our business!" Pa stacked some empty baskets and tossed them into the back of the wagon.

Sam eyed him through a narrowed gaze. Frustration pumped through his veins. "But Mary said they're making Kristin sleep outside in the wagon."

Pa didn't reply.

"It's our fault!"

"No, it's not. It's that crazy uncle of hers!"

As if on cue, Lars Eikaas came stomping down the road, accompanied by the sheriff and Ole Thomassen, his deputy.

"Any idea where Lars's niece ran off to?" Sheriff Brunette called to them. "I need to ask her a few questions about the incident earlier."

Sam debated whether he should say. Mr. Eikaas appeared sufficiently agitated already. He hated the thought of Kristin getting into more trouble on account of his family.

Pa sent him a glare then looked at the sheriff. "Did you try Miss Betsy's? My children were attacked between her place and the school."

"Just heading that way." The sheriff nodded. "Thanks."

Sam watched the men round the corner before tossing another stack of baskets into the wagon bed. Not even midday and they'd sold out most of their wares. The rest Mr. Hinshaw at the General Store agreed to purchase.

Pa came to stand beside Sam. "I got a message this morning.

The Menominee will have their hearing in Madison next month."

"That's great news!" Sam's features lightened with a smile.

"Of course, that doesn't mean anything other than the government is willing to listen to the Menominee's arguments."

"It's something, anyway." Sam straightened. "When will you be leaving?"

"Well…"

A commotion in the street stymied Pa's answer. Sam turned to see Mr. Eikaas tugging Kristin by the elbow. The skirt of Kristin's brown and red printed dress swirled around her ankles, causing her to suddenly trip on the hem, although, thankfully, she didn't tumble.

Sam stepped forward to intervene, but Pa held him back. "She's none of your concern, son. Besides, Sheriff Brunette's following them up the walk. You can see as plain as me. He's got his eye on Eikaas."

Just then Mr. Eikaas shifted his weighty frown, aiming it at first Pa, then Sam. He slowed his pace as he passed their wagon with Kristin still in his clutch. Perspiration stained the front of his gray shirt. "Stay away from my niece!"

"But, *Onkel*, I am trying to explain." Kristin tipped her bonneted head. "Someone told me that my good deed this morning removed all evil spells. They are gone now."

Puzzled, Sam raised his brows. First time he'd heard that bit of lore. Then he caught Kristin's surreptitious glance followed by a timid roll of her shoulder. He understood at once. A placating tactic. Good try.

Quickly he wiped his mouth to cover his grin.

"Is this true, Sundberg?" Mr. Eikaas squared his broad shoulders. "Any spells over me and my family are now gone?"

"Believe what you will," Pa said. "When did you ever listen to me?"

Mr. Eikaas snorted.

The sheriff moved around to Mr. Eikaas's other side. "Lars, your niece's actions today have brought honor to your family's name, not shame." The bearded lawman clapped him on the shoulder. "She did the decent thing by stepping in and helping the Sundberg children. Don't be so angry about the whole thing."

Confusion wafted across Kristin's face as she obviously struggled to understand what had just been spoken in English. Sam's gut reaction was to translate for her, but under the circumstances he thought better of it.

Mr. Eikaas grumbled and eyed the emptied wagon. "*Ja*, sure, and you might ask how the Sundbergs manage to sell their produce before noon." He gave Pa a glare. "Each week they park in the best spot at the market."

"It's our habit to get here before sunup, Eikaas."

He arched a bushy, platinum brow. "Or maybe you hex everyone and cause them to oversleep on market days."

"You're a madman." Pa waved a hand at him.

"And you are—"

"That's enough, gentlemen." The sheriff held up his hands. "Eikaas, move along now." He looked at Kristin and dipped the brim of his study brown hat. "Again, my thanks for your help this morning, Miss."

Evidently she understood a few words because she gave him a polite, parting smile before her uncle resumed hauling her down the street. His manhandling of Kristin irked Sam to no end.

"We will see to it your youngsters get home all right after school today," the sheriff promised.

As he and Pa shored up the details, Sam's focus remained on Kristin. She ran to keep up with her uncle's wider strides. Sam's instincts told him something had to be done to protect her, but what could he do?

Seconds later he glimpsed Peder Olstad's approach into the street. Sam realized Pa had been right. Kristin's welfare was none of his concern.

CHAPTER 7

*T*HE MIDAFTERNOON SUN beat down hard on Kristin, causing her skin to blaze beneath her lightweight dress. Underneath it she wore her new garments. Beads of perspiration trickled down her neck. How she longed for some shade and a cool drink of water.

Shortly after noon it became apparent that selling any more produce was not to be, and Uncle Lars turned the team of horses and the wagon toward home. He'd made mention to Peder that he had earned a few coins, but not nearly as much money as he hoped. Kristin glanced around her. Most baskets still contained Uncle Lars's harvest, although it now withered in the heat. She recalled the plump, juicy fruits and vegetables she'd seen in the Sundbergs' wagon, causing her to wonder what Uncle Lars did wrong—and what the other family did right. "Ask her why she was in Miss Betsy's store this morning," Uncle Lars called to Peder over his shoulder. "Did she make a purchase? And what did she use to pay for it?"

Peder fixed his gaze on Kristin and raised his brows.

As she bumped along in the back of the wagon, she debated whether to lie or come straight out with the truth.

"Aw, you know how women like to talk, Mr. Eikaas." Peder set his elbows on the side of the wagon bed and reclined. "My mother and sister can chatter for hours with neighbors and shopkeepers."

"*Ja*, it is true." Mr. Olstad smiled and wagged his head.

Uncle Lars muttered, and Kristin felt herself relax.

"You owe me," Peder said under his breath.

Kristin gave him a speculative glance. However, before she could inquire, the wagon lurched from side to side as it rolled past the orchard. Staring into it, she wondered why Uncle Lars hadn't picked a bushel of apples to sell this morning. Ripe red fruit hung on leafy limbs, and suddenly her mouth watered as she thought of the refreshing taste of tart and sweet on her tongue.

Dust from the road plumed in the wagon's wake, and soon Uncle Lars turned and drove the team into the yard. No sooner had he parked when Erik came running from the barn. The girls and Aunt Esther followed, and Kristin noticed their solemn expressions.

"*Far*, the cow…she is sick!" His blue eyes were wide with worry.

Uncle Lars jumped from the wagon and glanced at the boy then at Aunt Esther, who replied with an affirming nod.

Kristin climbed down out of the flatbed and found Inga and Anna staring at her. Were those accusations in their eyes?

Shaking herself, Kristin wondered if she had begun to feel overly self-conscious. Of course her cousins would not blame her for an animal's sudden illness…

Would they?

Peder met her gaze with a stern expression as he came toward her. Uncle Lars and Mr. Olstad made their way into the barn accompanied by Aunt Esther and the children.

"What sort of trouble is this?"

Kristin stared at him. "How would I know, Peder? I have been away from the farm most of the day."

"But you associated with the Sundbergs... *again*. And if this cow dies, your uncle might get so angry with you that he will throw my father and me off his property because we brought you here. Then what?"

"My aunt and uncle asked me to come. You did not bring me here." Exasperated, she placed her hands on her hips and tipped her head. "I thought you were my friend. You should defend me."

"My father and I need a place to stay until we can buy our own land, Kristin."

"And it may cost you more dearly than you know to stay here." *Like our childhood-long friendship!*

"Kristin..."

She ignored the warning knell in his voice and swung around. Then she stomped off, unable to help her display of temper. In the last few months it was never more apparent than now that Sylvia and Peder were quite different from each other. Sylvia, like Kristin, would fight for a friend. They had come to each other's rescue several times while on the playground or off. But Peder...

Come to think of it, Kristin didn't recall much about his character. But the lack thereof shone through today.

Kristin trudged through the dried cornfield. At its end stood a row of tree stumps and, beyond them, a pond. She'd never seen it before now, as her aunt had kept her busy with chores the last two days. Tall weeds grew around the side closest to her, but she could still see that the water looked cool and inviting. It beckoned to her, and suddenly she couldn't resist the urge to take a quick dip. What harm could come of it?

Squinting, she scanned the vicinity and saw no one, so she

sat on a stump and removed her bonnet, shoes, and stockings, followed by her dress, petticoat, brand-new corset, and camisole. She'd worn her newly purchased items so Uncle Lars wouldn't learn that she'd kept money from him. She was grateful that the Olstads distracted him.

Clad in only her drawers and chemise, she waded into the pond. Just as she anticipated, the water felt refreshing against her hot skin. She cupped her hands and drank, realizing she'd been as thirsty as she was hot. After submerging her head, she floated on her back and gazed up at the cloudless sky, marveling as she typically did at its vastness.

What would her future hold? It appeared dismal, at best.

An unnatural rustling in the brush caught Kristin's attention. Her senses on alert, she quickly looked toward the bank. Several birds flew toward the sky, but Kristin saw nothing else. She figured the sound had come from animals.

Another minute later, Kristin gave up her swim, dried off, and began to redress. She had chores to do, after all, like unloading the wagon. But at least she no longer felt as parched as Uncle Lars's crops.

As she hooked the front of her corset, she spied the apple orchard on the far side of the pond. Her stomach rumbled, and she figured it wouldn't hurt to pluck a fruit or two since she hadn't eaten any lunch. Perhaps she'd offer to make apple butter for Aunt Esther. Would that sweeten her up? Maybe *Onkel* and her cousins would come around too, and they'd finally start speaking to her again.

But why didn't her family harvest the orchard? Perhaps they weren't quite ripe yet. No harm in looking.

Once dressed, she gathered her shoes, stockings, and bonnet and walked around the edge of the pond to the orchard. She noticed the rivets of water, running to the ends of each row of trees. The lanes between the wide trunks were well maintained. It seemed an odd contrast to the rest of her uncle's property.

Finding a tree that she guessed she could climb with relative ease, Kristin secured her bonnet around her neck and then proceeded to collect apples. When her hat bulged with fruit, she climbed back down.

And that's when she heard a man clear his throat. She froze then slowly turned.

"Miss Eikaas." Sam Sundberg gave her a polite nod, although he didn't remove his floppy-rimmed hat.

"What are you doing here? If my uncle sees you, I will be in even more trouble than I am now."

"I was about to say the same thing."

Kristin tucked her chin. "I do not know what you mean."

"This is Sundberg property."

She blinked. "Oh, I–I did not realize…" She looked down at her bonnet, filled with apples. "I am so sorry. I had assumed this was part of my uncle's land."

"No harm done."

At his gentle reply, embarrassment like hot liquid ran down her neck and filled her chest. Most likely Sam had seen her climb from the tree and now she stood there, feeling like a thief, caught in the act.

"You may keep the apples," he said as if guessing her thoughts.

Kristin knew she couldn't do that. "Thank you, but my aunt and uncle would not allow it." She glanced up to see agreement play across his features.

"Well…" He removed his hat and raked his fingers through his hair. "I could use a break. Will you join me and eat an apple?"

She knew she shouldn't. She should turn and run back along

the pond. But somehow she couldn't get herself to refuse. Besides feeling physically hungry, she needed a friend. She felt so alone.

Before she could reply, Sam stepped forward and took an apple from her bonnet before sitting against the wide trunk of the very tree Kristin had climbed. He faced the orchard with his back to the shallow gulley that she now realized separated the Sundberg's property from her uncle's.

Against her better judgment, she sat down next to Sam, hearing the crunch of the apple as he bit into it.

Then she took a bite of hers.

"You said you are in trouble? Is that because of this morning's incident?"

She chewed and swallowed. "No, although it is part of it."

"I thought you said all the spells were gone now." With a chuckle, he bent his knees and rested his arms over them, brushing against her shoulder as he did so.

She slid a glance his way, briefly catching his gaze. "Your sister gave me the idea to say that."

"Brilliant, at least coming from a ten-year-old."

Kristin had to grin in spite of herself, although it was short-lived. "We came home to find that the cow is sick. She may be dying."

"That is a serious matter. But surely your uncle does not blame you."

"He has not said so directly. Not yet. But based on his past reactions, I fear that if the cow dies, I will be blamed." Letting go of a long sigh, Kristin lolled her head against the tree trunk. "I am beginning to feel as though I really am cursed."

"Hmm…greater is He that is in you than he that is in the world. No Christian is cursed."

Kristin recognized the truth. "*Ja*, you are right." Gratefulness plumed inside of her. "I needed reminding." She ate another bite of apple.

"Glad to be of some help." His gaze met hers before his eyes ever so slowly drifted down her face and lingered on her lips.

Kristin ceased chewing and swallowed the piece of apple in her mouth. She had a hunch, and not for the first time, that Sam wanted to kiss her. The thought caused tingles of anticipation to shimmy down her limbs.

She quickly looked away and her reason returned. Kristin would never kiss a man she barely knew. She wasn't that sort of a girl.

And maybe Sam wasn't the sort who went around kissing females. Perhaps she had merely been sloppy with her eating, and now traces of apple stuck to her cheeks. For now, she'd give him the benefit of the doubt. She liked Sam. He'd been polite, even kind to her.

Kristin hurried to brush any remnants off her face. "I am not accustomed to my uncle's temper." She decided to talk away her discomfort. "My father, his brother, was a very different man, soft-spoken and kind. He would do anything for anyone in need. He did not rush to judgment, but he could be rather stubborn."

Sam grimaced. "Your father is dead?"

Kristin nodded.

"I am sorry to hear it."

"I miss him and *Mor* very much. My little brothers too." She turned the apple in her hand. "Fever and smallpox ravaged our little village a few years ago."

"I am sorry, Miss Eikaas. I am sure that had to be terribly difficult for you."

"*Ja*, it was…"

Sam reached over, and before Kristin could guess his actions, he lifted the cross pendant she wore. His fingers brushed against her neck as he inspected it. "Very lovely." He stared into her eyes.

She swallowed her bite of apple. "*Takk*."

Sam tipped his head and grinned. "In English, please."

She could barely breathe with his close proximity. "Thank you," she eked out.

Suddenly the summer breeze carried her name on it. She froze, listening. Moments later, she recognized Peder's voice.

Sam peered around the other side of the apple tree. "Your *forloveden* beckons. Is he the one who gave you that pretty necklace?"

"No. *Mor* did." Kristin had heard Sam's sarcasm and now grinned. "And Peder is not my *forloveden*. He is not even my friend, so he can beckon all he wants."

"Did you two have a spat?"

"Whether we did is of no consequence. Peder is the brother of my best friend, Sylvia. We grew up together in Norway." Kristin let go of a sigh that felt both wistful and weary. "I wish Sylvia were here. I miss her very much. But soon she and her mother will come to America."

"You do not sound very confident."

Kristin exhaled audibly once more. "I no longer feel confident..." She tried to find the right words to express her tentative feelings. "The future does not seem quite as bright as it did last week. I could not wait to arrive, but now..."

"Give it time. You have traveled a long way. You are in a new country. There are many adjustments to make."

Peder called for her again. Kristin rolled a shoulder and ignored him.

Sam laughed under his breath before finishing his apple and

tossing the core. "What will Olstad do if he catches you over here? Tell your uncle?"

Kristin honestly didn't know. She felt as though she knew less and less of Peder with each passing day. "Peder is concerned that if the cow dies, my uncle might turn his anger on him and Mr. Olstad too. If *Onkel* asks the Olstads to leave, they will have nowhere to live."

"And what about you? What if your uncle orders you out of his home?"

"I am already sleeping in the wagon bed beneath the stars." She couldn't help the facetious lilt.

"I heard." Sam sounded none too pleased, causing Kristin to feel a measure of vindication. "Mary told me after she arrived home from school today."

Peder called for her once more. "Krist-tin!"

She tossed her apple core. "I had best go. Peder does not easily give up."

Sam stood and helped her to her feet, holding her hand seconds longer than necessary. "If you hurry to the other end of the orchard and cross near the road, there's a good chance no one will see you."

"Thank you." Kristin scooped up her shoes and stockings. "But first will you turn your back so I can put these on?" Her gaze flicked to her hands and the items she carried.

"Of course."

Rounding the tree, she leaned against the trunk and quickly pulled on her stockings, fastened them just above her knees, then laced her shoes. All the while she kept a close eye on her uncle's property, praying she wouldn't get caught here with Sam. It had been foolish of her to take such a risk, and yet the meeting lifted her spirits.

Turning, she saw Sam near the next tree, his back to her. As if he sensed her presence, he glanced over his shoulder before swinging fully around. "Finished?"

She nodded.

He pushed out a little grin. "Be careful."

"I plan to be." Gathering her skirt, Kristin took off through the grove. Dapples of sunlight flitted through the leafy canopy overhead and onto the sweet-smelling pathway. Kristin noticed how well tended the orchard appeared.

Reaching the last row of trees, she leaped across a narrow stream. She trudged up a small embankment and saw the back of her uncle's home. The next sight, however, was far more disparaging than even the wooden shack. Kristin watched as Uncle Lars, Mr. Olstad, and Peder dragged the dead cow out of the barn.

Sam cringed. In the distance he could just make out the men struggling to remove the cow's lifeless body from the barn. Losing their only cow would prove devastating for the Eikaas family. It meant no milk, cream, cheese, or butter—all necessary ingredients for preparing other foods too. He couldn't blame Mr. Eikaas for being upset about it.

But would the man blame Kristin?

Sam thought over these last minutes, sitting with her under an apple tree. If Pa found out, he wouldn't like it any better than Lars Eikaas. Still, Sam hadn't been able to resist her company.

Lord, forgive me for my blatant disobedience to Pa...

Glancing at his feet, he realized Kristin had forgotten her bonnet. Shiny red apples still bulged inside its ruffled rim. He squinted across the way and saw Kristin still dallying near the house. She'd placed her hands over the lower half of her face. Was she frightened? Of course she was. She'd said as much.

Lord, do You want me to step in? If so, how? And I'll need Pa's permission.

His thoughts in motion, Sam picked up the white bonnet. He recalled the beetle hidden in its folds last Sunday. He'd relished removing it. And Ma had said Kristin seemed like "a nice young lady" after getting to know her that day. What's more, Kristin wasn't betrothed as he'd assumed. The discovery had encouraged him in a way he didn't understand.

Smiling, an idea began to form. A way to help Kristin—and Ma too. He strode through the orchard and then walked the acreage to the barn.

Reaching it, Sam squinted into the structure's darkness. "Pa?" The sweet smell of hay mixed with the pungent scent of animal hides tickled his nostrils. "Pa, you in there?"

"Up here, son."

Bonnet still in his grasp, Sam walked to the ladder, climbed to the upper level, then found his way to Pa's office. He paused in the doorway. "Can I have a few words with you?"

"Of course. Come in."

As Sam entered, he caught a glimpse of his stepmother's willowy form in the corner armchair. He nodded a greeting and removed his hat. "Ma."

"I'll leave you two men to your business." She stood.

"No. Please stay." Sam glanced down at his booted feet. "What I have to say involves you too."

"All right." Ma tipped her head, and a lock of dark brown hair fell over her shoulder. She'd been having good days lately. But when her chronic condition flared, there were days when Ma could barely get out of bed. That's where Rachel had been such a help to her. "What are you carrying, Sam?"

Somewhat embarrassed, he handed her the apple-filled bonnet. "It belongs to Kristin Eikaas. I found her in the orchard this afternoon. She was picking apples. Apparently she thought she was on her uncle's property."

"Bah!" Pa pulled his chin back. "Lars probably said the orchard was his."

"No, I don't think so. I believe it was an honest mistake. Kristin apologized."

"She could have kept the apples, Sam," Ma said.

"She refused them, saying she'd be in even more trouble with her aunt and uncle if they found out she'd been on Sundberg property. Kristin has already been banished from that shack of a house and is sleeping in the back of Mr. Eikaas's wagon because of last Sunday—because of us."

"I thought we had this discussion this morning." Pa tipped his head in a challenging manner.

"Well, there's been a new development." Walking to the desk, Sam sat on its edge so he could face both parents. "As I'm sure you've heard, Ma, Kristin helped Mary and Jackson this morning."

"I told her all about it." Pa folded his arms.

"And Jack and Mary filled me in on the details." Ma smiled and sent Pa a coy glance.

He sent his gaze upward before looking back at Sam. "I plan to work with the school board to coordinate a volunteer lookout. It's a sorry shame my children were attacked so close to the schoolyard."

Sam dipped his head in agreement.

"But what's this got to do with the Eikaas girl?" Already Pa wore a stubborn tilt to his chin.

But Sam refused to be deterred. "The Eikaases' cow died just minutes ago, and Kristin is afraid she'll be blamed for that too—because of what happened this morning." He wagged his head. "You know how Mr. Eikaas can be."

"Sure do. That hot-headed man needs to take some responsibility for himself and his family."

"Seems that way, Pa." Sam eyed his father.

"Oh, that poor girl." Ma came forward and touched Sam's shoulder. "I sense her heart is in the right place."

"It is, but it won't be for long if Mr. Eikaas continues to punish her," Sam said. "She's lived through a lot of heartbreak." Sam raised his gaze. "Her family took ill and died in Norway."

"Yes, she told Agnes and me on Sunday." Ma's dark eyes trained on him. "And now here she is, living in a new country, unable to speak or read English. I'm sure she's confused…perhaps even frightened. It doesn't seem like she gets much direction from the Eikaases."

"She gets none from them." He recalled how he'd pointed out the way to Miss Betsy's this morning. She hadn't a clue where she was going.

"Son, it's none of our concern."

"Hear me out, Pa." Sam watched his father's shoulder's sink in resignation. "Kristin desires to make a new life for herself, but how will that happen if she's oppressed by her aunt and uncle, not to mention her cousins, who, I'm sure, wouldn't dare cross their pa. And the Olstads…" Sam pulled in a deep breath. "Kristin told me they won't defend her because they're afraid Eikaas might turn them out and they've got nowhere else to go right now."

Ma squinted and searched his face. "What are you thinking, Sam?"

"How about hiring Kristin as your house girl? The position is available, now that Rachel and Luke are married. Mary can help Kristin learn English." He grinned. "Mary wants to be a teacher someday. It'll be good practice for her."

"Well…" Ma looked at Pa, and Sam didn't miss the hopeful glint in her dark eyes.

A stubborn frown furrowed Pa's brow. "No!"

Sam moved his leg off the edge of the desk and stood. "Pa, if Kristin was Oneida or Menominee we wouldn't think twice about helping her. And Rachel…we took her in."

"He's right, Karl."

"No!"

Ma gave him a hard stare.

"No." Pa lost some of his vehemence, but his glare held Sam in place. "Even if we did offer her Rachel's old job, Eikaas will never agree to his niece working for Sundbergs. This is all nonsense."

Sam stood his ground. "But if we go over there with a cow, I'll bet Mr. Eikaas will listen."

"And I should give Eikaas one of my cows?" Disbelief and sarcasm laced Pa's words.

"Karl, please." Reproof filled Ma's voice. "This isn't about Lars Eikaas. It's about his niece. What if she's in danger? We all heard him threaten to horsewhip the young lady on Saturday—and just because she bumped into Sam."

"My sentiments exactly, Ma."

"The Eikaases allowed her to suffer with an inflamed foot." Ma's dainty chin went up. "Another day and it would have been infected. Think about this, Karl. Kristin has been ordered to sleep in the wagon bed. What is next?"

Pa grunted out an inaudible reply.

"Kristin can have Rachel's old room," Ma suggested.

Sam worked to conceal a grin, and he sent up a quick prayer of thanks that Ma agreed with him. Pa would likely soften now.

"A cow? I should give Eikaas one of my cows?" Pa snorted indignantly.

"What is a cow compared to a young lady's future, Karl?"

"That's right, Pa."

He grumbled and began to pace his makeshift office.

Then, all at once, he stopped and stared at Sam. "All right. We will offer the position to Lars's niece, not that he will allow it."

Ma smiled.

Relief welled up inside of Sam.

"But under one condition."

"What's that, Pa?" Sam squared his shoulders.

"That you go to Madison in my stead. I had just been discussing the matter with your mother when you walked in. With her ill health…"

"But now I will have Kristin—"

"We don't know that, Mariah." Pa's tone was even, steady. "I would prefer to be here and let Sam go with Chief Oshkosh and his men."

"When would I leave?" Sam wasn't opposed to the idea.

"Tomorrow morning if that Eikaas girl comes to work here."

"What?" Sam tapered his gaze.

"Oh, Karl, really." Ma laughed softly and folded her arms.

"You leave at the end of the month," Pa grumbled.

"What about the late harvesting and turning the fields over before winter?"

"I'll make do without you. There are neighbors who will lend a hand if needed."

Sam thought it over. "At the end of the month, huh?"

"Right."

He narrowed his gaze. "Pa, if this is about me associating with Kristin, you've got nothing to worry about."

"I think maybe I do. Every time I turn around, you're with that girl in spite of my warnings to keep your distance."

"Happenstance, Pa. Pure and simple."

"Hmm." He ground out the curt reply, stood there for several long seconds, and then strode toward Sam with purposeful strides.

"Son, we've talked about the kind of woman you should be looking for in a wife. We're praying to that end. We want a woman who is cultured and sophisticated. One who can advance the political career you've dreamed of. So far you've only dabbled in politics…which is another reason I'd like you to go to Madison. It's time, Sam." Pa set a hand on his shoulder. "Time for you to get serious about your future."

"I think so too, Pa." They had this discussion many times in the past. "But you're wrong about my having feelings for Kristin. I'm concerned for her welfare, is all. Just like I'm concerned about the Menominee losing their last parcel of land."

"Am I wrong, son? Am I really?"

A foreign emotion shook Sam to the core, and suddenly he couldn't look his father in the eyes and claim he wasn't, at least, attracted to Kristin Eikaas. She'd been on his thoughts far more than the Menominees' plight—even more than his chores on the farm.

"Mmm-hmm, I thought so." Pa inched his head to one side. "Well, need I remind you that the girl has no knowledge of American history, particularly Wisconsin history, and she can't read English, let alone speak the language."

"The same could be said of you once."

"That's different…oh, for heaven's sake, Sam, take hold of your common sense!"

Sam set his hands on his hips, not knowing how to respond. He hadn't acknowledged his attraction to Kristin, even if it was only to himself, until now. But he enjoyed the feeling of her in his arms as they danced. He liked making her smile, comforting her, and being of assistance, which she didn't get from her family. He admired her pluck and the glints of determination that entered her eyes. In addition, he had to admit that the idea of kissing her ripe and rosy lips appealed to him more and more, each time he saw her.

"The best thing is for you to leave for a while," Pa said. "A month...maybe two."

"Two months?"

Pa's hand slowly slid off Sam's shoulder. "Get your thoughts in line, son. While you're in Madison, you can gauge the first step in your career. Garner advice from men who're in the real political arena."

"We'll take good care of Kristin," Ma promised in that smooth, honeyed voice of hers.

Pa's features fell as if in defeat.

Sam grinned. "I'd like the Lord to find me a wife. I want to marry for love, not political gain." His smile grew. "As I recall, many people warned you not to marry Ma. But you followed your heart."

"That's different!"

Sam noted Pa's repetitive argument, proving it had no substance.

"There's not too much difference, Karl." Ma came to stand beside him and threaded her hand around Pa's elbow. "But let's set aside this debate for now. And there's time to talk about Sam's trip to Madison later. It's near suppertime, and we've got a cow to hitch to the wagon and take over to the Eikaases' place. Kristin will need time to pack her things and then unpack once she gets here."

"Lars will never agree to this arrangement," Pa growled.

Sam's equilibrium returned. "Well, we've got some persuading to do then too."

CHAPTER 8

*K*RISTIN HEARD THE jangling of harnesses and the thunder of horse hooves coming up the road leading to her uncle's cabin. She locked her trunk. Uncle Lars planned to drive her to the Wollumses since he had no place for her here. He said the reverend and his wife would have to deal with her now. And that was just fine with Kristin. She would rather live with the Wollumses.

Even so, sadness gripped her heart. Despite everything, *Onkel, Tante,* and her cousins were the only family she had. And the Olstads...

Kristin felt more angry than sad over Peder's and his father's behavior. Instead of defending her, they kept their silence. But, perhaps, going to the Wollumses' home would not be the worst fate imaginable. She liked the family very much.

But would they want her?

She strolled toward the shanty's entryway and saw Sam and his father coming up the dirt road in their two-seated wagon. Hand over her mouth, she gasped, glimpsing the brown cow tethered to the back of it. Sam must have said something about

ANDREA BOESHAAR

this afternoon's misfortune. But had he told his father about their meeting in the orchard?

Kristin's hand fell to her side and she nibbled her lower lip, watching the wagon's approach. Would she be in even greater trouble now? Perhaps they would think she was wanton for being alone with Sam in the orchard.

Entering the yard, Mr. Sundberg pulled his fine-looking team to a halt then braked the wagon. Uncle Lars immediately burst from the barn, carrying his long-barreled hunting rifle.

"Get off my property, the both of you!"

"Now, hold on a minute, Lars." Mr. Sundberg climbed from his perch. "I come to make you an offer."

Sam jumped down.

Kristin watched her uncle's features relax as he eyed the cow. "What kind of offer?"

"This here fine cow for your niece."

Kristin straightened. Surely Mr. Sundberg didn't mean to purchase her. For a cow?

Aunt Esther, Inga, and Anna suddenly appeared in the yard, wearing curious expressions. Peder and his father marched in from a nearby field while young Erik sat a ways off, toying with a grass snake.

Kristin remained stock still.

Mr. Sundberg continued. "We need a house girl now that Rachel is married."

Uncle Lars lowered the gun then pursed his lips, looking just like Poppa did when contemplating an important issue. Was he actually considering the idea?

But no! Everything inside her knotted tightly in blatant refusal. She did not travel from Norway to be a slave here in America. Not to the Sundbergs. Not to anyone!

"We will give her room and board, and you can keep this here cow…"

Kristin strained to hear the rest of the conversation but couldn't. Next she spied Mr. Sundberg walking to the back of the wagon and untying the animal. Kristin noticed how much healthier it appeared than the one that just died.

Aunt Esther, Inga, and Anna smiled at each other.

"Go ahead." Uncle Lars waved one hand in the air. "You Sundbergs are the ones who cursed the girl, so you might as well take her."

"No!" Kristin ran to her uncle. "My father would not approve of this arrangement!" She ground out each word.

"Kristin!" Sam's voice reached her ears. She looked at him and noted his wide-eyed expression. He shook his head ever so slightly as if warning her to keep silent. But how could she?

Uncle Lars raised the gun, pointing it in her direction. "You have no choice, *liten niese*. I only took you in because of family honor. But you are more trouble than you are worth!"

Looking down the barrel of his gun, Kristin's knees began to quake.

"Mr. Eikaas, please, put away the gun."

Sam's voice sounded close by. Then just as her legs would have buckled from fear, his hand cupped her upper arm and steadied her.

"We will leave right now. You can keep the cow." Sam pulled Kristin in the wagon's direction. "That cow is one of our finest."

"*Ja*, I can see that." Uncle Lars ever so slowly lowered the gun.

Kristin continued to follow Sam's lead until they reached the wagon. She stayed close, praying *Onkel* would not lose his temper and kill them both.

"We will give you a sow too, if you'd like."

"What?" Mr. Sundberg's voice held deep indignation. "Are you crazy, boy?"

"*Ja*, I would like a sow." Uncle Lars smirked.

"Then I will be back with it first thing in the morning." Sam turned, his face just inches from Kristin's. "Get up in the wagon. Quickly."

She didn't think twice about it. Suddenly being sold into slavery seemed a far sight better than living with her aunt and uncle.

Uncle Lars called for Peder. "Fetch her trunk, will you?"

Kristin had almost finished her climb into the wagon when Sam gave her an added lift into the seat. Mr. Sundberg sat beside her while Peder carried her trunk on his shoulder. Kristin refused to look at him or Mr. Olstad—or any of her family. They all treated her like a discarded old shoe.

Peder said nothing as he hoisted her trunk into the wagon bed. Sam climbed into the backseat, and moments later, Mr. Sundberg gave a flick of the reins. The wagon jerked forward. Clutching to the rail on the side of the seat, Kristin held back the onslaught of tears threatening from the backs of her eyes. She would never forget how her family forsook her this way. Then, again, she lost everyone she'd ever loved. Poppa and *Mor*, her siblings. Now the rest of her family had abandoned her. Kristin shuddered. What would happen to her now?

The evening sun penetrated the sleeve of Kristin's dress and branded her skin. She would never get ahead, working as a slave. Her dreams of someday owning a shop where she could display and sell her needlework vanished, and a dismal emptiness—as dismal as Uncle Lars's cabin—took its place in her being.

A short time later they reached the Sundbergs' yard. Mr. Sundberg slowed the horses to a halt and yanked on the brake. A black and white dog barked until Mr. Sundberg commanded him to stop. Mary ran to greet them, and after Sam helped

Kristin to the ground, the girl hugged her around the waist. Kristin nearly lost her composure.

"I am so glad you are here!"

Kristin pressed her lips together. She hadn't expected such affection. Bending, she pet the dog's head to conceal her emotions.

"Come. I will show you where your room is."

"My...*room*?" Kristin had somehow expected her accommodations would be equal to or worse than at Uncle Lars's. But she should have known the Sundbergs would be different.

Tugging on her hand, Mary led her into the house. "This is the mudroom."

Kristin saw that the room had been built around the well. An ingenious idea, really. The well was protected from the winter elements.

"Ma makes us wash up before we can enter the house. But I did already, and you look clean enough."

"*Ja*, I guess I am." She'd had her swim in the pond only hours ago and hadn't done much to get soiled since.

Mary led her down a flight of steps. Cool air whisked across Kristin's face and neck.

"This is the summer kitchen."

Kristin glanced around in amazement. A black cookstove occupied one wall. She smiled. A stove—a real stove! A block-top table stood in the center of the room. Cupboards lined the far wall. "Very nice."

"And over here..." Mary waved her farther into the basement. "This is your room."

Mary opened the door and showed Kristin into a quaint space. The walls were whitewashed brick and there wasn't a window. But she didn't mind. Kristin hadn't slept in a room this nice since leaving the Old Country.

A cot, complete with mattress, had been pushed up against one wall, and a small chest of drawers stood opposite it. There was even a place to hang her dresses, as a thick wire had been nailed between two low-lying rafters.

Sam burst through the doorway, balancing Kristin's chest of belongings on one thick shoulder. He set it down under the wire without a single grunt. Straightening, he glanced at Kristin. "Ma will be in shortly." His gaze wandered the room before coming back to rest on her. "So what do you think?"

Sheer and utter gratefulness enveloped her. "I think I will never be able to repay you for what you did for me, Mr. Sundberg."

"It's Sam." His smile was warm and genuine.

"Can we call you Kristin?" Mary asked with wide, hopeful brown eyes.

"Of course." She touched the girl's cheek, then looked back at Sam, recalling how he stepped between her and Uncle Lars's rifle. "You saved my life. *Takk*...I mean, thank you."

"I only did what any decent man would do." Chagrin flitted across his face. "If it is any consolation, I do not think your uncle would have really harmed you. Like Pa says, your uncle's bark is worse than his bite."

"I am not sure about that." Kristin hugged herself as a chill ran through her. She'd seen the hatred in her uncle's gaze.

"Well, do not let it trouble you any longer. You are safe here." Sam's voice held a note of promise that soothed her frayed nerves.

Mrs. Sundberg's willowy frame suddenly graced the doorway. "Welcome, Kristin."

"Thank you." She smiled then quickly lowered her gaze. She didn't know how to be a slave exactly, but she'd seen servants in Norway accompanying the rich with downcast looks. Once she'd heard from Sylvia that slaves must never look their superiors in the eye.

"May I show you around the rest of our home?"

Without looking up, Kristin gave a nodded reply. When Mrs. Sundberg moved away from the door, Kristin took her cue from Sam and followed with Mary in tow.

Upstairs they walked back through the mudroom. Kristin toured the main kitchen, which would be used more often now that autumn rapidly approached. In fact, something delicious wafted from the oven and two pots simmered on the stove. Kristin tried not to think about how hungry she felt. Her last meal had been a bite of repast just before dawn.

The tour continued. Adjacent to the kitchen was the dining room and, next to it, a quaint sitting room. Above the hearth's polished mantel hung the head of a great, dark brown beast. Just looking at it caused prickles of unease to climb Kristin's limbs.

"That's the bear Pa shot a couple of years ago." Jackson came up from behind them. "We did not go hungry that winter."

"A bear..." Kristin regarded the mounted thing. "I have never seen one up so close. I am glad it is not alive."

"Me too. Good thing Pa killed him with only two shots."

"Jack, where are your manners?" Mrs. Sundberg's tone sounded both warm and admonishing. In many ways she reminded Kristin of her own mother.

He quickly swiped off his floppy-rimmed hat. "Hello, Miss Eikaas."

Kristin noticed that one of his eyes was puffy and bruised from this morning's brawl. Other than that, he seemed all right. "Hello, Jackson."

Looking back at his mother, he asked, "When's supper? I am starved."

"In a few minutes." Mrs. Sundberg set her hand on Kristin's forearm. "I hope you have not eaten yet. I made extra so you could join us."

"No, I have not eaten yet." Her stomach rumbled as proof to the statement.

The Sundbergs laughed and Kristin's cheeks flamed.

"We will hurry and show you the rest of the house so we can get supper on the table," Mrs. Sundberg said. "Jack, go wash up."

"Yes, ma'am."

"And Sam, would you fetch your father?"

"Good as done, Ma." He gave Kristin a parting smile before leaving the room.

The heat in her cheeks spread downward into her neck.

A moment later Mrs. Sundberg led her across the front hallway and slid open a pair of paneled doors. "This is our parlor. We only use it for special guests or on holidays."

Mary piped in, "Ma and I like to sew in the sitting room at night. Sometimes Pa, Sam, and Jack go sit on the front porch."

Kristin grinned at the child's enthusiasm.

And then she spotted it. The spinning wheel in the corner, next to the far side of the parlor's hearth. It looked just like *Mor's*.

"It is beautiful!" She strode across the room and knelt beside the large wooden wheel.

"That was Sam's mother's." Mrs. Sundberg tipped her head. "My people did more weaving than spinning."

"Do you know how to spin?" Mary hunkered down beside Kristin.

"Oh, *ja*, my mother taught me."

Mrs. Sundberg smiled. "Then perhaps you can show Mary and me how to spin sometime."

"It would be my pleasure."

"For now, we had best continue with our tour. Supper is already a half hour later than usual."

They ambled upstairs where Kristin saw three bedrooms. Sam shared a room with Jack, and Mary slept in her own small chamber, not much larger than Kristin's room. The biggest room belonged to Mr. and Mrs. Sundberg.

"I am frequently ill, Kristin," Mrs. Sundberg told her. "Lately I have been feeling fairly good, but on the days when my malady takes over, I barely have the strength to climb out of bed." Her dark eyes bore into Kristin's gaze. "That's when I will have to count on you to help me and also care for my family."

"*Ja*, I will be glad to help."

Mrs. Sundberg smiled again, and Kristin realized she had forgotten about being a slave.

"I mean…*yes, ma'am*." She would commit those words to her English vocabulary.

Mrs. Sundberg led the way back down the narrow inside stairwell. In all, Kristin was impressed. While the home was hardly a mansion, it was a glorious sight compared to Uncle Lars's shack.

Back in the main kitchen, Kristin did her best to help Mrs. Sundberg and Mary with supper preparations. Unfamiliar with the layout, Kristin felt burdensome rather than of any use. But when the meal was ready, she made trips back and forth into the dining room, carrying in the plate of sliced pork, the basket of dinner rolls, a bowl filled with cooked red potatoes, and another containing an assortment of cooked greens. She'd learned that six days out of seven, supper consisted of repast. But on Wednesdays, when the men went to market in town, the meal was more like the noon dinner.

As she set the last bowl of food on the table, Kristin gave Sam a smile. He sat beside his father, who was seated at the far end of the table. Jackson sat across from Sam.

Mr. Sundberg cleared his throat, and Sam's gaze jerked to his father. Kristin thought something unspoken seemed to pass through the men, which caused Sam's smile to fade slightly.

Mary entered the dining room and seated herself, and finally Mrs. Sundberg walked in and did the same.

"Please, Kristin, sit down with us."

She backed away, shaking her head. "No, thank you, ma'am."

Mrs. Sundberg's easy grin reached her. She patted the seat of the chair next to hers. "Come and sit."

"It would not be fitting, Mrs. Sundberg." Kristin hurried back into the kitchen and, moments later, heard Sam ask the blessing over the food. She enjoyed the commanding sound of his voice, and as he prayed in English, she tried to pick out the words she knew. Thank you. Food. Bless. Miss Eikaas—

Her gaze flew to the doorway, leading to the dining room. Why had Sam included her in the dinner prayer?

Before she could think about it further, Mrs. Sundberg gracefully strode into the kitchen.

"Please come and eat with us, Kristin."

She shook her head. "I should be ready to serve if anything else is needed."

"We will let you know if more is needed. However, you must eat so you maintain your strength. There is much to do on this farm." She hooked her arm around Kristin's. "Come and eat with us. Rachel always did."

"She did?"

Mrs. Sundberg nodded.

Kristin decided that she must do as she was asked. She allowed the woman to guide her back into the dining room. Jackson kindly held her chair.

"*Takk.*"

"In English, please." Both Sam and Mary spoke at once.

Kristin stared, first at him, then Mary. She couldn't help a grin. "Thank you."

"You're welcome, Miss Eikaas." Jackson's overly polite manner caused Kristin's smile to grow.

"While you are here, I am going to teach you to speak English," Mary said, with a determined expression.

"Now, Mary…"

"Oh, sorry, Ma." She looked at Kristin. "If it is all right with you that I teach you, of course."

"I would like that, Mary." What a kind offer.

"I am almost eleven," the girl added, "and I am a very good student at school. I help the other children who are slower at learning. Someday I hope to be a teacher."

"You will make a fine teacher." Kristin felt touched to the core.

"We will all help you," Jackson said, "by making you speak English to us." He smirked in a jesting manner.

Kristin eyed him. He sat across from her, forking another bite of food into his awaiting mouth. She thought of her own brothers, now in heaven with God. The older one, Kjell, would have been about Jackson's age if he'd lived.

Shaking off her sad past, Kristin helped herself to a slice of pork, a spoonful of greens, and potatoes. Napkin in her lap, she lifted her fork and began eating. A different sort of spice gave her pause as she worked the vegetables around in her mouth. It wasn't hot, just strong and quite pleasant. She swallowed and picked up her knife to cut off a bite-sized piece of meat.

Around her everyone spoke in English, and it seemed as though Mr. Sundberg made some sort of announcement because expressions of surprise and wonder appeared on Jackson's and Mary's faces.

Mary looked across the table and met Kristin's gaze. "Sam is going to Madison," she said in Norwegian. "Madison is our state capitol here in Wisconsin. There is going to be an official hearing for the Menominee Indians, and Sam is going to help mediate."

"It sounds very important."

"It is." Mary bobbed her head. "And Sam might be gone until Christmas."

Kristin worked very hard not to show the inexplicable sense of disappointment winding its way around her insides. Sam had been her only real friend since she'd arrived in Brown County. Now he was leaving and would be gone for months.

But perhaps that was best. Kristin's gaze fell to the food on her dinner plate. She was, after all, his family's slave and in a social class well beneath the Sundbergs. No longer could there be friendship—or anything more—between Sam and herself. Besides, both her uncle and Mr. Sundberg forbid it.

Another wave of disbelief crashed over her. Her family had all but disowned her. The Olstads too. How could they?

When the meal was finished, Kristin noted that she'd cleaned her plate in spite of her toilsome musings. She must have been hungrier than she realized. Standing to her feet, she quietly collected the ironstone china, and when her arms couldn't carry a single additional plate, she made her way into the kitchen.

Mrs. Sundberg entered behind her. "We will make coffee now. I baked apple pies this morning. After dessert, we will wash the dishes."

"Yes, ma'am." She kept her gaze lowered, hoping she behaved in a manner worthy of her new post. What she feared more than anything was disappointing the Sundbergs. If they turned her out, where would she go? What would she do?

"You seem quieter than last Sunday when we visited. You must be tired today."

Kristin shook her head. "No, I am fine. I will work until you tell me to stop."

Mrs. Sundberg paused in the middle of cutting the first slice of pie, and Kristin glanced up to see her peculiar expression.

"Once the dishes are washed, your evenings are your own, Kristin." She smiled. "I suppose I should have said that. You see, Rachel had been with us for so long, I just forgot to state my expectations. I apologize."

"No need."

Mrs. Sundberg continued slicing the pie, and Kristin held out the first plate.

"We begin our day at dawn. Karl, Sam, and Jackson go out and do the milking and fetch fresh eggs. You can use that time to wash and dress."

"Yes, ma'am."

"Rachel usually made coffee, so I will give you that job. But, of course, I will show you how to use the stove first."

Kristin made a mental note.

"When the men and Jackson return from the barn, we make breakfast. There will be days that I will not be able to help you because of my…condition."

"You mentioned before that you are ill. But you look well."

"Thank you." The woman smiled. "I have had a series of good days lately. But when I have one of my episodes, I can barely get out of bed without help."

"I–I am sorry to hear it."

"It is the reason I need a house girl to help me, particularly on those bad days."

Kristin held out a second plate onto which Mrs. Sundberg

lopped another piece of pie. "I will do whatever I can to make things easier for you."

"I know you will." She turned and wiped her hands on her apron. Then she cupped Kristin's face. "That is why I am glad you are here."

The tenderness in Mrs. Sundberg's voice brought tears to the forefront, but Kristin did her best to blink them back.

"I will serve the pie now." She sidestepped Mrs. Sundberg, and with a plate in each hand, she reentered the dining room.

CHAPTER 9

*I*T DOESN'T TAKE a genius to conclude that Kristin is unhappy here, Pa." Sam bridled the horses while Pa straightened the harnesses. "I think she's trying too hard to please us."

"Better than not trying at all."

"I suppose." Sam straightened, waiting for Pa to catch up. "Can't she see she's got better accommodations here? We'll give her a chance at the future."

"I don't know what she sees, Sam. But I do recall warning you to stay away from her."

Sam knew it was so, and yet it proved almost impossible for him to avoid Kristin—not that he wanted to.

Above them, the golden leaves of clustered birch trees shimmered on the morning breeze. Together he and Pa hitched the horses to the wagon so it could be used for riding to church. When they finished, they sauntered to the house to put on their Sunday best.

Both men paused in the mudroom to wash their hands.

"At least she can make coffee the way I like it now," Pa

whispered. "Last three days I thought that brew of hers would take the hair off my chest. It was just that strong."

Sam chuckled. "Maybe you could tell her that—that she succeeded with the coffee. I think you've been awfully terse with her."

"Now, don't go making this my fault, Sam."

"I'm not. I'm only suggesting that you be nicer. Right now she probably can't see a difference between you and that ogre of an uncle of hers."

Pa replied with a look as mean as Kristin's coffee.

Sam only chuckled, causing Pa's features to relax.

"Pa, you've got godly convictions, and you passed your faith onto Jack, Mary, and me. I admire you for it."

Pa inclined his head. "I appreciate the accolade, son." He paused as if he wanted to say more but then moved toward the kitchen. "We had best get moving if we want to make it to church on time. You know how I hate walking in late."

"I know, Pa."

Leaving the mudroom, Sam ran upstairs and changed. Ma had ironed his chambray shirt and dark blue trousers. As was his habit, he buttoned a pair of suspenders to the waistline of his pants then slid them onto his shoulders. Finally he pulled on a dark jacket. Grabbing his Bible, he went back downstairs. He found the ladies waiting outside near the wagon. His gaze fell on Kristin. She looked fetching in her fitted brown dress

"Good morning." Sam reached the wagon, smiled, and set his Bible under the seat. "May I lend my assistance?" He bowed dramatically, garnering a giggle from his sister.

Then he glimpsed Kristin's timid grin and decided his theatrics were well worth the effort.

Ma took his hand, and he lifted her slight frame easily into the wagon. Next he swung Mary into the bed, causing her to squeal. He chuckled and extended his hand to Kristin. She placed her gloved fingers in his palm, and Sam boosted her into the second seat of the wagon, next to Ma. Seconds later Jackson came running from the barn, still sporting a blackened eye from the fight four days ago. He climbed into the back of the wagon. Pa strode out of the barn after him, his jacket slung over one arm.

"Karl, put on your good suit coat," Ma said.

"I will as soon as we get to church. I'm as hot as your cook-stove from searching creation for Jack."

"Sorry, Pa. I wanted to check my traps, and I lost track of time."

"Make sure it doesn't happen again." Pa climbed up into the wagon.

"Yes, Pa."

Sam hopped into the wagon just as his father gathered the horses' reins in one fist.

"Everyone ready?" Pa asked.

"Ready," Ma answered, with Jack and Mary echoing her.

Sitting back in the seat, Sam watched the scenery go by. He still had hay baling to do, but it dried nicely in the field. By this time next month, the winter squash and pumpkins would be ready to harvest.

"The crops are looking well, son." Pa turned to Sam and grinned. "You've done a fine job this year."

"Thanks." Sam didn't hold back a smile. Pa's praise meant a lot, particularly since he didn't dole it out often. That's why going to Madison in his stead meant a great deal to Sam. It meant Pa trusted him—well, at least to a point. It was obvious that Pa didn't trust him around Kristin. But that was Sam's fault, and he took full responsibility. Still, he couldn't seem to help it. When he worked in the fields or in the barn, Kristin permeated his thoughts, almost to distraction. Once he almost let the cows into the pigpen instead of out onto the grassy knoll behind the barn. In the evenings, Sam felt content to watch Kristin sew. She was amazingly adept in mending even Jackson's torn clothes.

But what did his happiness matter if *she* wasn't happy?

Pa nudged him, and Sam returned to the present.

"Did you hear what I just said?"

"No, Pa."

He grunted. "You've never been a daydreamer before." He leaned closer and lowered his voice. "What's with you, Sam?"

He thought about it while sucking in a deep breath. "I've got a lot on my mind."

"Well…" Pa straightened. "You'll be happy to learn that I contacted a friend of mine in Madison. I'm sure he'll be happy to let you stay there for a bit."

"Thanks." Sam's reply came out terser than anticipated, except he disliked his father's manipulation. If Kristin proved to be the wife Sam had been praying for, then there was nothing Pa could do to get between them. But Sam wasn't in any kind of hurry to marry. Neither was Kristin, it would seem.

He caught himself. Why was he entertaining ideas about marrying her anyway? He'd only met Kristin a week ago.

Sam shook off his wayward thoughts, although lately that particular line of thinking had become less and less manageable.

Pa flicked the reins and steered the team into the churchyard. Finding a place in the shade, he pulled the wagon to a halt and braked it.

Jack and Mary jumped down. Pa helped Ma alight, so Sam reached for Kristin, and hands on her waist, he helped her from the seat.

"*Takk.*"

"Excuse me?"

"Thank you." Kristin sent him a look of mild irritation.

Smiling, he turned and trailed behind his parents as they made their way toward the church's opened front doors. Within moments, however, he sensed Kristin hadn't followed. He whirled around to find her still standing near the wagon, her gaze downcast.

Enough was enough. Sam approached her. "Did I offend you?"

She brought her gaze up to meet his. "Offend me? No. How?"

"Well, I…" Sam didn't know how to explain. "Why are you not coming into church?"

Kristin's shoulders seemed to deflate. "I do not know what to do."

"I am not understanding." Sam leaned against the wagon.

"Where do I sit? That is, it is not fitting for me to sit with your family."

"Not fitting?" Sam narrowed his gaze, wondering what that meant. Had the Eikaas-Sundberg feud come to roost in her heart too? Was she ashamed to be seen with Sam and his family? Could that be the reason she appeared so unhappy of late? He decided to press the issue. "Why is it not fitting?"

Kristin's stare clouded with doubt. "Does a slave sit with her owners? I am afraid I don't know what is appropriate. Perhaps I should sit in the back row."

Sam blinked. "Slave? What are you talking about?"

"But of course you know that your father purchased me for a cow and pig. I came all the way from Norway only to be sold into slavery, although I must admit that, even in my low position, your family has treated me very well. Better than my own relatives."

"Kristin, I believe you have misunderstood the circumstances.

133

You are not a slave. My family has a moral opposition against owning slaves. We simply offered you a job, as my mother needs the help around the house." Sam shoved his hands in his jacket pockets. "It was my idea. I only wanted to help."

"And you have. I owe you my life."

"You owe me nothing, Kristin." Sam tried to drive in the point. He had helped Kristin the way he'd help anyone in need. "You work hard. I have seen you the past few days. You have more than earned your wages already."

"Wages?"

"Of course. In addition to room and board you will receive a small monthly payment. I thought Ma would have told you that."

"Perhaps she did…" She gave a single wag of her head before peering down at the tips of her leather boots.

"You have had a lot of information thrown at you. You cannot be expected to recall every detail. But, yes, you will earn a wage."

Kristin brought her gaze up to his. "I am so grateful, Sam."

"I know. We all know that. And you are doing just fine."

Relief spread across her features.

"Now, as for church, you are more than welcome to sit with us, although if you think it will provoke your uncle—"

"Ha! My uncle…what do I care if he is provoked? I will sit with you and your family."

"Very well." Sam felt pleased with her decision. He cupped her elbow and guided her forward. "Ma likes you. And Pa is getting used to your coffee."

Kristin put her gloved hand over her mouth, trying in vain to conceal a grin. "I am learning how to use that fancy stove in the kitchen."

"Yes, and we know it takes time."

Another couple of wagons pulled into the churchyard. The

Dinsmores and the Olessons called out greetings as they passed on their way to find a place to park.

Kristin paused near the doorway. "Thank you, Sam."

"You're welcome." He figured he'd do almost anything to get her to smile. "You look lovely today."

"*Takk*...and I feel so much better, now that I am not a slave." She looked suddenly awed. "And I will earn wages too."

"Your hard work is worthy of every coin." He widened his smile. "Come on. Let us claim our seats before the sanctuary gets too crowded."

~❦~

"The Lord bless thee, and keep thee. The Lord make his face shine upon thee, and be gracious unto thee. The Lord lift up his countenance upon thee, and give thee peace."

Kristin felt a special blessing pour over her as Reverend Wollums finished his sermon. Her dream of someday becoming a business owner wasn't as dashed as she thought. In fact, she'd moved a step closer to achieving her goal. With the money she earned from the Sundbergs, she would save for a shop. Of course, it would mean many years of saving, Kristin knew that. But at least she had real employment. She wasn't a slave.

When the service ended, Kristin filed out of the pew. She glimpsed her uncle and his family, along with the Olstads, and chose to ignore them. She'd been terrified when Uncle Lars pointed that gun in her direction. Neither Peder nor his father stepped in. Only Sam.

Outside, the sun had made its way out of the clouds, warming the late summer day. Mary and Jackson took off with their friends, and Mr. Sundberg and Sam were in a deep discussion with several other men. Kristin glanced to her left and saw Mrs. Sundberg talking with Mrs. Wollums. Unsure of where to wait, she decided to make her way back to the wagon. Perhaps someday soon she would have friends to talk with after church.

Kristin thought of Sylvia and wondered if, instead of saving for a shop, she should save for Sylvia and Mrs. Olstad's passage to America. The sooner Sylvia arrived, the better.

But Peder had been right. What would she and Mrs. Olstad find when they arrived here? Uncle Lars's accommodations were worse than the Olstads' in Norway. What would Sylvia and her mother think of America if they saw the impoverished way the Eikaases lived? Sadder yet, Kristin didn't think it had to be that way. If *Onkel* could build such a sturdy barn, he could put some effort into a house for his family.

Kristin reached the Sundbergs' wagon and leaned against it. Shielded by the shade of a large willow, she felt content to wait. But moments later she saw Peder sneaking around the tree.

She turned her head, refusing to acknowledge him.

"Kristin." His voice was low but insistent. "Kristin, *kommer hit*—come here."

She set her jaw and pretended she couldn't hear him. Did he really think that she would agree to meet him on the sly?

"I am sorry about your uncle's show of temper last week. I just want to make sure that the Sundbergs are treating you all right."

And what if they weren't? What would Peder do about it? Nothing!

Kristin folded her arms, still gazing in the opposite direction.

"Oh, fine, be that way." Exasperation tainted his tone. "But you are the most stubborn girl in all of America!"

She did her best not to grin.

A rustling sound, followed by a second man's voice, caught her attention. She gazed toward Peder and saw Sam standing beside him. They exchanged words that Kristin couldn't hear before Peder took off in a jog. Sam turned toward Kristin and rolled his broad shoulders as he strode forward.

"What did he say?" Kristin asked once Sam was within earshot.

"Nothing really." Sam glanced back over his shoulder. "I caught him off guard, and he did not appreciate it." Despite the fact, he grinned.

"Good. Now Peder knows how it feels to have someone sneak up on you. He does that to me all the time." Kristin gave a shake of her head. "He finds it amusing."

"Hmm…" Sam shrugged out of his jacket and put it and his Bible under the seat of the wagon. "Well, Mary and Jack should be along shortly. Pa told me to round those two up, and I gave it my best shot."

"They do not listen to their older brother?"

"Not even a little."

Kristin smiled at the happy sound of Sam's chuckles and realized that she liked him far better than Peder Olstad.

Then, all at once, she realized that *Onkel's* rejection had been a part of God's special blessing, bringing her to a far better place. She wasn't the one cursed at all. In time she hoped her relatives would realize it and perhaps even speak to her again.

CHAPTER 10

A WEEK PASSED IN a succession of hot days and cooler nights. Kristin fell into a comfortable routine. Mrs. Sundberg's health held out, so the woman felt strong enough to show Kristin how she ran her household. Kristin learned quickly.

Now today, Monday, she and Mrs. Sundberg lingered at the dining room table, planning the week's menus. Kristin discovered that keeping the men fed was priority. Sam and his father worked hard outdoors and expected hearty dinners at noon. She checked the food pantry to be sure they had all the ingredients needed for the next seven days.

"It is all there," Kristin said, bringing Mrs. Sundberg another cup of coffee.

"Good. And Jack snared a couple of rabbits this morning before school." Mrs. Sundberg smiled, looking pleased by another of her youngest son's accomplishments. "We'll make good use of them."

"Indeed."

The planning continued. In a while they would brush off the Sunday clothes and hang them outside to air out. Then they would soak the soiled clothes in preparation for tomorrow's laundry day. They'd feed the chickens and spend a couple of hours in the garden, gathering potatoes, beets, carrots, and onions. Then it would be time to make noon dinner, rabbit stew and freshly baked biscuits.

This afternoon would find them cleaning up after dinner, then scrubbing the kitchen cupboards. Supper would be served at six, and after dishes were washed and homework completed, Jackson would read while Kristin, Mary, and Mrs. Sundberg did mending. Mrs. Sundberg promised Kristin a portion of those wages earned as well as her own monthly salary. Kristin had caught some of the Sundbergs' enterprising spirit.

Kristin rose from the table. "I'll feed the chickens and meet you outside."

Mrs. Sundberg set her cup into its saucer. "I'll be out shortly."

"Take your time."

Humming, Kristin strode to the mudroom where she donned her bonnet before heading out to the barn. The chickens sensed her intentions and clucked at her heels. Entering the barn, she met Sam on his way out.

"Hello, Kristin." He inched his floppy hat higher on his forehead. "Anything I can help you with?"

"Oh, no, thank you. I am just about to feed my squawking little pets."

Sam smiled. "Do not get too attached. One might be Sunday's dinner."

"All the reason I had best feed them." Kristin smiled. "I came from a family of farmers and know better than to grow too fond of any of the animals. Although, I must admit, I learned that lesson of certain heartbreak the hard way. You see, I once fell in love with a piglet. The sweetest pink thing you would ever want to see. But when it reached maturity Poppa had it slaughtered and the meat smoked. I cried for weeks."

Sam grinned and sat on a covered rain barrel in the shade of the barn.

"And I could hardly choke down any pork that winter."

He lowered his head and chuckled. "Sounds like Mary. She is forever taking shines to the calves, baby rabbits, and chicks. Some she actually wraps in blankets and carries them around like they are real infants."

"They are." Kristin gave a little laugh. "I did that too. *Mor* used to say it's God's way of making women out of girls. He put that mothering instinct in us, so it is not our fault, really."

"Really?" Sam's semi-echoed reply held a note of laughter mixed with incredulousness.

Kristin couldn't hold back her mirth any longer. Sam's chuckles joined hers.

"You seem much happier of late."

"Oh, I am very happy. Your mother is very kind to me. She is teaching me many things about running an American household. *Mor* had taught me much, but I was nearing seventeen when she died. It was a year of a terrible fever... well, I cared for my family the best way I could."

"I am sure you did, Kristin."

All the gladness she felt only moments before turned to gloom. "I do not know why God spared me from the epidemic."

"He still had a purpose for you." Sam's voice was calm but insistent. "For instance, if your family had lived, you would not be here in America, helping my mother, who, you will see when she has one of her episodes, needs you desperately."

Kristin smiled. The idea that God had a plan for her made her feel special. But was it really true? How she could know for sure?

Mr. Sundberg suddenly appeared at the edge of the yard. "Sam!" He spoke in English, so Kristin didn't understand him. However, his tone said he wasn't pleased. Next she noticed the look of chagrin spreading across Sam's face like soft butter on hot bread.

"Excuse me, Kristin." Sam slid off the barrel. "Pa's been waiting on me. I sort of forgot."

"Of course. I am sorry to have kept you."

"Do not be sorry. I enjoy talking with you." He gave her a parting smile and, hat in hand, he walked toward his father.

Kristin watched him go, thinking she would definitely miss Sam while he was away in Madison.

Mrs. Sundberg stepped from the house, and Kristin finished feeding the pecking hens. She hurried to catch up with the other woman near the vegetable garden, and that's when Kristin noticed a pained expression on her employer's face.

"Is everything all right, Mrs. Sundberg?"

After a moment's pause, she shook her head. "I think an episode is coming on."

"Let me walk you back to the house."

"No. I should pick these vegetables first."

Kristin saw the look of determination in Mrs. Sundberg's brown eyes. "I will make you a deal." She took Mrs. Sundberg's elbow and led her to a grassy patch near a tall pine tree. "I will pick all the vegetables you want, and you can watch me from here. You can see how fast I am at picking."

Mrs. Sundberg squared her shoulders. "I am not an invalid."

"True. But from what I have heard, you become bedridden when your episodes are in full swing."

She rubbed her arms. "Oh, Kristin, I pray to God the pain leaves my body now and I don't get ill. I have been doing so well…"

"Then rest yourself while I gather the vegetables. When I am done, we'll go back to the house."

Mrs. Sundberg gave a grudging nod before lowering herself onto the grass.

Kristin drew in a breath of thick, hot, summer air. Some of the last of the season, most likely. She wasn't accustomed to this kind of heat and humidity, but she wasn't afraid of hard work.

Pushing up her sleeves, she bent over and began pulling carrots. When she'd finished one row, she looked to Mrs. Sundberg, who directed her over toward the onions. Basket in hand, Kristin walked several feet to where that vegetable had been planted. A short distance away she could see Sam rolling the drying hay. She waved to him. He smiled and returned the gesture.

Hunkering, she began pulling up onions. Perspiration trickled down her neck, and to get her mind off her discomfort, she imagined what it might be like to be a proprietress of her own shop—like Miss Betsy—except Kristin would offer threads, yarns, all different kinds of cording, material, and, of course, dress-making. She figured that in a city the size of Green Bay, more than one of the same sort of shop existed. Perhaps she could find out details, although she was hardly in a position to open a shop yet.

The sun continued to beat down hard, and the front of Kristin's fawn-colored dress dampened. She wiped the droplets of sweat on her face away with her sleeve.

When a row of onions had been harvested, Mrs. Sundberg waved Kristin over.

"I think you need to rest a while, Kristin. Your face is bright red, and it is growing hotter by the minute."

"*Ja*, and I could use a tall glass of water." Placing her hands on the small of her back, Kristin stretched and glanced off in the distance at the house. It wouldn't take her but a few minutes.

Looking at Mrs. Sundberg, she asked, "Shall I fetch some water for the both of us?"

"I'd like that."

"Would you like to walk back to the house with me? I can help you into bed."

"No, I feel good to sit right here in the shade."

Kristin smiled. "All right. But do not pick anything until I get back. I know you will be tempted, but resist."

Mrs. Sundberg laughed, and the sound was light and breezy to Kristin's ears. "You know me well already." Her smile grew. "I promise I will not move until you get back with the water." Her gaze moved to somewhere behind Kristin. "Perhaps you should bring enough for Sam too."

"*Ja*, all right. I will."

As Kristin made her way toward the house, she pushed back her bonnet, allowing what little wind there was to waft through her moistened hair. She'd braided it and pinned it in its usual band around her head. However, even wearing her thick tresses off her neck didn't make her feel any cooler today.

She entered the mudroom and walked to the well, filled the bucket, but then realized the pail would be too heavy for her to carry. Turning to enter the kitchen, she nearly collided with a bare-chested, tanned-skin man who was apparently on his way out. He wore soft-looking moccasins and a breechcloth over the most private part of him, and a sleeveless animal skin robe that hung open enough so Kristin glimpsed the handle of a long, sheathed blade in his leather belt. Her gaze went upward, and she saw his weathered face and deep brown eyes. His thick black hair had been tied back and was held in place by a piece of leather and adorned with feathers.

Kristin stood as still as possible as if waiting for a poisonous snake to strike.

The man spoke to her—in English! She understood when he made mention of Sam, Mariah, Karl. Was he asking where they were? Unsure, she could only shrug.

The dark-eyed man spoke to her again, and this time, reached for her hair. She jumped back and screamed and everything she'd ever read about the "savages" in America inflicting horror and death on white settlers came to mind.

"*Berør ikke meg*—do not touch me!" She slapped his hand away.

The native man's chuckle rumbled low inside his smooth, tanned chest. He spoke again, and Kristin screamed louder. She wanted to run, but the man had worked his brown fingers through the braid in her hair.

"*Vennligst ikke vondt meg*—please do not hurt me!"

He spoke to her in an urgent tone, and Kristin thought he said the word *friend*. But his hand remained in her hair, and each time she pushed him away, desiring to create more space between them, her hair pulled painfully.

"*La meg ga! La meg ga!*" She begged for him to release her. Still, he hung on fast.

Then all at once Sam burst through the mudroom door. His chest rose and fell, and Kristin guessed he'd sprinted from the field.

"Sam, *hjelp meg!*" Kristin covered her face, fearing a bloody fight. The native man possessed a knife, after all.

But Sam spoke to the man in a familiar tone and then chuckled. "Kristin, his ring is tangled in your hair. If you can be still for a minute, he can—"

"Ouch!"

"—pull it out."

The native man held out his hand, and strands from Kristin's head dangled from the metal ring he wore on the middle finger of his right hand.

Kristin massaged her scalp.

The bronze-skinned man said something and gave her a polite bow.

Sam cleared this throat. "Kristin, may I present to you Running Deer." Sam turned and spoke to Running Deer in what sounded like English. When Sam faced her again, he smiled. "Running Deer is my uncle—or step-uncle, if you will. He is my stepmother's brother."

⁘

"She is very beautiful."

Sam eyed his uncle speculatively, hoping the man hadn't gotten any big ideas about Kristin. Since his wife died last year, Running Deer had been searching for another woman.

"She is the one I saw swimming in the pond over a week ago."

"I figured, since you would have recognized the other Eikaas girls, Inga and Anna."

"Old Weasel Eyes's daughters?" Running Deer sent a glance upward. "Yes, I know of them."

Sam had to chuckle over the Oneida name for Lars Eikaas. He'd earned it over the years from ranting at the Indians who dared to cross his property line. Any damage done to the Eikaas farm came from Eikaas himself and not the Indians.

"But there was someone else watching the beauty swim like a white swan. It was a red fox, looking on from the bushes as one who hunts his prey."

"Peder Olstad." Sam thought his uncle's description fit. So the man unashamedly watched Kristin swim that day. *The cad.*

"But I kept my eye on the red fox. Made sure he did not do anything."

"I appreciate it." Sam hadn't ever liked the fact that Running Deer paused to actually watch Kristin. But he hated it more that Olstad was there too.

"She doesn't speak English, eh?"

"No, and I hope you're aware that you scared the liver out of her just now."

"How was I supposed to know she's here? No one told me you hired a new house girl."

"You haven't been around since last week."

His uncle grinned, and tiny crinkles appeared at the corners of his dark eyes. "I went north to hunt for bear."

Sam's interest was piqued. "Any luck?"

"None." Running Deer drew in a deep breath, and his eyes narrowed. "The trappers had gotten there ahead of me. They skin their animals, take the fur, and leave the rest to rot, unlike our people who make use of it all, leaving nothing to waste."

He'd seen and heard the same story before, so Sam knew his uncle spoke the truth.

"The number of animals they slaughter and leave littering the countryside would feed my entire village through the winter months."

"It's a shame." Sam put a hand on his uncle's shoulders. "But maybe I can help. Pa's sending me to Madison to mediate between the Menominee and a U.S. government committee that agreed to hear the band's charges involving their treaty. Perhaps I can bring up this matter of the trappers' wastefulness."

"Ugh! Sam…" Running Deer shook his head. "The more the white government gets involved, the worse it becomes for Wisconsin Indians and our brothers on the Plains. Maybe just keep your mouth shut." He grinned.

Sam replied with a helpless shrug and lowered his arm. "Just trying to help."

Running Deer clapped him on the shoulder. "Indians might get a fair piece if you were in charge of the white government. Your father is right. You should someday run for president."

Sam laughed. "That's Pa's ambition, not mine."

"A pity."

"Depends on how you look at it. But let's change the subject. I've been hearing enough about politics from Pa these last two weeks."

Kristin had run to fetch Ma, and now both of them entered the kitchen by way of the mudroom. Sam glimpsed Ma's tight features and guessed she was having a bad day. Even so, she smiled and hugged her brother.

"Have you met Kristin?" Ma asked.

"Yes." Running Deer eyed her in a way that caused Sam's gut to cinch. "She is lovely." He reached for the braid on her head, causing several hairpins to fall to the floor.

"Ouch!" Her hand flew to her hair, which had now come undone.

"Running Deer, you hurt her." Indignation grew inside of Sam. "Mind your manners, will you?"

"Mmm, soft hair." He held Kristin's long braid in his palm.

Sam read the fear in her eyes as she tried to pull away.

"Unhand her, Running Deer. You're scaring her."

He released her hair. "You are very beautiful," he told Kristin in English. "And your hair is like a rope of fine threads. I would be honored if you were my woman."

Kristin stared at him with a blank expression.

Ma turned to her and translated in Norwegian. A look of horror crept over Kristin's face.

"I don't think she likes you," Sam half-joked to his uncle, although he hoped to discourage him.

"Maybe not—not yet." Running Deer squared his shoulders

and slowly ran his hand down his smooth chest. "But I will show her that she has nothing to fear from me."

"Oh, no," Ma said with a wag of her head. "You are not wooing my new house girl. I need her."

Sam met Kristin's troubled gaze. Then slowly, she made her way to Sam's side.

"What are they saying?" she whispered in Norwegian. "I do not wish to be this man's woman."

"I realize that." Sam gave in to the urge to comfort Kristin and set his arm around her shoulders, hugging her to his side. "But do not worry. My uncle will not harm you."

Ma glanced at him, then Kristin, before looking back at Running Deer. "As you can see," she said in English, "you'll have to get into line if you want to court her." A twinkle entered her eyes.

"Hmm, yes…" Running Deer's dark gaze assessed the situation. "She runs to you, Sam. But we will see who she runs to in the days to come."

"It's not a competition."

"Good."

Sam didn't like the sound of this, especially since he was leaving in ten days. "Leave her alone, Running Deer."

"Do you and she have an understanding?"

Sam's gaze slid to Kristin, and he noted her puzzled expression. He wished he could lie, but he couldn't. "No." He looked at his uncle now. "We do not."

"I say, until you do, I am free to try and win her affection." Running Deer folded his arms, looking Norwegian obstinate, a trait he'd obviously picked up from Pa.

Sam didn't know how to argue the point. He glanced at Ma, deciding it was a good thing Pa wasn't here to see this. He'd send Sam to Madison at tomorrow's first light instead of at the end of the month as planned.

"Kristin, we had better start dinner." Ma changed the subject and spoke in Norwegian.

"Yes, ma'am."

"I have already skinned the rabbits. They are in the sealed pot that I lowered into the well so they would stay fresh." She looked at Running Deer, reverting to English once more. "You are welcome to have the rabbit fur."

"Many thanks." He tipped his head. "And may I join you for your noon meal?"

"Of course." Ma smiled. "But first, will you bring in some potatoes for the stew? Your surprise visit interrupted Kristin, and she didn't get finished in the garden."

"I will take her with me." Running Deer smiled at Kristin.

Sam felt her shrink closer to him. "I think not."

Running Deer snorted a reply and then marched out of the kitchen.

Ma laughed softly. "Sam, you're incorrigible," she said in English. "And Kristin?" Ma stepped closer to them and spoke in Norwegian. "Please do not be afraid of my brother. He will not force himself on you or hurt you in any way. However, you will have to let him know that his advances are not welcome."

"Advances?"

"He has taken a liking to you, Kristin." Ma spoke softly.

"So I gathered." She peered up at Sam, her blue eyes beseeching him to help her.

And he would too. "If Running Deer comes too close to you, just say *I am not interested in you* in English. Try it."

Kristin's pink mouth moved as she tried the words on her tongue. "I ern't interested you."

"Close." Sam grinned. "*I am not interested in you.* Keep practicing."

"I er not interested you."

"In you," Sam coached.

Kristin made her way to the well to fetch the rabbit meat. "I er not interested *in you.*"

"Good!" Sam smiled and glanced at Ma, who laughed under her breath.

"I guess that's one way to learn English," she said. "I am sure it won't be the first time she'll have to use that line against an overeager suitor."

Sam prayed that Kristin would never have a suitor—other than himself. And that she would never use that line on him.

He forced his thoughts to the present and took off his hat. Pulling out his soiled handkerchief, he rubbed the sweat from his brow and neck. "I'd best go finish my work while you ladies start cooking." He peered out the window at his uncle, clad in his sleeveless buffalo robe. Maybe he'd enlist Running Deer's help too—just to keep him away from Kristin.

CHAPTER 11

KRISTIN STEPPED OUT of the church the following Sunday morning, thinking summer made its last hurrah. Already the air felt thick and hot, and the white puffy clouds hung low in the blue sky. After greeting several people, Kristin made her way to the Sundbergs' wagon. At least it had been parked in the shade of a leafy oak tree.

As she waited for the Sundbergs there, she watched in amazement as Peder boldly approached her. "*God morgen*," he greeted her.

Kristin gave him curt nod. She still felt hurt, angry, and disappointed in Peder and Mr. Olstad for not coming to her aid nearly two weeks ago.

"Do you know that a savage has been following you?" Peder set his hands on his trim waist. "I saw him lurking around as you and the Sundberg women bathed in the pond last evening."

"You saw us bathing?" Indignation plumed inside of Kristin.

"I did not stare," he recanted. "I just…glimpsed you." To his credit, Peder shifted uncomfortably.

"Peder, you had no right to be anywhere in that vicinity. That is Sundberg property!"

"Lower your voice." Peder glanced around. "I only have a few minutes while your aunt and uncle speak to Reverend Wollums about Inga. It seems she has taken up with the blacksmith."

Kristin frowned. "Mr. Frantzen?"

"*Ja*, except he denies it."

Kristin believed the man over her cousin. But that wasn't her concern. Peder's spying was! "You are despicable. I should speak to the reverend about *you*!"

"Ah, but you won't." Peder's hazel eyes twinkled. "Because, if you do, I will have to tell your uncle that you did not give him all your inheritance. You purchased garments in town and still wear your mother's necklace."

Kristin inhaled sharply and touched the spot beneath her dress where the gold cross hung. "I used my own money in town and..." She tipped her head. "How did you know about my necklace?"

"I saw it once when we were on the ship. You were in your chemise, and—"

"Peder!"

"I walked into our cabin while you changed clothes, but quickly left again when I saw you were not dressed. Still, I glimpsed the necklace."

"*Mor* gave it to me. It was a gift."

"I wonder if your uncle will see it that way too."

Kristin refused to be intimidated. "What I have and what I do is no longer any concern of my uncle's. He all but disowned me."

Peder lifted one shoulder in a careless shrug. "But that is not what I need to tell you."

"Then state your business."

"That savage who follows you..."

"Running Deer? He's not a savage. He's Oneida Indian and Mrs. Sundberg's brother." Kristin had gotten somewhat accustomed to seeing the man around the Sundbergs' farm. "He hunts on the Sundbergs' land sometimes."

"Your uncle said the Sundbergs are getting ready to sell you to those Indians."

"That's preposterous." Kristin didn't believe a word of it.

Peder laughed. "I suppose it is." So he had been teasing, eh?

Kristin gave her head a shake. "Why do you torment me?"

All humor drained from his face. "Because it is your fault that I am here in this country, Kristin. It is your fault that I am living with your uncle in poverty, earning no wages. I had it better for me in Norway."

"Have you looked for work?"

"Your uncle keeps me too busy to hunt for a paying job."

Kristin understood his frustration. "Soon all the work will be caught up, Peder. You'll find work. And, here in America, you have a chance to be a landowner someday. That is your dream. Remember?"

"That dream has left me, Kristin." He pointed a finger at her. "And it is all your fault."

"Maybe not so much as you would like to believe." Kristin pulled herself up to her full height. "I did not force you to come to America. You chose to come. And I did not hear you defend me against my uncle's bad temper the day the Sundbergs came to hire me. Maybe they would have admired your tenacity and hired you too."

Peder took a menacing step forward. "How dare you blame this on me."

"And how dare you blame me!"

"I think of my mother and Sylvia. How will they ever come to this country? What will they find if they make the journey?"

The idea wound its way around her heart. Kristin shrank,

recalling, yet again, how she felt when she'd first glimpsed Uncle Lars's home.

"But you are very comfortable at the Sundbergs' home, aren't you?"

"*Ja*, I am—but it wasn't my plan to go there and work. Remember? My uncle said I was cursed and wanted me off his property. No one defended me, not you, not your father who acted like my own *far* after Poppa died. Is the incident coming back to your mind now? After all I suffered, why should I not be happy now?"

"You should be ashamed. Do you ever think of us? How we might be suffering?"

"No. I do not think of you. I am very busy, cooking, cleaning, helping with chores around the Sundbergs' farm.

"You are selfish, Kristin." Peder scowled. "And my suffering is a result. You made America sound so good to us."

"You read my uncle's letters, just as I did. Hate him. Not me."

"But you encouraged us, Kristin. Every day you fed us pieces of lies."

"Bah!" She threw a hand at him. "You hate me because you are a man filled with hatred. That is all."

"And I will hate you—forever. Because of you, I am like a man in quicksand with no escape."

"What a man thinks in his heart, so is he."

The paraphrased piece of God's truth seemed to rile Peder all the more. He raised his voice. "This is your fault!"

"Your situation is not my fault, Peder." She took a step back. "Nor is it my concern."

"And how do you imagine that I will get out of the bad situation in which I find myself? I have no money." Peder glanced over his shoulder and pulled something from his jacket pocket. Lowering his voice he moved toward Kristin. "Look at this." He unfolded the paper—a page from a newspaper. "It is in English, but there is a man here at church who read it to me. It is the *California Star* from April of this year and only one of many pages printed about the 'immensely rich' gold mines in the Sacramento Valley. The man I referred to is leaving for this territory by the ocean known as California. Men are getting rich very quickly there, and I would like to go with him, but how can I?" Peder's expression darkened as he refolded the page. "I have no money for the journey!"

"And that is *my* fault?" Kristin lifted a defiant chin, refusing to accept blame.

"*Ja*, you brought us here!" Peder came at her with his hands poised as if he'd like to strangle her.

"Hey! Leave her alone!" Jackson jogged over from where he'd been chasing around in the churchyard with some other boys. "Kristin, are you all right?"

Just as Jackson reached them, Peder spun around and gave the boy a shove. Not expecting it, Jackson landed on his backside.

Kristin shrieked.

Peder chuckled. "That will teach you to mind your own business, *half-breed*."

The boy worked to catch a breath.

"Peder, he is a child." Shock and rage welled up in Kristin. "Look, you have knocked the wind out of him. How could you?" She went to help Jack to his feet, but he waved her away.

Instead, he balled his fists and went after Peder. But Kristin jumped in between the two.

"No, Jackson. Stop!"

"He's part savage," Peder taunted. "He cannot help himself."

Kristin whirled on Peder, tempted to knock the man upside the head herself. "Do not speak to Jackson that way."

"It is true." Peder peered at the boy. "They call you half-breed, isn't that right, boy?"

"Get out of the way, Kristin." Jackson clenched his jaw.

"I will not!"

Then suddenly everything happened so fast.

Jackson charged Peder.

Peder raised his fists and shouldered Kristin out of the way. Except somehow his elbow connected with her chin.

The blow sent her reeling backward, and she landed hard on the ground. The sound of a freight train filled her head as the whole world went dark.

"Will you sit down, son? You're making me nervous!"

Sam stopped pacing and glanced at Pa. "Oh, all right." He headed for one of the several wooden armchairs lined up against the wall in Dr. Støen's office. "I'm just worried about Kristin."

"We all are, Sam." Ma's soothing voice caused some of the tension in his shoulders to ebb.

"Olstad ought to go to jail for this." The chair creaked beneath Sam's weight.

"Some people are saying that about your little brother." Ma sent a stern look Jackson's way. "Mrs. Hansen said he belongs in a home for wayward boys. It is, after all, his second fight in less than two weeks."

"The Hansens always side with the Eikaases," Pa muttered. "Still, that's no excuse for brawling."

Jack sat up a little straighter. "But I was defending myself and protecting Kristin. The first time I defended Mary and myself."

"Now look, son, we've told you all your life that ignorant people are going to call you names just because of who you are. You're to turn the other cheek just like the Good Book says."

"But when I do, the boys call me a sissy." Jack lifted a proud chin. "Running Deer said I'm Oneida, so I should act courageous and brave."

"Courageous and brave doesn't mean brawling, and you mustn't confront a full-grown man like Mr. Olstad." Exasperation lined Pa's forehead. "You're to respect your elders."

Jack sulked but managed to mutter a "Yessir."

Sam's heart ached for his brother—ached for all Indians. And the flame of indignation that burned inside of him was fueled all the more by this incident with Olstad.

Dr. Støen stepped from out of the back room, pulling the thick blue drape, which hung in the doorway, closed behind him. A husky, white-bearded man, he slowly came toward the waiting area.

Everyone stood.

"No broken bones." Dr. Støen smiled. "But Miss Eikaas has got quite an impressive bruise on her face."

"Like my black eye?" Jack asked. "It lasted more than a week."

Sam grinned at his brother's fervor.

"Yes, well, I'm sure Miss Eikaas's bruise will only look worse before it fades."

"Can we see her?" Ma asked.

"Yes, in fact, she's a bit sore from the fall and could use a little help dressing."

"Of course." Ma stepped around Jack.

"Can I come too?" Mary was right behind her.

Ma nodded then thanked Dr. Støen, and she and Mary disappeared into the back.

"Thanks, Doc." Pa shook the man's hand.

"Glad to be of assistance, Karl." Dr. Støen's thick lips curved upward beneath his snowy beard. "I'm just glad I was in church this morning when the accident occurred."

"Accident?" Sam didn't see it as such.

Pa shooed Jackson out of the office. "Wait by the wagon and don't get yourself into more trouble. Hear me?"

"Yes, Pa."

Sam took a deliberate breath. "An *accident*, Doctor?"

"That's what Miss Eikaas called it. She blames herself. She said she should have run to get you, Sam, or you, Karl, but instead she tried to break up the argument herself."

"It was an all-out fight." Sam's ire was up. "And Olstad, an adult, started it—with a twelve-year-old boy!"

"Most unfortunate." The physician's eyes narrowed, and his steady gaze held Sam's. "To tell you the truth, I'm growing tired of all the divisiveness in our little church. It's downright distracting, not to mention ungodly. The missus and I are going to start attending services elsewhere. We told Reverend Wollums that this morning. And I've got to tell you…" Dr. Støen gave a single wag of his head. "There are plenty of folks who sympathize with my wife and me. They'll likely be leaving too."

"Sorry to hear it." Pa folded his arms. "Seems to me all this mess began when the Eikaases moved here from Muskego. The man's a troublemaker, and it's *he* who ought to find another place of worship."

"I might agree with that, Karl. I've treated Lars for some cuts and bruises over the years, due to his scrapes with other men in town. It's never his fault. Always someone else to blame. Unfortunately, anger is contagious, and his has become a virtual epidemic in our small Norwegian church."

"It's a plague, all right." Sam thought it began with small congregations and spread to governments that swindled land away from Indians.

"His niece is quite different, isn't she?" Dr. Støen rolled down his shirtsleeves. "A lovely, well-mannered young lady."

"Yes, she is." Sam gave Pa a pointed look.

Pa snorted.

Dr. Støen looked suddenly disappointed. "Karl, you keep up this hatred between you and Lars Eikaas, and you'll have apoplexy."

"Oh, now, Doc...I've tried to make amends with that stubborn ol' mule. Look! I've taken in his niece, given her a job!"

Dr. Støen stroked his beard. "I don't know what more can be done. The reverend feels the same way. It takes all his strength just to keep the peace between the divided congregation." With a hooded glance at Pa, the doctor walked to his desk and retrieved his dress jacket. "Reverend Wollums is thinking of moving on himself."

"What?" Pa was obviously taken aback. "After we built that fine church and parsonage for him?"

"Brick and mortar don't make a church, Karl. Believers do."

"I know that." Pa folded his arms, looking as stubborn as ever. "I don't need another sermon today."

"All right, but if you'd been listening to Reverend Wollums this morning, I wouldn't be lecturing you right now. The hatred's got to stop."

"I agree! No argument here!" Pa shifted and appeared suddenly more thoughtful. "Maybe if we invite the Wollumses to dinner and discuss this matter..."

"That'd be a start, I'd say." Dr. Støen shrugged into his jacket. "Now, if you'll excuse me, I'm going to join the missus over at the hotel's eatery for a noon dinner."

"Enjoy," Sam said. "And thanks again."

The doctor gave him a nod and a friendly slap on the back. "Nice to see you again, Sam."

"Same here." After the doctor left, Sam turned and looked at Pa. "Are you ready to call a truce now?"

"Son…" Pa picked up pacing where Sam had left off. "I've been ready to make peace with that mule-headed Lars Eikaas for years." Pa stopped. "But, I'm telling you, he won't have it. Know why? He's got a guilty conscience. I still believe he stole those silver spoons I acquired in a trade for a team of horses."

"But we can't prove it, so let the Lord be the judge."

Pa grumbled. "*Ja, ja…*" He reverted to his native language. "But coin silver is worth more than a dollar an ounce these days. Those spoons would be worth almost thirty dollars!"

"I know, Pa. But the fact is they're gone. So let the matter go."

Pa raised his hands in a helpless gesture.

Sam arched a brow. "And I would like you to know that I hope to court Kristin when I return from Madison." He'd been praying—no, dreaming—about courting her for days now, since his uncle showed interest in Kristin.

"Now, that's a whole 'nother matter." Pa walked up to Sam so they nearly stood chest-to-chest. "You don't want to marry that girl. She can't speak a lick of English."

"On the contrary. She can say, 'I am not interested in you' quite well." Sam couldn't subdue a short chuckle.

Pa found no humor in the attempt at levity. "We will have this conversation at another time and in my office at home." He growled the statement. "But get ideas of courtship out of your head or I'll—"

"You'll what, Pa?" Sam knew his father loved him, so he had no problem challenging his implied threats. "You'll disown me?"

"Of course not. Don't be foolish."

"Throw me off your land? Disinherit me?"

"Don't give me any ideas." A facetious note rang in Pa's voice.

In spite of himself, Sam felt a grin threatening.

"Seriously, Sam, I've lost enough people in my life. Friends. Family. Your mother…" Pa stared at the half-curtained windows facing the main road. "I don't want to lose you. I want the best for you." He tipped his head and met Sam's gaze. "And marrying an Eikaas isn't the best."

Sam shook his head. "Like you said, we'll have this conversation at another time and in your office at home." With that, Sam strode to the door, opened it, and left the doctor's office for the wagon, parked on the street.

CHAPTER 12

ROM HER CHAIR on the Sundbergs' covered front porch Kristin watched the dark clouds gathering in the distance.

"God willing, we'll see some rain and a reprieve from today's heat." Sam sat on the edge of the white porch, his feet on the first step and his forearms dangling over his knees.

"*Ja*, that would be nice." Kristin ran her fingers across her jaw. It hurt to talk.

"Would you like another cool rag?" Mrs. Sundberg leaned over and touched Kristin's wrist. "Mary will fetch it."

"Sure I will." The girl glanced over her shoulder from her place beside Sam.

Mr. Sundberg and Jack were tending to the animals.

"I think I am fine for now. Thank you." Kristin hated to be an object of copious attention, but that's all the Sundbergs had done today; they had seen to her every need. Never had an employer treated her with such kindness. She knew she could never repay this family for everything they'd done for her.

"I still say Olstad ought to be jailed for assaulting you and

Jack," Sam said. Still in his Sunday best, he'd rolled up his sleeves to the elbows and removed his black ribbonlike tie.

"No, Sam. I think that would only make matters worse. Peder is so angry with me." Kristin felt a shudder coming on despite this afternoon's heat. "I am shocked by his intense hatred. We grew up together. His sister is my very best friend. How can he say he hates me?"

"Maybe because it is easier to blame someone else than face his situation head-on." Sam gazed at the growing storm clouds. A roll of thunder warned of their approach. "Kristin, you did not shackle the man and force him to come to America. Peder and his father made their own decisions based upon your uncle's letters. If there is anyone to blame, it is Lars Eikaas."

"True. My uncle is not a good man—like my father was. I realize that now. Even though Poppa had talked about his brother and the trouble that seemed to follow him, I believed *Onkel* had turned his life around because of his letters. He made it sound as though he had a farm as productive and as attractive as…as yours." Kristin thought it over. "In fact, he may well have described your place in his letters."

"But surely Lars knew you and the Olstads would see the truth with your own eyes upon your arrival in Brown County." Mrs. Sundberg sat forward wearing a curious frown.

"But by then *Onkel* knew he would have my inheritance." Kristin looked at her and then Sam. "As you know, a woman cannot legally inherit anything in Norway. I realize now that Uncle Lars wanted everything my parents left—but it only amounted to my poppa's gold watch, which, I believe, *Onkel* promptly sold."

"That devil," Sam muttered.

"But perhaps Lars will use that money to make improvements to his home and property." A sympathetic chord sounded in

Mrs. Sundberg's voice. "We should give him the benefit of the doubt."

"Why?" Sam turned toward his mother, skepticism written on his face. "Mr. Eikaas has not done much since he arrived here five years ago. We supplied the lumber for his barn, and the community pitched in for its raising. Then Mr. Eikaas picked up scraps of wood and erected that shanty of his. Each winter everyone worries Mrs. Eikaas and children will freeze to death. Now fall is coming, and soon another winter will be upon us. He has not done preparations to the house as far as I could see when we picked up Kristin a couple of weeks ago."

Kristin had already feared every word of Sam's remark, and how blessed she felt to be here with the Sundbergs!

"Perhaps now that two able-bodied men are visiting him, they will help Lars rebuild his home." Mrs. Sundberg gave Kristin a hopeful smile.

"It will take more than lumber and nails to make my relatives a home. *Mor* always said that a house is not a home and that it is a woman's job to make it such." Kristin wondered if *Tante* did what she could with what she had. However, there was no love inside those four unhewn walls. Little wonder Inga set her mind on escaping in any way possible. Even if it meant lying and entrapping poor Mr. Frantzen.

But, of course, that was mere speculation on Kristin's part.

"I am sure you miss your family very much," Mary said.

"I do." Kristin talked about her younger brothers and her parents. Poppa had farmed and worked part-time at the post office. *Mor* had taught her how to use a spinning wheel and sew.

Finally she realized how much she'd monopolized the conversation.

"I am terribly embarrassed for babbling on like a little brook."

"Why?" Sam grinned. "We enjoy it—helps us to become better acquainted with you."

"We sheered our sheep this spring." Mrs. Sundberg narrowed her gaze, and Kristin sensed she pondered an idea. "I wonder if we have more wool in the barn. Karl sold some in town, but…"

"I'll go see, Ma." Mary sprang from her chair, ran down the porch steps, and sprinted across the front yard in her good Sunday dress.

Mrs. Sundberg clucked her tongue.

Kristin felt a tad confused.

Mrs. Sundberg turned to her. "If we have more wool, would you like to spin it? You may use Sam's mother's spinning wheel." She glanced at Sam for confirmation.

He gave a nod of approval.

Kristin smiled in a way that sent a painful jolt through her head. "Oh, *ja*, I would like that very much." She couldn't help a wince. "I can spin it into yarn or thread, whichever you desire."

"Good. However, you need another cool rag for that jaw." Mrs. Sundberg rose. "I'll be back shortly."

"I'll get it, Ma." Sam stood.

Mrs. Sundberg held out a forestalling hand before she walked gracefully to the door. She lifted the hems of her printed dress and entered the house.

Sam took a few long strides and then sat on the porch rail. "I think if my mother can look down from heaven and see us, she would be pleased that you will use her spinning wheel."

Kristin smiled, careful not to move too quickly and hurt her injured jaw. "It is my pleasure. It will bring me happy memories of my own mother."

Sam returned her smile before glancing at the storm, growing ever closer. "You know, when you spoke about Olstad's hatred and how it was so difficult to understand, I started thinking about Ma's people, the Oneida, and the Menominee, and the hatred they face daily. You saw firsthand what happened to Jack and Mary as they walked to school. And what happened with Jack today."

"More hatred?" Kristin frowned. "But Peder has no reason to hate Jackson."

"Well, I do not believe Olstad knocked my brother down for no reason. And it wasn't just because Jack butted into Olstad's so-called business."

"I suppose you are right." Peder's disgraceful behavior sickened Kristin.

"You heard him call Jack a savage and a half-breed. Olstad hates my brother because of who—make that *what*—he is. Oneida Indian."

"Sam, it makes no sense. First and foremost Jackson is a boy like any other. He is a soul, whom our heavenly Father deeply loves."

"Prejudice doesn't make sense to people like us, Kristin. We're people who can see beyond any particular race. Perhaps it is a gift, because the Good Book says the Lord Himself doesn't look at a man's appearance but at his heart."

Kristin recognized the truth and gave a nod. "I never thought of it that way." But she did suddenly see Sam as possessing all the potential his father boasted about. Earlier Mrs. Sundberg had told Kristin that Sam's father had big plans for his son's future—and that future involved a leadership role in this country's government. Kristin could envision it for Sam. He had a mild temperament and the courage to speak the truth.

He chuckled. "Why are you staring at me like that?"

Kristin blinked. "I apologize. I did not mean to be rude." She felt her cheeks flame with embarrassment. "I just realized that what your father wants for your future seems to fit you perfectly. I think you will someday be an important man, Sam."

He laughed. "My father is ambitious for me, no doubt. The truth is that I don't have to be a politician in Madison or Washington to make a difference in this world. I would be happy to bridge the prejudicial gap in my local church—in this community." He pressed his lips together in momentary thought. "All I know is that I want to fight against it somehow."

"You will make a difference, Sam, because that is where your heart is."

"Part of it, anyway." Another rumble of thunder caused Sam to glance off in the distance before he looked back at Kristin. "Where is your heart?"

"That is a good question." Lowering her gaze, she watched her left forefinger trace a square in the fabric of her blue, green, and white plaid dress. "My dreams to build a life for myself in America have blurred." She shook her head, so as not to give Sam the wrong impression. "But I am not unhappy." She brought her eyes back up to meet his.

"Good." Sam's deep-blue gaze pierced through to her soul. "I want you to be happy, Kristin."

"I am—for the most part."

"But you wish things were different between your family, the Olstads, and you?"

"No. How can you ask me that? Those people are dead to me. My uncle would have liked to kill me. I saw it in his eyes."

"Kristin, I know you've been hurt, but you must forgive them."

"Never!"

"Ma likes to say that unforgiveness is like drinking poison and expecting the other person to die."

"Hmm…"

"Unforgiveness will only eat you up inside, little by little."

Kristin didn't know how to reply. On the one hand, she believed Sam, but on the other, she felt such deep, abiding anger at her uncle and his family as well as the Olstads.

"Years ago Pa and his best friend, John Sylvester, were ambushed on their way to the trading post. Pa had married Ma, and she was expecting Jackson. Well, when Pa didn't come home when he said, Ma began to worry. No one in our settlement at the time would listen to her because she was an Indian, so I had to find the Territorial marshal and report Pa's disappearance. Days later Pa was found, barely alive. Sauk Indians, specifically some leftovers of Black Hawk's warriors who wandered back up into the Menominee Nation to wreak havoc on the white settlers, beat Pa and John, stole their furs, took their horses, and burned everything else. John was killed. My father survived."

"That is horrible!" Kristin had heard such stories about the brutal "savages" in territorial America.

"It is horrible, all right, but Pa doesn't hate those men. Never did. He forgave them."

"And the Indians? Were they ever brought to justice?"

Sam shook his head. "Not in American courts. They were brought up before a tribal counsel and released."

"That does not seem very fair."

"No…" Sam stared at the floor of the porch. "But the Sauk felt their braves had a right to attack. You see, back then, Black Hawk, a fierce Sauk leader, opposed the treaty that pushed his people west of the Mississippi River. Anger ran rampant. Hatred developed out of that anger."

"But is there not enough land in America for everyone?"

"I guess there is. But it is the principle. The U.S. government thinks it is savvy business to get the Indians to cede their land. When the Indians discover it, they feel tricked—cheated."

Kristin could understand how they would.

"They have been ousted since Europeans entered this country, even though they are willing to share their land. However, sharing has not been good enough for American leaders. The Oneida, for instance"—Sam shifted his weight and looked back at Kristin—"were originally from the state of New York. More than fifty years ago, they signed a treaty giving up millions of acres so the Erie Canal could be built. My mother was an infant when her people arrived in Wisconsin. Years later, her people made a pact with the Menominee and Winnebago Nations to share the land among them. The Sauk and Fox Nations lived in the southern half of Wisconsin and have, little by little, lost their land to the government also. They are angry. My father understands this and, for that reason, refuses to hold a grudge against them."

"But there are those," Kristin said, putting all the pieces together, "who resent the Indians for fighting to keep their land."

"Yes, you are correct."

"Like my uncle." She blew out a breath, trying to think how a solution would be reached. "You have a lot of work ahead of you, Sam."

He chuckled. "So it seems."

From out of the corner of her eye, she saw a flash of movement. Mr. Sundberg came into view and walked onto the front lawn.

"Sam?"

He spoke in English with a heavy frown lining his forehead. Kristin didn't understand the rest of what he said. But gauging from Sam's reaction, he wanted to speak with Sam privately.

"Excuse me, Kristin." Sam spoke in Norwegian. "Pa needs my help in the barn."

"Of course."

She watched as Sam descended the porch steps and walked with his father across the front lawn.

Mrs. Sundberg stepped from the house and handed Kristin a cold wet rag. Setting it against her throbbing jawbone, Kristin released a sigh. "Feels good."

"I thought it would." Mrs. Sundberg's dark eyes trailed her husband and Sam as they strode to the barn.

Another growl of thunder, louder this time, resounded from above.

"A storm is coming, sure as the dawn." Mrs. Sundberg sat back in her chair. "It will clear the air."

Kristin wondered if she referred to the impending conversation between Sam and his father or the thundershowers moving in.

<hr />

"Your ma told me that Kristin wanted to use the spinning wheel." Pa fetched one of Ma's tall baskets. "I sold most of the wool already. Just have this here bundle left." He lowered the tightly woven container from the upper level of the barn and into Sam's waiting arms. "It has been to the carding mill already. I think your mother was saving it for batting. But there's plenty more." Pa climbed back down the ladder. "Tell Kristin she can have this bundle to spin, if she's so inclined. I don't mind."

Sam felt impressed. "That's real nice, Pa."

"*Ja*, well…" He muttered the rest of his reply.

"I'll be sure Kristin gets this." Sam balanced the basket on his shoulder. It didn't feel heavy, just awkward to carry.

"Sam?"

He turned.

"I don't guess I have to remind you to keep your eye on the prize and don't get distracted."

"Oh, I've got my eye on the prize, all right."

"I don't mean the Eikaas girl."

Sam swallowed a chortle.

"Sam, you're a man of twenty-one years, and Wisconsin is a brand-new state. There will be openings in all branches of the legislature, and with your smarts, easy manner, and good looks, you're sure to be elected."

All laughter aside, Sam strode to where his father stood. "Pa, you raised me right, in the admonition of the Lord, and now you've got to trust me. You said yourself that I'm a man. That means I have to make my own decisions. I'm willing to go to Madison. I'm looking forward to seeing what God has for my future—and I'm not sure if Kristin is a part of it or not. But that's between the Lord and me."

Pa narrowed his gaze. "Even Moses went to his father-in-law for advice. Don't discount my words, Sam. This Eikaas girl will do your future no good."

"Because she's an Eikaas?"

"Because she has no influence, not to mention she has no idea of how the United States government is comprised."

"She's intelligent. She can learn."

"But you don't know this girl!" Pa lifted his hands, emphasizing his point.

"I guess that's what a courtship is for, right?"

Pa let out an exasperated groan.

"Unless you can think of a biblical reason, not a political one, that I shouldn't court Kristin, then you've got no argument. No case against her, other than your own prejudice."

"What? I don't have a prejudiced bone in my body."

"Perhaps, then…" Sam chose his words carefully. "…you have a spirit of unforgiveness, which taints your view of Kristin."

"That's ridiculous! And how dare you question my faith and my spirit."

Sam exhaled. "I meant no disrespect. I want your blessing, Pa. And I want to court Kristin. Won't you, at least, pray about the matter—as I am?"

Pa's lips formed a firm line of disapproval before he marched out of the barn.

Still a no. Couldn't Pa see that he behaved like a hypocrite?

Somewhat discouraged, Sam followed, carrying the wool. Dark clouds now concealed every trace of daylight, and a flash of lightning split the sky. Just as they reached the back door of the house, fat raindrops began to fall.

"We'll get our rain, all right." Pa paused in the mudroom and glanced out the wove-wire screen, covering a third of the door. Because of the overhang, the rain didn't spray into the house.

"Crops need the water." Sam had been praying for rain. He walked around his father and placed the basket of wool in a dry corner of the mudroom. Then he traipsed through the house and out onto the front porch.

The first sight that greeted him was Running Deer standing near Kristin with three fox furs, dangling from a bow-supported line.

"What are you doing?" Sam leaned one hand against the house and stuck the other on his hip. As usual, his uncle wore a buffalo-skin robe, breech cloth, moccasins, and "dingle dangle" around his neck, as some whites called it.

"I am offering a great gift to my woman."

"She's not your woman." Sam had tired of this game already.

"Running Deer," Ma said gently, "Kristin already said she's not interested in you."

Sam hid a grin.

Pa sauntered out onto the porch and stretched. He did a

double take when he saw Running Deer. "What are you doing here?"

"I can't come to visit my family?"

"Of course you can. You're welcome anytime. You know that." Pa set his hands on his hips. "I just didn't expect you, is all."

"He's offering a gift to Kristin." Mary reported the situation with wide eyes. "I went to fetch wool in the barn but couldn't find Pa. Instead I ran into Running Deer, and he told me he wants Kristin to be his woman."

"Is that right?" Pa's eyes darted to Sam.

Sam ignored the silent goad.

Pa snorted back a chuckle.

"Look what he's giving her." Excitement rimmed Jackson's tone as he ran one hand over the reddish-brown furs. "Three fox skins. They're worth a lot of money, aren't they, Pa?"

"Three months' worth of wages, at least." Pa glanced at Running Deer. "You really think your people will accept a blonde-haired, blue-eyed woman as your wife?"

"They will if I say so." Running Deer tipped his head. "They accepted you as Mariah's husband, didn't they?"

"Yeah, Pa." Sam slapped his father on the shoulder blades. "They accepted *you*."

"That's different." Pa grumbled the reply and tossed a warning glare at Sam.

He laughed.

Running Deer turned to Kristin and again offered the fox furs. "Translate for me, Mary."

"All right."

Sam disliked his little sister's eagerness.

"I give these furs to you, Kristin, as an offering of my affection." He bowed and held out the skins. "I ask for nothing in return. So take them."

Mary translated in Norwegian, adding correctly that if Kristin refused the gift, Running Deer would feel a great insult.

Sam watched as a mix of reluctance and apprehension pinched Kristin's lovely features. But she accepted the furs and thanked Running Deer in English.

"You're welcome."

He inclined his head.

Kristin gave him a slight smile as she touched the furs. "My, but they are luxuriously soft, aren't they?"

Mary reverted to English. "She likes them, Running Deer."

And that was all it took. The native man's stature increased by at least two inches.

"Heaven help us," Sam muttered.

Now it was Pa's turn to laugh.

Beyond the porch the rain came down in sheets.

"Will you stay for supper, Running Deer?" Ma asked.

"No, I must return to my own home." He turned and looked at the inclement weather. "This storm will not stop soon, so I will go now."

"Be careful." Ma hugged him before cupping his face with her hands.

"I have nothing to fear. This is not an angry storm. It was sent to nurture our crops."

Ma's smile was skeptical at best, and Sam knew why. Running Deer didn't profess to be a Christian. Rather he'd formed his own opinions and beliefs about God, and they changed as frequently as the Wisconsin skies.

Running Deer took his leave. As soon as he left the porch, he sprinted through the downpour toward the road. Sam knew he'd keep up the pace all the way to his cabin, over a mile away. As a kid, Sam often tried to outrun him as only a five-year difference spanned their ages, Sam being the younger. But, despite his best efforts that led into adulthood, Sam never won a race with his uncle.

Turning his gaze to Kristin now, Sam caught her eye. She sent him a tentative grin along with an uncertain shrug. Sam smiled, praying the gesture would help to assuage her insecurities and fears.

And, in that second, he knew the race to win's Kristin's heart was one he couldn't abide losing.

CHAPTER 13

*T*HE STORM INTENSIFIED, and Mr. Sundberg suggested everyone go inside the house.

"Want to play a game of draughts, Pa?" Jackson was on his heels as his father entered the sitting room.

"Oh, I suppose so."

Kristin stood holding the fox furs, wondering if Running Deer had made it to his home before the thunder and lightning erupted from the heavens.

"Allow me to take those to the mudroom for you, Kristin." Sam took the bow supporting the three animal hides. Only then did she realize how heavy it had been to hold.

"Thank you, Sam."

"If you would like, Pa can take them to town and sell them for you. Running Deer will not be offended."

"That is a good idea." Kristin didn't know what else she'd do with fox skins.

Mrs. Sundberg tapped Mary on the shoulder. "Come and help me set out some repast for supper." Together they strode to the kitchen.

Kristin followed. "May I help?"

"No. You rest. I will need your help tomorrow."

"*Ja.*" Kristin knew Mondays were quite busy. She sat down on the deep burgundy-upholstered settle and watched Jackson set up the board game. "Where did you learn to play such a game?"

"I met a Canadian trapper years ago," Mr. Sundberg began, "and he taught me the game. We played all night because I could not stand to let him win." He chuckled. "Years later I saw this game for sale at the General Store, and I bought it."

"And Pa taught Sam, Mary, and me to play with him."

"I am still trying to win." Mr. Sundberg smiled, and crinkle lines appeared at the corners of his eyes.

In that moment the man didn't seem so cross and overbearing to Kristin. Perhaps he didn't dislike her, as she'd assumed, but rather disliked her Uncle Lars. And who wouldn't?

Sam returned and eyed the game. "Draughts, eh?"

"I will play you next, Sam, after I beat Pa."

"Hey, now…" Mr. Sundberg frowned. "We have not even begun, Jack. How do you know I will lose?"

"You usually do." Jackson smirked.

Kristin found herself smiling at the banter. She was grateful the Sundbergs spoke Norwegian so she could understand what they said.

Sam returned and seated himself beside her.

Kristin noticed Mr. Sundberg's heavy frown as he glanced their way. But Sam didn't seem troubled in the least.

Mr. Sundberg spoke English to him. A warning? Kristin scrutinized Sam's expression as he replied, then gauged Mr. Sundberg's glowering countenance.

"You think we should not sit together?" Kristin stood, peering directly at Mr. Sundberg.

"I do not feel it is wise, no."

"Well, then we do not. This is your home, Mr. Sundberg."

Sam pushed to his feet. "This is my home too." Hands on hips, he glared at his father.

Mr. Sundberg, however, concentrated on his game and didn't reply.

Kristin moved to a nearby chair just as thunder exploded and lightning pierced the darkened sky.

"It is quite a bad storm." She hoped to alleviate some of the tension by changing subjects.

Sam lit a lamp before leaving the sitting room. Kristin watched the board game, unsure of what to think. It seemed obvious that Mr. Sundberg disproved of her budding friendship with Sam. Was it because she was his wife's house girl and lower than their social class? Or was it because she was an Eikaas?

Minutes later Sam returned, carrying a basket. He exited once more then came back with his mother's spinning wheel.

Setting it near the hearth, he looked at Kristin. "Pa found a bundle of carded wool and said you can spin it if you would like."

Hope bubbled up inside Kristin and came out as a little laugh.

"It was Pa's idea." Sam glanced over his shoulder. "Right, Pa?"

He looked up. "Help yourself to both the wool and spinning wheel."

Kristin smiled. "Thank you. This is a most precious gift." She removed the basket's lid and felt the rough woolen fibers between her fingers as she scooped out a handful. Sitting down near the spinning wheel, she began to roll and twist a twelve-inch lead on her lap. After supper she would begin to spin. She would remember everything *Mor* had taught her. But more importantly, her finished products would forever be a reminder of *Mor*.

―❦―

"Lars Eikaas is the biggest fool in Brown County."

"Lower your voice, Pa." Sam nodded toward the basement steps. "Kristin might hear you."

"She doesn't know English."

"She can pick out certain words." Sam sent Pa a warning look. "She understands."

Pa took a sip of coffee and inclined his head toward the sitting room.

Sam followed him through the quiet house. Everyone else was in bed and sleeping—all except him and Pa. It would seem they both had too much on their minds to relax just yet.

"Lars could have made a fortune on that girl. She spins... well, just as good as your mother did."

"High praise, indeed." Sam lowered himself into an armchair. "I've heard you mention how gifted my mother was at the spinning wheel."

"And it's so." Pa stood by the opened window. The wind had shifted and a pleasant breeze wafted in.

Sam glanced at the spinning wheel, feeling pleased it was in use again. He had to admit too that he was glad his gift outweighed Running Deer's.

"I think I've prepared you for your trip to Madison as best I can." Pa stared into his coffee cup for a long moment before looking at Sam. "I heard back from my friend John Evans. He's got a stately home not far from the Capitol building."

It sounded good to Sam. "I had assumed I'd stay with Oshkosh and his men."

"No..." Pa appeared thoughtful. "I think it best you stay with John and his dau—" Pa coughed. "Excuse me. John and his family."

"All right." Sam trusted his father's judgment. After all, Pa was usually the one who did the traveling as well as the negotiating.

"You'll enjoy this adventure, Sam. I can promise you that." A faraway gleam entered Pa's blue eyes. "You'll dine with educated men who smoke fat cigars and talk about current events. They recline in rooms with rich, dark paneling, leather chairs, and entire walls dedicated to bound books." Pa's gaze returned to Sam. "I never learned to read English well."

"What?"

"Oh, I speak English fluently, but reading…" Pa shook his head.

"But when I was a boy, you and I read the newspaper together every night. Then we'd discuss various issues."

"Who read the newspaper?" Pa arched a brow.

Sam thought about it, remembering. "I read the newspaper." He'd never realized it before. "You would ask me to read the articles." He grinned. "I thought you were just making me practice my reading."

"My intention was twofold, you might say."

"I never knew that about you, Pa."

He gave a deep shrug. "I learned to speak English as an adult—when we first came here from Norway. I had no reason to learn to read. I was a widower who needed to earn a living and support myself and my young son. The skills I acquired, even some farming techniques, were thanks to the trappers and the Indians who taught me. As for the negotiations I've made, they've been verbal and penned by Territory officials. But now that Wisconsin is a state, a more learned man will be needed." Pa gave a single nod. "You are that man, Sam."

"I'm flattered you think so." Sam stood. A niggling inside him couldn't be ignored. "But I'm not sure politics is for me."

"You haven't tried it yet."

"I know. And I'm willing. It's just…"

"This is all new to you, Sam. It's normal to feel some anxiety."

"It's not that, Pa." Sam didn't think he had an anxious muscle in his body. "It's—"

"That girl!" Pa's expression darkened. "Putting a little distance between you two won't hurt. I'd say you're leaving at just the right time. Wish it were sooner!"

Sam felt the same old frustrations coming on. But discussing them with Pa didn't seem to make a difference. *Lord, was there ever a stiff-necked man such as this one?*

"Good night, Pa." Sam left the sitting room and made his way to the stairwell. How could he influence an entire committee if he couldn't even sway his own father?

The room he shared with Jackson felt hot and stuffy, despite the wind's shift. Sam opened the window wider then climbed onto the lower bunk and stretched out. Felt good. Staring at the ceiling, he silently prayed, *Lord, my future is and always has been in Your hands. You said let any man ask for wisdom and it would be granted unto him… well, I'm asking. For wisdom and for Your Holy Spirit to guide me to Madison, help me to complete the job I'm sent to do, and bring me back home safely.*

Sam's eyes fluttered closed, and that's the last thing he remembered until the pinks of dawn shone through the window and the smell of Kristin's strong coffee signaled that his chores awaited him.

⊶♥⊷

Kristin began her Monday morning a bit tardy, and as a result, she hadn't yet pinned up her hair before she made the coffee. Her bruised jaw felt more sore this morning than yesterday, and the purplish mar from Peder's elbow had grown in size. Still, she'd managed to get herself dressed and planned to retreat to her room and tackle the task of winding her waist-long hair around her head once Sam and his father poured cups of their morning brew. But for now it would have to hang in a long, fat braid down her back.

Lighting the woodstove, she recalled the dream she'd had this morning. *Mor* and Poppa and her brothers were alive and healthy. They smiled and waved to her from Norway.

But, alas, it had only been a dream. And even though a couple of years had passed since their deaths, Kristin's heart still ached for her family.

From her periphery she saw a movement and turned quickly to see Running Deer, stepping from the shadows. He appeared no worse for wear after his jaunt through yesterday afternoon's storm.

"Good morning," she said, practicing her English.

"Good morning to you."

A nervous flutter filled Kristin's insides as the Indian man came slowly forward, wearing a lopsided grin. What did he want this time? A cup of coffee?

Reaching for an empty cup, she held it out to him and pointed to the pot.

Running Deer shook his head and stepped even closer. The musky scent of his body reached her nostrils as he grabbed hold of her braided hair. She froze. Did she call for help? But Mrs. Sundberg said her brother wouldn't harm her.

In spite of her best efforts to remain calm, Kristin's chest rose and fell with mounting fear. When she saw him unsheathe his knife, terror gripped her. Would he slit her throat?

Kristin opened her mouth to scream, but nothing came out. Trepidation choked her. She closed her eyes, trembling.

She felt a tug on her scalp. Running Deer pulled and pulled.

"Stop! Stop it!"

Suddenly it was over. When she opened her eyes, the Indian

man stood, smiling and holding six inches of braid in his tanned fist.

"You...you cut my hair!"

He pointed to the odd-looking *halskjede*—necklace, which rested against his bare chest. Long teeth, a bone, and several beads dangled from a leather string. It appeared he would now add Kristin's braid.

"What's going on in here?"

Kristin saw Sam and immediately ran to him. "He cut my hair, Sam. Look!" She showed him the portion now missing. With the end piece gone, her hair fell into kinky waves.

Sam's arm went around Kristin's waist, and she felt instantly protected in his embrace. He spoke to Running Deer in a restrained voice while Kristin collected herself.

Running Deer responded, and Kristin heard the laughter in his tone. He thought violating her in such a manner was funny? *Mor* always said no man should touch her hair until after she was married.

The conversation between Sam and Running Deer continued. Kristin heard the challenge in the Indian man's voice now.

Sam glanced down at Kristin. Their gazes met. Then, all at once, Sam's mouth captured hers in an unexpected but ever-so-sweet assault. She closed her eyes. Then all too soon, he pulled his head back.

"Sam?" Her voice was but a whisper.

He faced Running Deer again, and this time the Indian man didn't reply. He stood there eyeing first Sam, then Kristin, before hurling the piece of hair he'd severed at Sam's feet. Next, he spun on his moccasin-clad heel and left the house.

Relief mixed with profound confusion stole over Kristin. "What just happened, Sam?"

"I told my uncle you were not interested in becoming his

woman. He asked me again if there was an understanding between us—you and me. I told him that, yes, there is. That's when I kissed you." His eyebrows dipped in all seriousness. "Forgive me for being so forward."

"Is there an understanding between us, Sam?" The words fell off her tongue before she could think better of asking the question.

"I want there to be." His features relaxed. "I have been praying about courting you proper when I return from Madison. Would you...that is...would you allow me to court you?"

Kristin lowered her gaze but couldn't keep a broad smile from forming. Looking back at Sam, all she could do was nod.

Releasing her, he stepped back. "Promise me you will pray about the matter, Kristin. I must be honest. My father is against a match between us."

The truth stung. She looked away. "Then perhaps it is not meant to be." A deep sadness saturated her being—much like what she'd felt when her family succumbed to the fever epidemic.

"That is what we need to discover through prayer. If a match between us is meant to be, we can proceed in the confidence Christ gives us, in spite of whoever is against us. Besides, the Lord is able to change Pa's heart."

"It seems daunting." Kristin wasn't certain she was up to such a task. She suddenly felt weary and discouraged.

Sam took her hand. "We can do all things through Christ who strengthens us."

She recognized the passage of Scripture. She believed it. "All right. I will commit this matter to prayer."

The light in Sam's eyes brightened. He bowed regally over her hand and placed a kiss on her fingers.

His actions brought another smile to her face. "May I pour you a cup of coffee, Sam?"

"Yes. Thank you." He let go of her hand.

"And pour me one too." Mr. Sundberg sauntered into the kitchen, pulling on his suspenders. He glanced from Sam to Kristin and back at Kristin, this time taking note of her loosely hanging hair.

She hurried to the stove. Suddenly it seemed she had to fear more from Mr. Sundberg than she ever did from Running Deer.

CHAPTER 14

*T*HE END OF the month arrived, and at the first pinks of dawn, Sam knelt on his bedroom floor and packed his clothes and gear into two saddlebags. The last few days had gone by in an industrious blur, but he'd managed to bale most of the hay. Pa and Jack could see to the rest. Last night he and Kristin were invited to dinner at Luke and Rachel's house. With Mary along, they were well chaperoned since the girl chattered on nearly nonstop.

A smile played on Sam's lips as he recalled the outing. He felt like Kristin completed the half of him that he'd been missing.

The sound of Jack's yawn brought Sam's thoughts to the present. "Wish I could go with you." Jack stretched. "I hate school."

Sam grinned. "You'd better not hate school. Someday you'll have to take my place in politics. You'll be the one in Madison."

"Where are you going to be?"

Sending his brother a glance, Sam lifted his shoulders. "Don't know quite yet."

Jack jumped from the top bunk. "Maybe you'll be married to Kristin."

"I wouldn't mind it." Sam chuckled, feeling his face redden with chagrin. "Now get dressed and do your chores so you can wash up for school."

"Oh, all right." Jack pulled on his trousers. "Pa went fishing. Maybe he'll catch some trout for breakfast."

"That'd make a tasty sendoff." Sam broadened his grin while anticipation of his journey pumped through his veins with each heartbeat. He couldn't wait to work alongside the Menominee chief, Oshkosh, and plead the Menominee Nation's case to the government committee.

Once more Sam felt honored Pa decided to send him. Still, he hated to leave Kristin. He had lain awake most of the night with his thoughts, like a pendulum, swinging from her to his impending trip to Madison.

Kristin. Sam recalled her wide eyes and broad smile yesterday afternoon when Pa gave her the money for the fox furs he'd sold in town. The gift Running Deer had given Kristin had been worth even more than Pa estimated. When Ma asked what she thought she'd do with the money, Kristin began talking about someday owning a shop—a dress shop. Not the usual dress shop, but more of an accessories store. Crocheted collars, knitted shawls, felted wool, yarns, and threads…

As Kristin described her vision, Ma seemed to understand. Pa had waved an impatient hand at the ladies and headed toward the barn.

"You would be in high demand, I should think," Ma had said.

"*Ja*, you think so, Mrs. Sundberg?"

"Hmm-hmm." Ma nodded before peering at Sam and speaking in English. "I will have to keep this secret from Miss Betsy. She'd want to hire Kristin away from me."

Sam had chuckled, noticing Kristin's blue eyes flitting from him to Ma.

Moments later she lifted her pretty chin. "I will not work for Miss Betsy. I am happy here, at least for now."

Sam had laughed while Ma lowered her dark gaze and pressed her lips together in an expression of chagrin. It appeared that in the months Kristin had traveled from Norway to America, along with her weeks here in Brown County, she had learned to pick out enough English words to figure out the meanings of some conversations. Sam knew Kristin would master the English language as quickly as Pa had.

The conversation about a shop continued. Kristin, Ma, and Mary shared daydreams of operating a fancy store. Sam sat by, listening, and got a sense of Kristin's ambitious nature as well as her hopes for the future.

"Almost finished, son?"

Sam peered over his shoulder to find Pa at the doorway.

Shaking off his musing, Sam stuffed the last of his belongings into the saddle bag. "Yes. All set." He stood and hefted the heavy leather satchels over one shoulder.

Pa reopened a flap and inserted something. "I added three pouches of our finest tobacco. Give them to John for me. A thank-you gift."

"Sure, Pa."

"I'm proud of you, Sam."

He smiled, knowing his father rarely doled out compliments. Pa had plans and goals of his own, and Sam was glad to be a part of them. Yet lately the Lord seemed to be making the point clear that Sam needed to search out his own path for the future—one in which God Himself would walk alongside him. Staking his own claim of land, farming it, marrying Kristin, and raising a family. Lately Sam couldn't help but set his mind along those lines. Somehow whenever he thought and prayed about these dreams, a peace like he'd never known came over him.

"Ready to go?"

Sam inclined his head. "Ready as I'll ever be, I guess."

Pa led the way out of the room and downstairs to the kitchen. Ma walked with them outside to the barn. Sam would pack up before eating breakfast.

"I packed dried beef and biscuits for the journey." Ma said. "I also filled your canteen."

"I appreciate that, Ma. Thanks." Sam placed the food and water in one of the leather bags and then saddled his gelding.

"Chief Oshkosh and his men will meet you in Madison." Pa went on to recount the plan.

"I got it, Pa." They'd been over all these details before.

"And you'll find John Evans's home easily, I think."

"I'm sure I will."

"He's expecting you by Saturday afternoon."

"Plenty of time." Sam planned to arrive in time to go to church on Sunday.

"The meeting at the capitol is on Monday—first thing in the morning."

"I'm aware of it, Pa." Sam finally turned to him. "Relax. I'll be fine."

The corners of Ma's lips went upward in a gentle grin. "He's right, Karl." She threaded her arm around Pa's elbow. "Sam is a capable man."

"Of course he is."

"But I think he should stay and eat a good breakfast first."

"Naw, on second thought, I'll just say my good-byes and go." Sam suddenly saw no point in prolonging the inevitable.

Walking over to where Jack milked a cow, he tousled the boy's hair. "Behave yourself. No more fights."

Jack looked at him askance and nodded. "Yeah, I know. Turn the other cheek."

Sam knew that wasn't the easiest of the Lord's commands. "And keep up on your studying."

"I will." Jack smiled. "Bye, Sam."

Reins in hand, Sam led the gelding from the barn. Near the entryway, he glimpsed Pa's grinning approval. It both pleased Sam and fueled his desire to continue with the Indian mediations his father began some time ago.

Now to bid farewell to Mary and Kristin. He tethered the horse in the shade and patted the animal's neck. "I know Mary's inside. Where's Kristin?" His gaze wandered the yard.

His folks glanced at each other. "Forget about her, Sam," Pa said.

He inhaled deeply. "We've been through all this."

"No." Pa stepped forward. "Your mother came fishing with me this morning. We were on the other side of the pond. We saw her with that younger Olstad fella."

"Peder Olstad?" That didn't make sense.

"That's him." Pa nodded. "She met him at sunup, on the sneak, and your Ma and I...well..." He looked at Ma, who lowered her gaze.

"Well...what?" Sam brought his chin back defensively.

Pa gave him a leveled look. "They embraced, Sam. Perhaps their meetings are habitual. Who knows what that girl does on her own time."

"Oh, Karl, please!" Ma pulled her arm from his. "Such innuendo is—"

"Mariah, I told you I'd handle this." His gaze slid to Ma.

She pressed her lips together.

Pa squared his shoulders and looked back at Sam. "Kristin Eikaas is playing you for a fool."

Sam gave a mild shake of his head. He didn't believe it. And Ma's pained expression said he *shouldn't* believe it.

"Where's she now?"

"In the orchard, I think," Ma said with a demure dip of her head. "She mentioned to Mary that she planned to bake apples."

"Just an excuse." Pa scowled. "She really went to meet that Olstad boy."

"We'll see about that." Sam walked around his horse, and Pa caught his arm.

"You've got important people waiting on you, son."

"I realize that." Tamping down his impatience, he stared hard at his father. "And I'm about to go talk to one of those important people now."

Pulling his arm free, Sam set off for the orchard. But five strides later, Kristin rounded the corner of the house. She held up the hem of her white apron, which she'd filled with apples.

"*God morgen*, Sam."

"In English, please." He would miss teasing her while he was gone.

"Good morning." Her tone sounded sassy at best, but then a more somber light entered her eyes. "I picked extra apples. Perhaps you would like to take a few with you to eat on your journey."

"I would. Thanks." Sam glanced over his shoulder at his folks. "May I have a word with you?"

"Oh, *ja*, sure."

Kristin led the way into the house. In the kitchen, Mary stood at the table and rolled trout in flour.

"Almost ready for frying, Kristin." Mary smiled at both her and Sam.

"Good." Unloading her apron into a basket on the counter, Kristin barely had time to turn around when Sam cupped her elbow and led her to the sitting room.

"*Hva er i veien*—what is the matter?"

He suddenly didn't know how to begin. She stared up at him in wide-eyed innocence.

"I like the way you are wearing your hair now."

She patted the thick bun at her nape. "Your mother trimmed it evenly for me. I guess it is not so bad that Running Deer cut my hair."

Sam took her hand. "Kristin," he said, lowering his gaze, "I will come right out with it. My parents saw you with Peder Olstad at dawn." He looked up. "Is that true?"

"*Ja.*" No look of guilt entered her gaze. She wet her lips and Sam felt the muscle in his jaw work. "I gave him the money from the furs."

Sam leaned back and frowned. "Why?"

"Because…" Her gaze flitted around the room before settling back on him. "Peder wants to go to a place called California, but he has no money. A man from church will be leaving for there soon, and Peder wants to go with him."

"Who? What man from church?"

"I do not know his name. Peder did not say. But he did tell me that he hated me for the way he is trapped at my uncle's place, living in poverty. I felt God wanted me to help him out. Give Peder a good start…like the one I have been given because of your kindness."

A certain light in her eyes let Sam know she wasn't fibbing.

"Also, Peder said my uncle's house was damaged in the storm on Sunday along with a side of the barn. I asked Peder to help with the repairs, using a little of the money I gave him." Kristin wagged her head. "But I don't think he will do that."

"You are very generous, especially since neither Olstad or your uncle deserves any kindness from you."

"And I agree. I really did not want to help my uncle—or Peder. But Sam"—she pulled her hand from his—"I did it for my cousins. They are only children. And I did it for my best friend, Sylvia. What would she think of me if she learned that I had money and didn't help her brother and father? What would she say if she discovered that I live in a nice home, protected from the rain and wind, while Peder and Mr. Olstad live in a smelly barn? Sylvia would be so disappointed in me."

"I understand." Sam honestly did too—or at least he was convinced of part of her reasoning. "Kristin..." He covered her hands with his. "Ma and Pa saw you and Peder...embracing."

"It is true." Her gaze hardened, her eyes the color of Lake Michigan during the wintertime. "Peder was so happy I gave him money that he hugged me."

Staring into her Kristin's face, Sam found no reason to doubt her.

"Do your parents still assume Peder is my *forloveden*?"

"Perhaps." He didn't know how else to describe his father's unflattering speculations without wounding her.

"Maybe that is why he does not approve of me. He thinks I made a promise to Peder. But it is not so."

"I know." Sam felt a rush of relief. "Pa will come around. Give him a chance, all right?"

"All right." Her eyes looked suddenly misty. "I will miss you, Sam. I did not know how much until right now. Ever since I arrived here, you have been my...*helten*."

Her hero. Sam smiled, feeling like maybe he didn't want to go after all.

Except he knew he had to.

Standing on tiptoe, Kristin put her hands on his shoulder and kissed his cheek. "Hurry back."

A powerful urge to take her in his arms and kiss that pretty pink mouth again—and really kiss her this time—gripped him.

It took every shred of willpower not to give into it. "I will," he eked out. "I will hurry back."

"Kristin." Mary's voice sailed in from the kitchen. "The fish are ready and I cored the apples for baking. But what goes inside of them?"

"Cinnamon and sugar." Kristin blinked and looked toward the kitchen. "Coming, Mary." With one last glance at Sam, she sidestepped.

His one arm caught her around the waist. "Kristin?" He needed to ask, as ridiculous as it might seem. "Did you ever kiss Peder Olstad?"

"Never." Her gaze met Sam's. "Oh, he tried to steal kisses when we were children, but I was always stronger than he." A smile tugged at her mouth. "I think I still am stronger." She fingered her bruised jaw. "Peder caught me off guard last Sunday."

"Careful so it does not happen again."

"No, it will not!" Determination was etched on her every feature before she turned on her heel.

A chortle simmered inside of Sam as he watched her making her way to the kitchen. Maybe he wouldn't leave quite yet. Ma had been right. He ought to have a hearty breakfast to see him off.

Kristin pushed the supper around on the plate with her fork. Sam had been gone only three days, and already she missed him greatly. When she'd gathered vegetables Friday and again yesterday for their noon dinner, she'd looked off into the distant fields and expected to see him. But he wasn't there. At church this morning there was extra room in the pew, and now, at the dining room table as they ate repast, Sam's chair sat vacant beside Jackson. Kristin wondered what he was doing. Had he arrived in Madison safely? Funny to think that it had only been a week ago that she'd enjoyed a buggy ride with him and dinner at the Smiths' house. That sunny autumn afternoon felt like years ago.

Kristin glanced at Mrs. Sundberg's empty place at the table. The woman had taken to her bed right after Sam left on Thursday. The entire family seemed solemn in her and Sam's absence. Mr. Sundberg began to talk in English, so Kristin didn't know what he said. If she tried hard enough, she might be able to figure it out. However, she felt too weary. Caring for Mrs. Sundberg and overseeing the children, plus keeping up with the housework, had become overwhelming. Still, Mary insisted that every day, after school, Kristin practice the English words that Mary wrote on her black slate. Kristin indulged the child while she prepared supper each evening.

Sy Sew

Kjole Dress

Sko Shoe

Vannkoker Kettle

Komfyr Stove

Cook Cook

Jeg vet ikke I don't know

Kan Jeg få litt hjelp? May I have some assistance?

Norwegian wasn't so different from English. Kristin had been practicing the words and simple phrases on her own while she knitted in the sitting room after everyone retired at night. Beginning tomorrow, Mary planned to give her a brand-new list of words and easy phrases.

Kristin smiled inwardly. *Mary will make a fine and determined teacher…*

"Kristin?"

She shook herself and glanced at the subject of her thoughts who sat beside her. "*Ja*, Mary?"

The girl reverted to Norwegian. "Pa made mention of the fact that Mr. Olstad, the younger one, was not in church today. And there does not seem to be any man in our congregation who departed for the California Territory."

So Peder lied. Kristin raised her shoulders in a helpless gesture. "All I know is what Peder told me a couple of weeks ago before fighting with Jackson." She glanced at Mr. Sundberg.

"Apparently Lars's lying nature rubbed off on your... *venn.*"

"Peder is *not* my friend—or anything else for that matter."

Mr. Sundberg's features came together in a simmering frown. "There are children present at this table!"

"And so they too can hear the truth from my own lips."

"Pa, let her be." Jack sent an annoyed glance at his father. "Everyone knows she likes Sam."

Kristin felt her cheeks growing pink. However, they would never match the purplish red on Mr. Sundberg's countenance.

Many moments of silence ticked by. Once more Kristin pushed the food on her plate around, suddenly unable to eat.

Mr. Sundberg spoke once more. "After service this morning Ole Larson told me he spotted Peder Olstad entering one of the taverns on Friday night. It appears, Miss Eikaas, that *your friend* is drinking away the money you gave him. Quite the waste."

Jack and Mary grew wide-eyed, and Kristin masked her indignation. She wasn't about to spout off to Mr. Sundberg again and threaten her position. What's more, she refused to set a poor example for the children. As far as Mr. Sundberg knowing about the money she gave Peder, Sam told her that he explained last week's *misunderstanding* to his parents. Mrs. Sundberg, like Sam, believed her. Mr. Sundberg, judging from his behavior, did not.

"In all due respect, Mr. Sundberg, what Peder does with his funds is and always has been, his choice." Kristin laced kindness around each word, although news of Peder's behavior stung. She had thought better of him. She believed he wanted a chance at a new life. "All I can say is my conscience is free and clear. I did what I could to help my best friend's brother and father. What happens next is neither my concern nor my responsibility."

Mr. Sundberg didn't reply but took a bite of his meal of meatballs, potatoes, and gravy.

"Who cares what that *onde mannen* says or does?" Jackson asked in between mouthfuls.

Peder? An *evil man*? Sadness pervaded Kristin's being. Before arriving in Brown County, Kristin would have never guessed Peder would be thought of in such terms.

Excusing herself from the table, she carried her plate to the kitchen. She wanted to buckle under the weight of animosity in this home, which had grown tenfold since Sam left. Instead, she pushed back her shoulders and set her jaw. She had a job to do here, which included running upstairs and checking on Mrs. Sundberg.

Taking to the steps, she reached the bedroom. She knocked then waited for a reply before opening the door. Even in the drapery-darkened quarters, Kristin saw the woman had eaten only a bite of one meatball.

"Mrs. Sundberg?"

The woman's eyelids fluttered open and she put her hands on either side of the wooden tray, as if realizing it still balanced on the tops of her legs. "Kristin." She sighed. "I must have dozed off again. You prepared a tasty meal."

"How do you know? You barely touched it." Gathering her skirt, Kristin carefully sat on the edge of the bed. "Take a few more bites."

"I cannot. I am too tired."

She ignored the protest and forked a small piece of potato into Mrs. Sundberg's mouth.

"Mmm...I so enjoy potatoes from our garden."

"I do as well. What makes them grow so well?"

She lifted one shoulder. "Fertile soil." She took a deep breath. "I scrape uneaten vegetables, egg shells, potato peels, old coffee grounds, and such, into the wooden barrel beside the barn. Every so often, I add more dirt. But no meat or bread goes into the mix. When the barrel is full, Karl brings me another, and I fill that one up too. Come springtime, he rolls those barrels onto the fields and spreads their contents over the soil before Sam plows. Afterward seeds are planted." She smiled. "You can see for yourself that our harvest is bountiful."

"I should say so."

"My people use that method of fertilization too."

"There is proof it is effective." Kristin forked another bite of gravy-slathered potato into Mrs. Sundberg's mouth. When no further protests came, she fed Mrs. Sundberg a third bite of food—a part of a meatball this time.

"Mmm... the taste of onion in the meat...delicious."

"Good." Kristin fed her another little piece.

"That is all." Mrs. Sundberg turned her face away. "I cannot eat another bite."

"Very well." Kristin lifted the tray and stepped toward the door. But the heaviness in her heart compelled her to retreat to Mrs. Sundberg's bedside. Setting the tray on a nearby table, she sat down once more. "I don't like to see you in such a state."

"I will be better soon. My condition waxes and wanes."

"I pray it wanes soon."

Mrs. Sundberg gazed at her and smiled. "Thank you, dear heart. It is good to have you here to help me."

A spirit of doubt clouded her thinking. "I do not believe Mr.

Sundberg feels the way you do. In fact, he behaves as if he does not want me here at all. Sam told me that this was his idea—me working for you." She scrutinized Mrs. Sundberg's expression. "Your husband would rather I not be here. Is that true?"

"He and your uncle…there is great strife between them." She ran her pink tongue along her bottom lip. "I am going to tell you something—something very personal. Go and close the door."

Kristin did as the woman bid her and returned to the side of the bed.

"I feel I can trust you, Kristin, so I will tell you this. My husband believes your uncle stole numerous silver spoons, although it has never been proved. Nevertheless, Karl holds the transgression against Lars Eikaas and refuses to forgive him."

"Oh, my…" Kristin's hand found its way to the base of her neck.

"And your uncle…" Mrs. Sundberg closed her eyes. Her voice sounded weary. "He despises my people and other Indian nations in Wisconsin. He feels we are inferior to whites and should not own land or anything else of value. And regarding the theft incident…well, Lars took great umbrage when the sheriff questioned him about the silver and denied all accusations. He then set out to ruin Karl's character and reputation in Green Bay, saying it was immoral for him to marry me. He even told Reverend Wollums that I should not be allowed to attend church with whites."

"That is not right. Scripture tells us that God does not look upon the outside of a person, but sees her heart." Kristin felt humbled as the words fell from her tongue.

"Yes. The good news is many people discount what Lars says— although some side with him."

"So that is the reason Mr. Sundberg dislikes me?"

"That is partly so." After an audible sigh, Mrs. Sundberg

opened her eyes. She reached for Kristin's hand. "More is the fact that Sam is in love with you."

Kristin sucked in a breath. The news was really no surprise, but hearing the words still took her aback. Love? Could it really be so?

"Sam's feelings have foiled Karl's plans."

"Plans for Sam to become an important man in Wisconsin?"

"Yes."

Things were beginning to make more sense. "But what if God's plan is not the same as your husband's?" Kristin found herself hoping it was so.

Mrs. Sundberg gave her hand a gentle squeeze. "That is what has Karl fuming. He has an unforgiving spirit and an unwillingness to concede to God's will." She rolled her head to and fro on the feather pillows that propped up her willowy frame. "He is a contender by nature. So I pray for my husband all day long. Even more so since my condition has flared." She paused and gazed at Kristin. "Perhaps that is the reason God allowed me to be ill—so I would have the time to pray longer and harder."

"Thank you for sharing this insight with me. It answers many of my questions." She pulled her hand away and stood. "I will pray too." Then, silently, Kristin added, *My prayer will be that Sam comes home quickly!*

CHAPTER 15

SO, WHAT DO you think about your visit thus far?" John Evans gave Sam a friendly rap on the shoulder blades.

"To say I'm impressed, sir, would be an understatement." Sam glanced around and, again, took in the rich, dark paneling of the library, the heavy velvet drapes, and the many volumes that lined the built-in oak bookshelves. Everything was just as his father had described.

"Please, sit down." Mr. Evans held out a long, thin hand, indicating the leather-upholstered chairs near the massive desk. "I'm glad your trip was uneventful."

"It was." He'd met with Oshkosh and his men and rode most of the distance with them. "I hope it's no imposition that I arrived later than planned." It had been dark when Sam pulled up to the gate last night.

"None whatsoever."

Sam eased into the cushy chair. "Your pastor preached a thought-provoking sermon this morning."

"Yes, we're fond of Reverend Michaels. His daughter and mine are the same age." Mr. Evans folded his tall, slim frame into the chair opposite him. "You might recall that I mentioned my daughter, Samantha, will be arriving home shortly." He chuckled. "Sam and Sam will dine at my table tonight."

Sam grinned at the joke, adding a slight nod. "I do remember your saying so."

"I would have said more this morning, but…" Mr. Evans waved his hand in his air. "My friends and acquaintances always have something to tell me, as you witnessed this morning after church. And my neighbors frequently stop to say hello while on their Sunday strolls."

"You are a man in great demand."

"Well, I don't know about that." He grinned and changed the subject. "Tell me news of your father." Mr. Evans crossed one leg over the other. His suit appeared to be cut from the finest cloth, causing Sam to feel like a regular yokel. But he couldn't change the fact he wasn't as monetarily wealthy.

"Pa is well. Thankfully crops have been good this year."

"And what of that undignified neighbor?" Mr. Evans dipped his head slightly. "Is he still so ornery?"

"Mr. Eikaas? I'm afraid he is." Sam lowered his gaze to his brown trousers and brushed a smudge off his knee. "I'm surprised Pa mentioned Mr. Eikaas."

"Yes, well, we conferred about a possible investigation into those missing silver spoons of your father's."

"I guess I had my head in my bookwork when they disappeared. What's more, my parents rarely discuss controversies in front of us kids—not unless they involve mistreatment of Wisconsin Natives."

"Which is what has brought you to Madison now." Mr. Evans smiled, stood, and ambled over to a polished table on which a crystal brandy service stood. "You would like a drink?"

"No, sir. I don't imbibe."

"I should have known. Like father, like son." Grinning, Mr.

Evans poured a small amount into a tumbler. "Sam, are you aware that your mother and my late wife, God rest her soul, were childhood friends in Norway?"

"No." In that instant, Sam felt rather ashamed for not knowing more about his birth mother. "I don't remember her and regard my stepmother as my mother."

"It's only natural."

The reply soothed Sam's conscience.

"Your father and I actually met in the courtroom. We were on opposing sides, but I marveled at his tenacity."

Sam had heard the story before.

"I invited Karl to dinner one evening, and my wife joined us. As we got to know one another, my wife pointed out the ironic connection. How sad she was to learn of your mother's death on the journey to America."

"It's not an easy voyage, so I hear." Sam immediately thought of Kristin and all she must have endured.

The maid suddenly appeared at the entryway. "Beg your pardon, sir, but Miss Samantha has just arrived home."

"Wonderful." Mr. Evans glanced at Sam. "Excuse me for a few minutes."

"Of course."

After the slender man strode into the mansion's foyer, Sam pushed to his feet, stretched, and made his way to the enormous bookshelves. Authors such as James Fenimore Cooper, Edgar Allan Poe, and Charles Dickens were among a collection in one section. A host of law books occupied another. And the last section of shelves housed curious reads, like *The Condition of the Working Class in England in 1844.*

Sam pursed his lips thoughtfully. In all the books he scanned he didn't see one religious publication. Nor did he find a Bible.

Mr. Evans returned. "Samantha is dressing for dinner. She

had an enjoyable time at her friend's cottage on Lake Monona. We're sure to hear all about it as we enjoy our meal, which will be served promptly at eight." The man peered at his gold pocket watch then tucked it back into his waistcoat.

Sam returned to his seat. He quelled the rumblings in his stomach. They ate much earlier back home. By eight o'clock the women would be sewing and chatting, and he, Pa, and Jack would have seen to the animals for the night.

He wondered what Kristin was doing right now. Perhaps she was spinning again. He smiled inwardly.

"A pleasant thought?"

Sam shook himself, embarrassed. "Quite." He stared across the way at Mr. Evans and watched as his host reclaimed his seat.

"So, tomorrow will be a busy day. Tell me, have you talked with Chief Oshkosh yet?"

"Briefly when we stopped to water the horses, although we weren't able to discuss much. I plan to see Oshkosh and his men first thing in the morning. I'll be at the capitol bright and early."

"I'll be sure Cook has made a breakfast for you before you leave. Sam and I—that is my daughter Sam and I—usually breakfast about eight. Lunch is at twelve-thirty, tea at five o'clock, and dinner at—"

"Eight." Sam smiled.

"You're a fast learner." Mr. Evans chuckled lightly.

The conversation drifted back to the meeting tomorrow. Mr. Evans enlightened Sam of some of the questions the committee might ask and coached him how to answer correctly.

Sam made mental note.

A rustling sound interrupted their discussion. "Ah, there you are, darling." Mr. Evans rose and strode to the library's doorway. "Sam Sundberg, may I present my daughter, Miss Samantha Evans."

Sam politely pushed to his feet. "It's a pleasure, Miss Evans." He took in her off-the-shoulder evening gown that revealed more of Miss Evans than he cared to see. His face felt suddenly aflame, and Sam realized just how backward he must appear.

The young lady strode gracefully forward and held out a gloved hand. Her green eyes boldly appraised him. "Mr. Sundberg…may I call you Sam?"

"Of course." Taking her hand he bowed over it politely.

"And you may call me Sam." She laughed, sounding like a twittering sparrow. "Sam and Sam." She turned to her father, her hand still clasped on Sam's. "Papa, Sam and Sam."

Mr. Evans chuckled too. "Quite the irony, I'd say."

Miss Evans glanced back at Sam, searching his face. He gathered she liked what she saw because she drew nearer. Her thick, floral perfume tickled his nose.

Sam took a polite step back just as the grandfather clock in the corner chimed. "Eight o'clock. I don't suppose you want to keep your dinner waiting."

"No, no…Cook will have a conniption," Mr. Evans said. "Come along."

Relief coursed through Sam…until Miss Evans coiled her arm around his.

⚜

In her basement room Kristin dressed, stepping into a chambray dress that proved plenty sturdy for doing chores and cooking. Once she'd hooked the many front closures, she donned a white apron and tied it in the back. Earlier Mrs. Sundberg had come downstairs just after Kristin lit the stove and announced she felt much better. Happiness pulled at Kristin's mouth. She'd been worried about Mrs. Sundberg.

After brushing out her hair, Kristin strode into the kitchen to make coffee for Mr. Sundberg. Once more she missed Sam's presence. Today was the day of the meeting, and she prayed God would put His words in Sam's mouth.

Setting the coffee onto the stove to brew, Kristin went back into her room and braided her hair. But it was too short to wind around her head, thanks to Running Deer, so Kristin made a ball and pinned it at her nape. By the time she returned to the upstairs kitchen, Mr. Sundberg stood at the stove, pouring himself a cup of the steaming coffee.

"Good morning." Kristin felt her heart begin to hammer, since she didn't quite know what to expect from this man. He was as ornery and unpredictable as *Onkel*. And, just like her Uncle Lars, Mr. Sundberg disliked her.

He grunted out a greeting and left the house.

Kristin sucked in a breath, allowing it to fill her lungs and calm her nerves. More and more she realized how much Sam had been a necessary buffer between her and those who disliked her. If he did as good of a job today at the meeting as he'd done for her, the outcome would surely be in the Indians' favor.

***

Sam lowered himself onto the hard bench, two places down from the Menominee chief, Oshkosh. In between them sat Oshkosh's representative, Soaring Eagle. In the row behind them, a dozen braves were perched with erect posture and attentive expressions. The Menominee had set aside their own garments for the white men's clothes and looked quite respectable for this very official and important meeting.

Sam eyed the committee. He didn't recognize any of the

seven men. Something about the way their gazes roved over the Indians, never making eye contact, gave Sam a sense this conference wouldn't go the Menominees' way. After speaking with Mr. Evans yesterday before dinner, he realized how little he knew federal law. Certainly he could plead the Indians' case, explain why they felt the amendment to the treaty was wrong. However, he couldn't wield the law like Mr. Evans did during their conversation.

At that instant the object of his thoughts appeared. Sam stood and made introductions. Mr. Evans shook each Menominee man's hand before greeting the committee members. Sam suddenly felt a little more hopeful.

When Mr. Evans returned, he motioned for Sam to move over on the bench. Seating himself, he placed his leather case on the table in front of them. "Had you not departed so abruptly after dinner last night," Mr. Evans said in a low voice, "I would have had the time to offer my counsel in today's meeting."

A sense of chagrin filled Sam. "My apologies. I am afraid my journey caught up with me."

In truth, it was Mr. Evans's daughter whom Sam wished to escape. For whatever reason, Miss Evans had taken a liking to him and quickly changed her plans to include him—plans that Sam had no desire to be a part of, like escorting her to the symphony, a harvest ball, and some neighbor's fall garden party. Sam just wanted to do his best at this meeting and get himself back home.

"So you don't mind my interference this morning?" Mr. Evans arched a brow.

"On the contrary. It would be most welcome. Thank you."

Before more could be said, the meeting was called to order. Mr. Evans stood and introduced Chief Oshkosh, whose round, somewhat pudgy face almost disguised the fact that Oshkosh was no stranger to the battlefield. Soon he'd be no stranger to bureaucracy as well.

Next Mr. Evans introduced Sam. Then he sat down, giving Sam the floor.

Pushing to his feet, Sam sent up a prayer for wisdom. He'd been on his knees at the predawn light, but another petition certainly wouldn't hurt.

"Sirs..." He addressed the committee. "As you may know, the Menominee have been ordered to cede the remainder of their land for a reservation west of the Mississippi River, in the Minnesota Territory, specifically the Crow Wing River area."

The men nodded.

"However, the Menominee feel they were both pressured and ill-represented when they signed the treaty in 1831 and its subsequent amendment. While they have agreed to share their land with first the Oneida, originally from New York, and then with white settlers, they never intended to give it up entirely."

"Now see here!" An older man with a corrugated countenance held one finger in the air. "The Indians were paid some one hundred and forty-six thousand dollars for five hundred thousand acres. They took government money for it. It's ours." He lifted his gavel.

"Just a moment, Thaddeus." Mr. Evans stood. "Let's not be hasty. The last thing we need in our new state is more war with the Indians." He walked around the table and toward the committee. "I beseech you and the rest of this distinguished committee, lend an ear to young Mr. Sundberg here."

The men grudgingly agreed.

Pivoting around, Mr. Evans nodded at Sam.

Taking a deep breath, he relayed the Menominees' request. "Due to an article in the amendment that changed the boundary lines, and the fact that they were not redrawn to the full understanding of the Indians at the time the treaty was signed, the Menominee Nation hereby requests to keep the land it now occupies."

"That's out of the question," one committee member blurted. He didn't even look up from the papers on the table at which he sat.

Mr. Evans stood. "Well, then, we will take this matter to a higher jurisdiction."

The reply smacked like an insult. Still, Sam translated to Soaring Eagle.

He replied to Sam who, in turn, addressed the committee.

"Sirs," Sam began once more. "Chief Oshkosh asks that if you cannot see your way to allowing the Menominee Nation to reside on the western half of their land, where they are presently living, you would, at least, allow them to stay for the next five years. This would give the Menominee time to make an exploratory trip to the Crow Wing River area before the Nation is relocated there."

The men of the committee murmured amongst themselves.

"Wonderful stall tactic," Mr. Evans muttered to Sam. "Good work, son."

"Wasn't me. I merely translated to English what Soaring Eagle told me."

"Nevertheless..."

Sam exchanged a glance with the Menominee man on his right-hand side. Was that amusement dancing in the brave's dark eyes?

"We must confer about this matter," said the committee chairman. "This meeting is adjourned until Friday morning, when we will give you our answer."

After a moment's pause, Mr. Evans turned to shake Sam's hand. "Well done, Sam."

"A week? They really need a week to think about this?"

"I'm sure they need to contact the federal government before they grant the request. But I think we've got a chance here. I commend you for waxing so eloquently."

Sam shook his head. "I really didn't do anything other than translate." He turned to the chief and his men and stated the outcome of today's meeting.

They mumbled among themselves before filing out of the hearing room.

"We will see you here Friday morning, then." Chief Oshkosh spoke to Sam directly and in perfect English.

Stunned, Sam clasped the man's right hand. "Yes, I will be here."

"Thank you for your help." Soaring Eagle too spoke English and shook Sam's hand. Then he and Oshkosh took their leave.

Sam laughed and gave Mr. Evans a sideways glance. "Guess I wasn't needed after all."

"Not true. You see, there are men on the committee who are quite prejudiced against the Indians. If they had their way, they would run the Indians up into British Canada and let the English deal with them." Mr. Evans grabbed his leather case and slid it off the table. "Had a white man not done the Menominees' talking for them, I doubt we'd be awaiting an answer. The matter would have likely been immediately cleared from the committee's docket."

Sam marveled at how easily he'd forgotten that hatred abounded. "Then I'm glad I was here."

"Indeed. And now you'll be staying the week." Mr. Evans gave him a friendly slap on the shoulder. "I'll have time to show you around our state's capitol and introduce you to members of the legislative branch."

"I'd like that. Thank you."

"Oh, and I know Samantha will be pleased too."

The smile on Sam's face withered. "Mr. Evans, I—"

"Sam and Sam." He chuckled.

Nonharmonic chords of dislike sounded inside of Sam each time he heard the equation. To him, the phrase was far from amusing. However, he didn't want to hurt Miss Evans's feelings, and he certainly wouldn't offend his host.

Squaring his shoulders, he sensed an impending skirmish. Sam only hoped he could talk his way around it without causing insult or injury. Out in the echoing, marble hallway, Sam prayed this week would pass quickly.

CHAPTER 16

$\mathcal{K}$RISTIN WORKED HER needle in and out of the fabric of Jackson's torn shirt. The afternoon rain had moved out, and now the October sunset flared gloriously in the western sky.

"Let us continue our lessons," Mary said.

Sitting on the front porch, Kristin smiled to herself, thinking that young Mary was a relentless instructor.

"Say '*kornet er gul*' in English."

"Um…" Kristin had to think. "Corn is yellow."

"Correct!" Mary clapped, and Kristin laughed softly.

"Now, '*himmelen er blå.*'"

"Sky is blue."

Mary smiled and clapped her hands again.

Her actions tickled Kristin.

A rider on horseback suddenly appeared on the soggy road, leading to the area between the house and barn. He slowed his horse as he neared.

Kristin paused, needle in hand.

Mary stood. "It is the sheriff! I will fetch Pa from the barn."

Setting aside her sewing, Kristin rose from her chair and

entered the house. She found Mrs. Sundberg in the kitchen, preparing the freshly laundered clothes for tomorrow's ironing.

"The sheriff is here."

"Oh?" She stepped back and wiped her hands on her apron. "Will you make a pot of coffee and pull out the leftover biscuits? We'll serve them along with some apple butter. In the meantime, I will greet our guest."

"*Ja,* of course." Kristin set about the task.

She could hear Mr. Sundberg's voice boom outside. Was he angry? Minutes later he stomped into the house. He glared at Kristin, and her eyes grew wide. What had she done now?

Mrs. Sundberg and the sheriff came in shortly afterward and settled at the dining room table. Kristin carried in a tray containing the coffeepot, cups, biscuits, spoons, and a small dish of apple butter. She set her burden down on the table a bit harder than intended and sent her employers an apologetic look.

Cool fingers came to rest on Kristin's wrist. The simple gesture, along with Mrs. Sundberg's gentle expression, let Kristin know no harm had been done.

"So you think these silver spoons are the ones that were taken from your home years ago?" the sheriff asked.

Kristin's gaze flew to the ruby-colored velvet bag in Mr. Sundberg's fist.

"*Ja,* these are the ones. I can tell by the silversmith's stamp on the back." Mr. Sundberg opened the bag and inspected each little spoon.

Kristin had seen such spoons before. From what she understood, people who wanted to avoid paying income tax took their coins to silversmiths and had them made into spoons. The government didn't tax spoons, after all. Only coins.

As she left the dining room, Kristin heard Mr. Sundberg ask, "Who found them?"

The sheriff stroked his beard. "A pawnbroker in town."

Kristin shooed Jack and Mary from the doorway where they stood eavesdropping. "Up to your rooms and do homework."

"Shh—" Jack put his forefinger on his lips.

Before she could shake her head at the children's naughtiness, Mr. Sundberg shouted for Kristin to return to the dining room.

Her heart hammered, but she made her way back, feeling as if her shaking legs might give way. What did she have to do with stolen coin silver?

"Tell her, Sheriff." Mr. Sundberg stood, his face reddened with anger.

"Miss Eikaas…" Sheriff Brunette's gaze was inquisitive but not condemning. "Mr. Errens, a pawnbroker in town, said a blonde-haired, blue-eyed young woman traded in these stolen spoons for cash. He added that she was Norwegian."

Kristin needlessly wiped her hands on her apron. She already sensed where this was going, but she waited for the sheriff to finish.

"We don't have a large Norwegian population here in Green Bay, so the young lady in question could be any number of—"

"You!" Mr. Sundberg pointed a finger of accusation at Kristin. "You are doing your uncle's dirty work."

"That is not true!" Kristin let her apron fall. "I have not spoken to my uncle since I began working for you."

"But you consorted with the younger Olstad. He is probably in on it too!"

"Simmer down, Karl." The sheriff motioned for Mr. Sundberg to be seated. "I have been to the Eikaas place, and Lars said he knows nothing about the silver—still claims he never did."

"He lies." Hard lines appeared around Mr. Sundberg's mouth.

With a deep breath, the sheriff folded his hands on the table.

"Miss Eikaas, I need to ask some questions. Do you know anything about the stolen silver? Did anyone ask you to take it to Mr. Errens's shop?"

"No." Kristin face flamed with indignation, although her voice shook with the fear of being accused of such a crime. "I had no part in this incident."

Mr. Sundberg's hand came down hard on the tabletop. "She is an Eikaas and lies like her uncle."

"Karl, please do not get so upset," Mrs. Sundberg pleaded.

Mr. Sundberg's blue eyes slid to his wife, then back at Kristin. She glimpsed the hatred in his gaze.

"Sheriff, this girl here gave Peder Olstad money last week."

Sheriff Brunette glanced at Kristin.

"It was my own money—from furs that Running Deer gave me."

"Karl?" the sheriff asked.

"Well, that part is true, but I think it is safe to say Lars used the two of them as go-betweens. And it is obvious Lars needs the money to fix his barn and that sorry excuse of a house before the bad weather hits."

The sheriff wagged his head. "The Olstads are not involved. Both father and son left on Saturday at sunup. I know that because I, personally, saw them out of town. Peder got into some trouble Friday night at a tavern. A man was killed."

Kristin inhaled sharply.

"It was clearly self-defense. However, it wasn't the first time that I've had a run-in with the young man. I asked him to leave Green Bay, and he agreed. His father went with him, and as I said, I rode them out of town."

"Where did they go?" As angry as she'd been with Peder, it was disheartening to hear he'd left without saying good-bye. What would she tell Sylvia now? Would she ever see her best friend again?

"They are headed out West—California, maybe. Peder has got ideas about gold-digging."

"*Ja*...he said as much to me." Kristin murmured. She stared at the black laces in her boots.

"See!" The accusation in Mr. Sundberg's voice could not be ignored.

"Mr. Sundberg"—Kristin lifted her chin—"Peder mentioned California to me the day he hurt Jackson. Please believe me when I say I have done nothing wrong."

"And how could she, Karl?" Mrs. Sundberg rose to her defense. "She has been helping me every day." She looked at the sheriff. "I had one of my episodes."

"Sorry to hear it." The sheriff turned momentarily pensive before pushing back his chair. "Well, Karl"—he stood—"it appears Miss Eikaas has an alibi. I believe she is innocent of any crime."

"But—"

"To tell you the truth, I hated to bring up the matter of this missing silver again. It has divided our small Norwegian church and affected our community. I wish Reverend Wollums would do something. I wish I *could* do something. The contention between you and Lars Eikaas is...shameful."

"But my family has been greatly wronged." Mr. Sundberg got to his feet once more. "I am surprised you cannot see the connection between Lars stealing these silver spoons and his niece taking them to a pawnbroker."

"There is no evidence to back up your theory, Karl." The sheriff gathered the spoons and put them in their velvet bag. They clinked together as he dropped them in. "I will keep these locked up for now. I realize you want your silver back, but Errens paid out on them. Until I discover the identity of the young lady in question, I must keep the silver under lock and key."

"Well, see that you do." Mr. Sundberg looked away, his angry expression leveled at some point on the dining room wall.

The sheriff glanced at Kristin. "Miss Eikaas, may I have a word with you, please?"

"Take her to jail is what you should do!"

"Karl, please..." Mrs. Sundberg stood and walked over to him. She rubbed his shoulder as if to calm him.

Kristin thought the woman ought to slap him for how he behaved. Nonetheless, Kristin trailed the sheriff out of the house.

They walked in silence to where his horse had been tethered to a nearby post.

The sheriff donned his black hat. "I am sorry about all this, Miss Eikaas." He packed the silver into his brown leather saddlebag.

Kristin worked her lower lip between her teeth and managed a nod even though she felt like sobbing. If only Sam were here to help and protect her.

"The missus and I have a home in town and...well, maybe it would be best if you stayed with us or the Wollumses until Karl cools down." He faced her. "It is amazing he hired you to be Mrs. Sundberg's house girl, but—"

"It was Sam's idea. He wanted to help me."

A certain knowing light entered the sheriff's eyes. "I see. Well, Sam is in Madison now, and I hear it could be a while before he returns."

"Mrs. Sundberg needs me. I must stay...for her sake."

"If you say so." He mounted his steed. The animal snorted and tossed his chestnut-brown head when Sheriff Brunette pulled the reins toward the road. "I suppose if you can beat off school bullies, you can handle Karl Sundberg." A grin inched across his bearded face. "But if you change your mind, you can seek refuge with my wife and me or with the Wollumses."

And then do what? She couldn't hide from her uncle and Mr. Sundberg forever. Still, it helped to be offered an alternative. "*Takk.*"

After a polite tip of his hat, the sheriff spurred his horse down the road.

Kristin stood there for several long minutes, watching the lawman ride off. She glanced at the Sundbergs' house next, knowing she must force herself to go back inside. Closing her eyes, she desperately wished that Sam would return... soon.

***

The pungent scent of Miss Evans's perfume caused a vicelike squeezing between Sam's ears. She said the fragrance was *Lilies of Paris* and an expensive gift from her father, who had purchased the bottle in Chicago. However, Sam knew he'd never smelled any kind of lilies like the ones she wore tonight.

Miss Evans shifted in her chair, sending another flowery plume his way. Sam winced as the throbbing at his temples increased. Escape was impossible, with her seated on his right-hand side and Mr. Evans on his left. At the front of the room an orchestra played a loud, dissonant number that did nothing to ease his headache.

Finally the intermission came, and Sam made straight for the balcony doors. He breathed in deeply of the cool, October air, trying to clear the scent of Miss Evans's floral presence. The autumn night breeze carried a sweet aroma of its own—one Sam recognized.

The wind from a sudden rainstorm this afternoon had scattered tree leaves. Harvest colors littered lawns and walkways.

The clean, damp, earthy smell always signaled a reminder to Sam to make hay before the weather turned bitter cold and a foot of snow buried the landscape.

"There you are, son."

Sam turned to see Mr. Evans step out onto the balcony, carrying two short glasses.

"Since you're being antisocial, I brought the punch to you." Holding out the tumbler, the man smiled. "Apple cider. And not to worry. The only alcohol involved here tonight would be that in the flask Mr. Jones happens to be carrying."

Sam chuckled and decided the cider might help to alleviate his headache. He sipped the sweet-tasting mix. "Mmm, very good. Thank you." He cleared his throat. "My apologies for being, as you said, antisocial, but I can't seem to shake my headache."

Mr. Evans pursed his lips and frowned. "Too bad."

"It'll abate." Again, Sam wished he were home. Ma knew better than he what herbs would help. She had remedies for most ailments—except her episodes.

"It's probably tension. I understand the importance of this morning's hearing. You're feeling it too."

"Yes, perhaps." Although his daughter's perfume hadn't helped matters.

"You're a serious young man."

Sam grinned. "What makes you say so?"

Mr. Evans regarded him from beneath arched brows. "Your reaction to Samantha, that's what. Most young men are drawn to her beauty and amused by her charm. You seem indifferent."

"I mean no offense, Mr. Evans. Your daughter is lovely." Sam paused to carefully choose his words, then gave up and decided to let honesty dictate. "There's a young lady back home whom I'm interested in courting."

"Ah..."

Sam spared the details as Mr. Evans already knew of the contention between Pa and the Eikaas family.

"Your father is aware of your intentions?"

"Yes, except, unfortunately, he doesn't approve."

"I didn't think so. During your father's frequent visits he and I often discussed the possibility of matching you and my daughter." He drained his glass.

"Is that right?" Like so many puzzle pieces coming together, Sam thought he saw the entire picture. "You and my father? Discussed a possible match between me and—"

"Sam and Sam." Mr. Evans chuckled.

Sam fought the urge to roll his eyes at the wearisome quip. He pondered, yet once more, his father's objections to his pursuance of Kristin.

Sam and Sam.

Suddenly a lot of strange things made perfect sense.

CHAPTER 17

KRISTIN AWOKE TO voices talking directly above her basement room. She recognized them at once, Mr. Sundberg's angry tone and Mrs. Sundberg's gentle voice of reason. Climbing out of bed, she lit a lamp and checked the time. It was early, so she knew she hadn't overslept. She wondered if either Jack or Mary had taken ill.

Pulling on her housecoat, she lifted the lamp, yawned, and made her way upstairs and into the main kitchen. The Sundbergs weren't there and their voices had quieted, so Kristin assumed they'd gone upstairs. She lit the stove and prepared the morning's usual pot of coffee. Then she returned to her room and dressed for the day.

Two more thoughts crowded Kristin's mind as she brushed her hair. First, Sam had been gone exactly one week, and second, ever since the sheriff had come by with the spoons, Mr. Sundberg's attitude toward her had grown increasingly hostile. Thankfully yesterday had been Wednesday, market day, and Mr. Sundberg left before Kristin arose. She didn't see him until supper that evening. He'd stayed in town all day, perhaps hoping for some word from Sam.

A knock sounded, and Kristin set down her hairbrush and strode across the small room. Placing her hand on the knob, she turned and opened the door. Mrs. Sundberg stood there and pushed out a sad-looking smile.

"I must speak with you."

"Of course. Come in."

The woman entered, and Kristin sensed something was very wrong. "Are Jack and Mary all right?"

"Oh, they are fine. They can sleep a bit longer this morning because Karl will drive them in to school." The Oneida woman, whom Kristin thought of as a friend, averted her gaze and spoke to the plank floor. "Kristin, I am afraid we must let you go."

A wave of disbelief hit her, knocking her off balance. She lowered herself down on the bed.

"The tension in my home is, well, not healthy for any of us. As it is, I feel another episode approaching. I slept very little last night."

"And that is my fault?" Kristin asked, a bit defensively.

"No." Mariah met her gaze squarely. "But Karl is my husband, and my loyalties in this house cannot be divided. I want Jack and Mary to look up to their father with respect. However, they defend you against him. So do I. The fact does not change Karl. It infuriates him."

"Because he is wrong. For all the reasons we spoke about on Sunday evening."

"Correct." Mrs. Sundberg whispered her reply and glanced over her shoulder at the half-opened door. "But only God can change a man's heart. As Karl's wife, my duty is to see to his happiness and that of my children's welfare."

Stunned, Kristin could only blink. "Are you sending me back to my uncle Lars?"

Mrs. Sundberg shook her head. "No, I want peace in my

household again, but not at the price of your safety. You will live with Mrs. Brunette and the sheriff." Once more, Mrs. Sundberg lowered her dark eyes. "The Wollumses would take you, but they might be leaving Green Bay." Meeting Kristin's gaze again, she added, "The divisiveness in our church is driving our good reverend and his family away."

Kristin was sorry to hear it, and yet she refused to take blame. "I have done nothing wrong, Mrs. Sundberg. I have not spoken to my uncle since he pointed his gun at me and Sam came to my rescue that day."

"I know you are innocent of the charges my husband makes against you. But he believes them, and I cannot persuade him otherwise. And now...my health is waning again. I felt it coming on late last night."

"Sit down beside me, Mrs. Sundberg." Kristin scooted over.

"No, thank you. You must quickly pack. Karl will want you ready to go after breakfast. He does not want Jack and Mary to be late for school. We will tell them that you are moving on to another job—a better one in town."

"A lie?"

"No. You will be working for Mrs. Brunette."

"I see." A rigid formality stole into Kristin's voice and made its way to her heart.

Mrs. Sundberg walked slowly to the door. "I'll be praying for you."

"I do not want to hear about your prayers. You said yourself that they do nothing. Look at your husband. Do your prayers change him? No. Look at our small church." Kristin gave a wag of her head. "I do not think God is here in America."

"Oh, but He is, Kristin." With her eyes brimming with tears, Mrs. Sundberg swallowed hard. "This is not a punishment. You will see."

Looking away, Kristin stood and walked to where her few dresses hung. She refused to grace the statement with a reply. Instead, draping her garments over one forearm, she moved to her trunk, opened the lid, and dropped them inside.

Mrs. Sundberg quietly left the room, closing the door softly behind her. Kristin stood there, staring at it, feeling her self-worth deflate, second by second. She felt abandoned, by her parents and brothers, Uncle Lars and Aunt Esther, and even by the Olstads. Could Peder and his father not have left a short note for her, saying good-bye? And now Mrs. Sundberg—and maybe even God too.

Kristin decided the Brunettes were the ones getting the real bargain. They were about to acquire a free maid, house-keeper, and cook—all because Kristin had been turned out of two households and had nowhere else to go. True, the sheriff seemed like a kindhearted man, but she supposed time would tell.

Beneath the lamplight she resumed packing. Maybe she judged the sheriff too harshly just now. But everyone was nice upon the first few meetings. What if the sheriff proved as ornery as Uncle Lars—or as stubborn and hateful as Mr. Sundberg? Worse, the charges that she had been party to a theft would likely follow her everywhere she went.

Smells of breakfast cooking wafted down into her room, but Kristin didn't feel like eating and continued to collect her things. When she finished, she sat down on the cot and just waited to be told when to go out to the wagon. Mr. Sundberg would have to carry out her trunk. What would Sam say when he discovered his family rid themselves of her? Would he, like Mrs. Sundberg, go along with his father's illogical biases in order to keep that curmudgeon appeased?

Oh, Sam…please come home!

At long last the Sundbergs came for Kristin. Mr. Sundberg grunted as he lifted Kristin's trunk.

"I have appreciated all you have done here," Mrs. Sundberg said. "I want you to know that."

Together they walked to the wagon, where Mr. Sundberg now sat waiting, his back turned, shoulders stiff.

Kristin didn't speak. To do so would mean dissolving into a pool of tears.

"Please do not be angry with me."

Angry? Kristin had always thought Mrs. Sundberg was quite adept at discerning emotions. But the woman missed the mark entirely just now. Crushed, heartbroken—that's how Kristin felt. Not angry.

"Good-bye." Mrs. Sundberg held out her arms, but Kristin turned away. What an ultimate betrayal, an embrace!

Mrs. Sundberg stepped back and then moved to place kisses on her children's foreheads. After a quick farewell to Mr. Sundberg, she returned to the house, moving slowly, already in evident pain.

Kristin banished the concern from her heart. Mrs. Sundberg wasn't any of her business. Not anymore. She climbed into the wagon bed without speaking to Mr. Sundberg.

"You can sit here with me," Mary offered, patting to the place beside her in the backseat. Jack climbed up in front with his father.

"I prefer right here, thank you." Kristin squared her shoulders and prepared herself for the bumpy ride into town.

On the way, sensing the mood of their father, the children were unnaturally quiet. And with a mind cluttered with doubts and fears, Kristin didn't feel much like talking anyway.

At last Mr. Sundberg halted the wagon in front of a weathered wood-sided home. A split-rail fence ran the perimeter of the property.

Sheriff Brunette sauntered out the front door, followed by his smiling wife. Kristin thought her fate with the couple might not be as horrible as she first imagined. As a conversation in English between them and Mr. Sundberg ensued, Mary tugged on Kristin's arm.

"Will you walk me to school?"

Kristin did her best to ignore the girl.

"Plee-eeze?"

Kristin rolled her eyes at the ten-year-old's pleading.

"It is just down the street, Kristin," Jack said. Tossing a glance at his father, he called a good-bye before sprinting across the road and disappearing down the way.

"Jack plays ball on the playground until Teacher rings the bell to come inside."

Again, Kristin didn't respond to Mary's explanation.

"Walk me to school? Please."

"Oh, all right." Kristin expelled a huff laden with great inconvenience. But it was lost on Mary, who beamed.

Kristin lifted her hems and carefully picked her way across the mucky lane.

"Maybe I can stop and visit you after school sometimes." Mary looked up and squinted into the morning sunshine.

"I am sure we will both be too busy for visits."

"Maybe on Sundays, then."

"Maybe." Kristin thought she could concede that much.

The heels of their boots thumped rhythmically against the wooden walkway as they passed shops, including Miss Betsy's Foundations & Pinnings. Kristin had learned what the sign above the door read. Reaching the playground, Kristin paused.

"Have a good day, Mary."

Unabashed, the girl hugged Kristin around the waist. "Do not worry. We will see each other again soon."

"Perhaps you are right." Kristin's eyes grew misty. "Now go. I see your teacher is about to ring the bell."

Mary took off running. She waved as she climbed the steps to the door.

Kristin waved back. Then she glimpsed Jack. His shirt had come untucked and his hair looked mussed. He saw Kristin and tossed her a gesture that resembled a mock salute. In spite of herself, she smiled and waved good-bye. She would miss both children very much.

Spinning on her heel, she made her way back to the Brunettes' home. Autumn sunshine spilled across her path. But as she passed Miss Betsy's shop, an idea sprouted. Should she? Dare she?

She slowed her pace and glanced at the heavy lace, which covered the tall windows. Her dream had always been of owning a shop, but perhaps working in one would suffice.

Making her way up the four wooden steps to the door, Kristin let herself in. Tiny bells jangled, signaling her entry. Miss Betsy walked in from the back of the store.

"Good morning."

"*God morgen.*" With her nerves tingling, she forgot herself.

Miss Betsy paused. "Oh, yes, I remember you." She spoke in Norwegian, and her smile produced more etchings on her wrinkled face. "Miss Eikaas, isn't it? You purchased some undergarments not long ago."

"*Ja*, and I wondered..." Kristin shifted and ran her tongue along her lower lip. "I wondered if you had a position to fill here. You see..." She paused again, unsure of how to describe the situation in which she now found herself.

"It did not work out at the Sundbergs' place for you?" Miss

Betsy tipped her head. "I did not think it would. You are an Eikaas. They are Sundbergs."

"It worked out fine with everyone except Mr. Sundberg." Kristin didn't mean to share so much so soon. "I mean no disrespect to him, of course."

"Of course." A little grin threatened at the corner of Miss Betsy's mouth. "In truth, I always thought that your uncle and Karl Sundberg were the two most stiff-necked men in Green Bay, Wisconsin."

"*Ja*, I would have to agree." Surprisingly, it didn't please Kristin to admit it.

"Well, I am sorry, I cannot afford hired help."

Kristin replied with an understanding nod. "*Takk*." She made a slow spin for the door.

"Although..."

Kristin's gloved hand paused at the polished brass knob.

"I recall the way you mended Mary Sundberg's dress that day, and you would be an asset to my business."

The compliment meant little at this point.

With disappointment sitting like a knot in her throat, Kristin pulled the door open. But maybe a good position awaited her with the Brunettes. Or perhaps the sheriff could find her work at another shop.

"I could offer room and board, but that's all."

Kristin halted and glanced at Miss Betsy. "Room and board?"

"You could help with the mending I routinely take in. And, of course, assist me around the shop."

"*Ja*, I could do that." Kristin closed the door with more enthusiasm than necessary.

"Maybe someday I could afford to pay you, but not now."

"That is fine with me. I accept your offer."

The older woman's face lit up. "*Ja*?"

"*Ja!*"

Miss Betsy smiled. "It is settled then." Additional crinkles appeared at the corners of her hazel eyes. "We will share the apartment upstairs. It is small, but you will have your own bedroom."

"*Takk.*"

"Come along. I'll show you around. It will be so good to have someone to talk to." She linked her arm with Kristin's. "Oh…and I always eat my meals at the Main Street Café. Your meals will be included in the room and board part."

"Many thanks," Kristin said in English.

"Well, now, that is pretty good. I'll teach you more English so you can talk to the customers."

"I would like that very much."

"Do you need to ride out to the Sundbergs and pack your things?"

"No." Kristin explained the situation. To her added relief, Miss Betsy didn't think there would be any opposition from the sheriff or his wife.

"Yes, indeed." Miss Betsy drew in a deep breath. "I believe our arrangement will work out to the benefit of all involved."

"I do too." And at that precise moment, Kristin sensed she'd found a trusted friend in Miss Betsy Biddle.

❦

Friday morning a hush fell over the hearing room, and Sam felt himself tense as the lean-faced chairman prepared to read his committee's decision.

"It is hereby agreed, by this officially appointed committee, that the Menominee Nation will, in fact, cede the western portion of its land as per the signed 1831 treaty in exchange for the Crow Wing area west of the Mississippi River."

229

Sam felt a lead ball of discouragement drop straight through him.

"Furthermore," the committee chairman added, "an extended time period in which the Menominee are to be removed from the aforementioned United States property is set at five years."

"Perfect," Mr. Evans whispered to Sam. "We'll file petitions and use every lawful tactic to delay the removal."

Sam saw the outcome as anything but *perfect*.

"Stand and thank the gentlemen for their time," Mr. Evans prompted quietly.

Sam pushed back the chair and got to his feet. "Sirs, I want to thank you for your time here today and…" He glanced at Mr. Evans then at Soaring Eagle and Chief Oshkosh. He just couldn't leave this matter as it was. "I would like to inform you all that I plan to take this issue all the way to Washington if need be. I'll go straight to the president, if I must. The Menominee were essentially bamboozled, and that makes even the best of politicians look like thieves to these people—and to others."

The distinguished committee members drew back, bushy eyebrows arched in surprise. Mr. Evans cleared his throat and Sam took the hint. He'd said enough. He sat down.

But the chairman grinned, looking amused. "I would expect no less from Karl Sundberg's son." He stood. "This meeting is now adjourned."

As the committeemen dispersed, Sam slowly rose. He turned to Soaring Eagle. "I'm sorry I couldn't do more."

"You have done plenty." No trace of emotion was evident on the brave's weather-lined face.

Chief Oshkosh stepped around his representative and regarded Sam in a steady gaze. "Our people have time now to survey Crow Wing and determine if the land is suitable.

Meanwhile, we will take you at your word, Sam Sundberg. You are a friend to the Menominee."

Sam inclined his head, honored that the chief deigned to speak directly to him yet a second time.

The Indians filed out of the hearing room, and Sam finally turned to Mr. Evans. "My apologies if I embarrassed you among your colleagues."

"Nonsense! I go toe-to-to with politicians all day long." He chuckled. "However, I have made up my mind about one thing."

"And that is?"

Mr. Evans squared his shoulders. "I want you to work for me, Sam. I need a protégé, a young man who doesn't intimidate easily." He set his hand on Sam's shoulder. "That young man is *you*."

CHAPTER 18

$\mathcal{A}$ PLUME OF DUST swirled up into the late afternoon sunshine as Kristin swept the walk in front of Miss Betsy's shop. After working here for nearly two weeks, a kind of realization began to dawn. Kristin missed being needed. Oh, she missed the Sundberg children and Mrs. Sundberg. She missed Sam terribly. And while there was always something in and around the shop to keep Kristin busy, by the end of the day she didn't find that certain sense of satisfaction like she did when her work had been essential in order for a household to function. But, even so, Kristin wasn't unhappy. She and Miss Betsy had become good friends.

Kristin thought back on the day she'd arrived at Miss Betsy's. As expected, Sheriff Brunette had given his blessing, and when Kristin viewed the room in which she'd stay, she truly did feel blessed. A real bed jutted out from the far wall—not a pallet or a cot, but two mattresses. Straw comprised the bottom one and the top had been stuffed with horsehair. Together they were piled onto a white-metal frame and were covered with soft linens and a pretty quilt. Lacy curtains graced a single window, and a braided rug lay over the plank floor in front of a small hearth. Kristin had nearly shed tears of joy.

Overall, the apartment above the shop was small. It consisted of a large sitting room with a table, matching chairs, and three armchairs, as well as the two bedrooms. There wasn't a kitchen in the place, and Kristin longed for the day she could cook a meal again. But, for now, the café down the street sufficed.

Kristin continued sweeping. Down the road she heard the jangling of wagons as the last of the Wednesday farmers' market wound down to a close. She'd known all morning that the Sundberg wagon wasn't far off, and she wondered if the family had heard from Sam. Shouldn't he have been home by now?

Footfalls on the boardwalk alerted Kristin to another passerby. She stopped sweeping and glanced up to see Aunt Esther making her way toward Miss Betsy's, the last building on the block. As she neared, Kristin thought her aunt looked worn out and weary.

"Good afternoon." Kristin spoke in English.

"*God ettermiddag.*" Her aunt added a curt nod before narrowing her gaze. "I heard you work for Miss Betsy now."

"That is correct." Kristin was surprised that her aunt spoke to her.

"Your uncle wonders what you did to make the Sundbergs let you go."

"Of course he does. However, it is not what I did, but who I am. An *Eikaas.*" Kristin thought she saw an expression of understanding flit across her aunt's face and pursued the conversation. "Did you help Uncle Lars sell produce today?"

"*Ja,* the last of our squash and several pumpkins. But we didn't sell too much. Never do."

Kristin pulled the broom up closer. "I understand that your, um, cabin and barn were damaged in the storm last month."

Aunt Esther replied first with another quick bob of her head. Then, after a moment's pause, she added, "We have no way to repair the damage. But it is good that the Olstads left. Now we live in the barn."

A small part of Kristin's heart ached for her relatives, especially her cousins. However, she mostly still believed that her aunt and uncle deserved their hardships—and more.

Aunt Esther climbed the few steps and entered the shop.

But now it was Kristin's turn to wonder—what was *Tante* doing in Miss Betsy's? Surely she didn't possess the funds needed to make a purchase.

And surely she doesn't believe that I should pay for her items! After all that had happened, Kristin couldn't squelch such a thought. Maybe *Tante* heard about the money she had given to Peder and thought there was more—and that it ought to be spent on her.

Setting the broom aside, Kristin hurried into the shop after her aunt.

Miss Betsy had already greeted her. "How may I help you today, Mrs. Eikaas?"

"I want some things…for my daughters and me." She strode to one of the bureaus and ran a calloused hand down a soft chemise. "I want store-bought things, like I have never owned before."

"Well, of course, Mrs. Eikaas." Miss Betsy cast a curious glance to Kristin.

She replied with a helpless shrug.

"Is it a special occasion?" Miss Betsy queried.

"*Ja*, you might say so." Turning around, Aunt Esther lifted a proud chin. "My daughter Inga is getting married soon. Her *forloveden* gave her money—a gift—for her trousseau. Inga wants Anna and me to have pretty...*unmentionables.* She sent me to buy them." A prim expression surfaced on her face. "I think such extravagance is...well, sinful. But, as Inga pointed out, it is not as if I have time to sew these garments, and they are badly needed."

"Why, of course. I understand. And nobody needs to know what is under your skirts." Miss Betsy smiled, sending additional crinkles across her lined cheeks.

Aunt Esther looked a bit taken aback by the remark. It was an expression Kristin had frequently seen in Miss Betsy's shop, as speaking publicly about ladies' undergarments was disgraceful. However, Miss Betsy knew her business well, and this was the place in which to discuss women's foundations.

"So, who is the lucky man that Inga will marry?" Miss Betsy made small talk as she sized up Aunt Esther and began gathering the usual. A shift, a corset...

"Mr. Oskar Frantzen, the smithy."

Several of Miss Betsy's curls swung as she shook her head. "I do not know him, but I am sure he is a good man."

"*Ja...*"

Kristin wasn't surprised to learn the identity of Inga's *forloveden.* She found a girl's chemise and held it out to Aunt Esther. "How about this one for Anna?"

"Oh, *ja.* Good."

Minutes later Kristin followed Miss Betsy to the back room, where they assisted Aunt Esther in removing her clothing. Her present undergarments were threadbare and badly stained, and, even with all the attempts made at modesty, Kristin glimpsed red sores on her aunt's skin where the stays had poked through her corset.

"Ah, this is what heaven must feel like." *Tante* murmured after she'd donned the new foundations.

"I am glad you like them." Miss Betsy looked pleased. "We will just burn these old garments."

"*Ja*, it is all they are good for."

Kristin helped her aunt finish dressing. The perpetual crossness that lingered on *Tante's* features seemed to smooth away. A gentler light seeped into her eyes, and little wonder why. Kristin thought she'd be crabby too if her pinnings continually jabbed her.

And then there was the barn in which *Tante* was forced to live. Kristin pondered her aunt and uncle's situation as she walked to the front of the store. Did Reverend Wollums know of their need? Perhaps the congregation would pitch in and help frame up a new house.

Silently *Tante* stepped up to the counter. Miss Betsy tallied the purchases and Aunt Esther extracted a coin purse from her skirt pocket.

"We will see you at church on Sunday, Kristin?"

"No, I am afraid not." Was her aunt attempting to reach out to her? "I have been attending services with Miss Betsy here in town." It seemed easier that way for many reasons.

"Well, at least you are attending church." Aunt Esther removed a large bill.

Kristin recognized the currency's value. Her eyes widened.

A smile spread across Miss Betsy's face. "Can I interest you in something more for the bride-to-be? Bedroom attire for the honeymoon, perhaps?"

A blush worked its way up to Kristin's face.

Aunt Esther cleared her throat. "No, I think the everyday items you have selected for Inga are fine for now."

Kristin hurried to wrap the packages in brown paper. She tied them with twine.

"Come back anytime, Mrs. Eikaas." Miss Betsy saw her out the door. She returned to the counter. "My, my..."

Kristin didn't know what to say. What a generous gift Mr. Frantzen must have bestowed on Inga. And so good of Inga to share!

Miss Betsy recorded the sale before setting the money into a lockbox beneath the counter. "We did a good business just now." The corners of her lips curved upward. "After supper tonight, we can treat ourselves to dessert."

<hr />

The next morning Mary Sundberg burst into the shop on her way to school.

"Kristin! Kristin! We got a letter from Sam yesterday!"

Setting down her dust cloth, she wiped her hands on her brown, bibbed apron.

"Sam thought he would be home by now, so he did not bother to write until last Sunday afternoon."

Prickles of warning climbed Kristin's spine. Why had Sam decided to remain in Madison? "Tell me what his letter said."

The excitement brought Miss Betsy from the back room.

"A letter arrived from Sam," Mary repeated.

"Well, don't just stand there, child." Miss Betsy put her hands on her hips. "Talk!"

"All right." Mary gulped down a breath. "The hearing for the Menominee did not go as Sam had hoped, but the outcome is all right for now." She lifted her hand, listing off each point. "Mr. Evans's home is a stately one, and the capitol is large and impressive."

"Mr. Evans? Your father's friend?" Kristin had heard the name before.

Mary confirmed the question with a quick nod. "Sam is staying with him and his daughter. In his letter, Sam stated that they attended a symphony, a ball, and a fancy party."

"They?" Kristin's unease grew stronger.

Again, the girl bobbed her head. "He and Miss Samantha Evans. Sam wrote that her expensive perfume tickles his nose."

Kristin folded her arms. "Is that so?"

"And Pa said if Sam married Miss Evans, they would be *Sam and Sam*." Mary tossed a glance upward. "Silliest thing I ever heard."

Marry? Miss Evans? A painful knot swelled in Kristin's chest.

"And Mr. Evans offered Sam a job in Madison, so he's staying the rest of the month while he considers the offer!"

Kristin exchanged glances with Miss Betsy, who showed Mary to the door.

"That is a lot of information. Thank you for sharing it. Now run along to school so you will not be late."

"Yes, ma'am. Bye, Kristin."

"Bye." She barely choked out the reply.

So, Sam changed his mind about courting her…

"I would not jump to conclusions." Miss Betsy moved away from the door.

Kristin stared down at the dark plank floor. Over the past couple of weeks she'd confided in Miss Betsy about her deep feelings for Sam and the words of promise he'd spoken to her before he left.

"As spry as she is, Mary is still a little girl."

Kristin brought her chin up quickly. "Miss Evans's expensive perfume tickles his nose?"

A flash of uncertainty entered Miss Betsy's eyes. "Hard to misinterpret that, isn't it?"

"No doubt Mr. Sundberg gives his blessing on the match and the new job. After all, he hates me."

"Oh…" Miss Betsy waved her hand in the air. "I have known Karl for years. He can be as stubborn as a goat. Thank goodness Mariah is a gentle soul." Miss Betsy tapered her gaze. "And I have known Sam since he was a boy. One word to describe him is…honorable." She set her palms on Kristin's upper arms. "You just need to have faith."

"Faith?" Kristin pulled away. "Everyone I love abandons me. Maybe God has too! Maybe I am cursed, just as my uncle said!"

Despite her efforts to hold them in check, tears leaked onto her cheeks. Covering her mouth, Kristin ran to the back room so if a customer entered, she wouldn't be seen crying.

Miss Betsy followed. "There, there…"

Seconds later, Kristin found herself sobbing against the older woman's shoulder.

"Let it out. That's right. A good cry cleanses the soul."

Long minutes ticked by. Finally Kristin's tears were spent.

"All you have to do is count your blessings." Miss Betsy led her over to where two chairs sat near an opened window that looked out to the schoolyard. "You are not cursed at all. Think of how God spared you from the disease that ravaged your village in Norway."

"Yes, but—"

"And God protected you on your journey here to America. Others died, trying to reach our shores."

"I know, except—"

"God's hand of mercy separated you from your uncle's tyranny and Karl Sundberg's bitterness. Remember, Kristin? Dwell on all God's goodness and grace."

She tried. She wanted to think of all the good things in her life. But somehow they seemed overshadowed by one regrettable event after another.

Miss Betsy continued. "When I was a child, it was just my father and me. My mother had passed. I never had any siblings. Papa brought me here from Ohio. I left all my friends and comforts. Then, only months after we settled here, Papa was killed while trapping. A tragic accident. It took awhile, but I overcame the sadness...or so I thought.

"When I came of age, I wanted desperately to get married, as most young ladies do. But the right man never came along. The years went by and by. No husband. No children. I felt so alone and, yes, abandoned up here in the Wisconsin wilderness.

"That is when a dear friend, the woman who owned this shop before me, reminded me that I am never alone. She explained that happiness is not in ourselves—or in another person. Joy comes from God."

"*Ja*, I know..." Growing up, Kristin had heard as much from the pulpit.

"But do you know that when our Lord hung on the cross, He cried, 'My God, My God, why hast thou forsaken me?' You see, your feelings of abandonment are not foreign to our Savior. And as He suffered there, He saw your face, just as He saw mine."

Miss Betsy's words reached an abysmal chasm in her soul, and Kristin's tears returned, this time for an altogether different reason. Had she ever thought of the Lord's crucifixion and death in such a...a personal way?

"And that is only the beginning. God raised His Son up from the grave on the third day. He is alive and with us today." Miss Betsy closed her eyes. "Praise be to God!"

Somehow Kristin didn't feel much like praising.

Miss Betsy must have sensed it. "Talk to Jesus. Tell Him about all the hurt you are carrying inside."

"But..."

"He can handle it, dearie. He is God."

Suddenly a dam of emotion ruptured. With tears gathering in her eyes, Kristin bowed her head. She prayed, although if she would have spoken the words aloud, they wouldn't have made any sense. Still, she knew the Lord understood each and every utterance of her broken heart.

Mor, Poppa... she cried for her deceased parents and brothers. *Uncle Lars...* she mourned at his mistreatment of her and for selling Poppa's treasured gold pocket watch. The *Sundbergs...* they abandoned her when she needed them most. *Sam...* he'd been her hero. Now he too left her.

"No one cares about me." Kristin managed to eke out the words through a sob.

"God cares. He loves you, dearie. Accept His love. Tell Him you do."

Kristin knew she didn't deserve to be loved by a holy God. She had learned that much in her confirmation classes. But had she ever accepted God's love?

Please, God, I want to be loved by You. You are the only One who can help me, guide and direct me... take this pain from me.

Minutes passed and Kristin quieted.

"With His stripes, we are healed."

Miss Betsy's words were a soothing balm. Kristin's tears came to an end. She dried her eyes with the ends of her apron.

"Better?"

"*Ja.* Better." She had to admit, she felt unburdened. "Such self-pity. How shameful of me."

"No. You are a young lady who has weathered some storms

of life. But they brought you to this point. And now you can continue onward with joy, knowing God walks alongside you."

Kristin's newfound feelings were unexpected and foreign. Yet they were strong and sure. "I have never been more certain of God's presence as I am now."

Miss Betsy smiled, and all the wrinkles in her cheeks narrowed and multiplied. Kristin saw joy reflected in the older woman's countenance.

"God is good." Miss Betsy's succession of little nods threatened her hairpins. She hugged Kristin around the shoulders. "Now, go upstairs and wash your face. Rest a bit." She stood. "In a while we will walk to the café and have our noon dinner."

⁕

Sam walked slowly down the tree-lined lane. A gust of autumn wind stole the last of the colored leaves from their branches. The sun felt warm on his face, although the chill in the air made him glad he'd worn his overcoat when he left the Evanses's stately home this morning.

For most of the day Sam had been at Mr. Evans's office researching the documents he possessed. He patted the papers tucked inside his dress coat's breast pocket. Who would have thought? Never had he dreamed…

His steps quickened. Enthusiasm pumped through his veins. But then Sam checked himself and relaxed his stride. He was in no rush to return to the Evanses's home this afternoon. He lifted his gaze to utter a silent prayer and noticed that the late October sky looked as blue as…*as blue as Kristin's eyes.* It was a day worthy of a good long stroll.

Thoughts of Kristin resurfaced, and Sam decided that thinking about her brought out the romantic in him, unlike a certain other young lady whose company he had been forced to keep lately.

Which was why he chose to walk so slowly back to the Evanses'. He couldn't abide more simpering parlor talk before dinner tonight.

What's more, he'd promised to give Mr. Evans his answer about the job position today.

Truly, there wasn't ever a doubt in Sam's mind as to what he'd decide. But then his conversation with Soaring Eagle last week proved confirmation.

Again Sam patted the folded papers in his breast pocket. The gift. The amazing gift!

As a token of gratitude, Oshkosh had bestowed on Sam a deed for some acreage located between Appleton and Manitowoc, east of Lake Winnebago—or *Ouinipegouek*, as the Fox Indians called it. The name meant *people of the stinking water*, as Lake Winnebago was reported to have a strong fish odor during the summer months. But, looking at the map, Sam's property was far enough away that any stench wouldn't be troublesome.

Sam had told Soaring Eagle to relay his thanks. However, due to the Indians' land dispute, he'd had Mr. Evans's clerk check into the deed. It came back free and clear. The best Sam could figure, the Menominee chief acquired the land in some sort of trade agreement with the original owner.

But now Sam owned the property. It was all registered in his name and a copy scribed for the state's records. He planned to politely refuse Mr. Evans's job offer, which wouldn't be easy, as Mr. Evans wasn't a man who enjoyed taking no for an answer. It had been the primary reason Sam hadn't declined his offer sooner, not that he was lily-livered. Simply, he hadn't wanted to risk his father's reputation.

But there was no help for it at this point. Sam had prayed—and prayed hard. He knew what he had to do.

And then there was Miss Samantha Evans, the Madison socialite. It hadn't taken long for Sam to figure out that she was husband hunting. Mr. Evans's offer, therefore, served as a means to keep his daughter well provided for, should Sam have been overcome by her feminine wiles.

Which he hadn't been. In all truth, he found the young lady a bit too forward for his liking. He much preferred to be the one doing the...*hunting*. What's more, he'd already found what he was looking for in a wife. He knew that now more than ever.

So he would take his leave tomorrow. He'd spend a few days surveying his new property before heading to Green Bay. In spite of the fact that he wasn't lawyer material, he'd be happy to continue representing the Menominee in any way he could. He relayed the sentiment to Soaring Eagle and added that he'd share his land with any Wisconsin natives who desired to hunt or fish on it, so long as their actions brought no danger to him or his family.

A family. Yes, that's what Sam had in mind. Perhaps come springtime he'd be ready to marry, build a house...

Sam realized he was about to pass the Evans's home. Pausing for a brief and silent prayer for wisdom, he took to the stairs. At the top he breathed in deeply, opened the front door, and stepped inside.

CHAPTER 19

*R*IVULETS OF SUNSHINE spilled through the window as Kristin checked her reflection in the looking glass. She tied her light-brown bonnet loosely beneath her chin then pulled on her white gloves.

"Are you ready for church, dearie?"

Whirling around, Kristin smiled at Miss Betsy. "Ready." She admired her friend's dark green brocade dress. One of Kristin's ivory crocheted collars encircled the neckline. "How lovely you look."

"Why, thank you. Now that November is here and the weather has turned, I can wear this dress. It is much too warm for summertime."

"Which reminds me…" Kristin strode to where *Mor's* knitted shawl lay draped over the end of the bed and pulled it around her shoulders.

A warm smile spread across Miss Betsy's face. "Your crocheted dress collars, doilies, and knitted shawls are selling well in the shop. So affordable and yet so elegant. I am pleased."

"Oh, *ja*, I am too." Kristin hugged the wrapper *Mor* had made more tightly to her, glad to earn a bit of money for herself. It made her feel less dependent on others but, at the same time, more dependent on God. She now saw her abilities as gifts from Him. "And I have my mother to thank. She taught me how to spin, weave, knit, crochet, sew…"

"There's no end to your talents." Jovial crinkles around Miss Betsy's eyes increased. "But we will be late if we do not hurry."

They took to the steps that led down to the hallway between the shop and side door. There, they exited.

"What a beautiful morning!" Miss Betsy inhaled deeply.

Kristin glanced at the sky. A few white puffy clouds drifted by. She too breathed in—at least as much as her stays allowed.

But then she caught sight of a dark brown gelding. A patch of white marked his nose and a black mane fell along his muscular neck. Staring at the horse, she stepped forward, toward the wooden walk. She'd swear the Sundbergs had a horse just like that…

Ugh!

She slammed into something—or someone—and the air left her lungs.

He caught her arms. "Kristin!" A wide smile. "We always seem to run into each other."

She felt mesmerized by the boldly handsome blond with eyes as deep blue as the sea. She struggled to inhale, wondering how many times she'd seen his face in her dreams.

"Sam…"

Releasing her, he swept off his hat. "So good to see you, Kristin."

Her lips quivered, but no words formed.

"Welcome back, Sam." Miss Betsy's voice caused Kristin to blink.

Regaining her composure, dozens of questions filled her mind.

Kristin deliberately stepped back. She straightened her shawl and glimpsed the puzzled dip in Sam's brow. But, for the life of her, she didn't know what to think—or say. Last she'd heard some woman's fragrance tickled his nose.

"We are just on our way to church," Miss Betsy continued.

"I know. That is why I am here. I thought I might escort you two beautiful ladies to service this morning."

Kristin couldn't look up at him, but she felt Sam's penetrating gaze. Her cheeks turned fire-hot from his stare. And yet she couldn't help wondering why he didn't attend the Norwegian church with his family.

"Oh, the more the merrier. Right, Kristin?" Miss Betsy gave her arm a tug.

"*Ja*, of course…"

They started walking, and all the way down the block, around the corner, and up the next street, Kristin couldn't seem to untangle her thoughts. Why had Sam come back? Didn't he accept the job his father's friend offered him?

And what about that other woman?

Once at church and inside the sanctuary, Kristin followed Miss Betsy into their usual pew. Sam removed his hat and seated himself on the end, next to Kristin. More worshipers entered the opposite way, and soon Kristin found her arm pressed up tight against Sam's. Of course, Miss Betsy could scoot over if she wished.

Kristin discreetly adjusted the side of her bonnet and sent Sam furtive glances. His skin had a healthy glow to it, and the set of his clean-shaven jaw exuded strength and confidence. How unfair that he should appear relaxed when she felt so distressed. And why did it feel so uncomfortably warm in church this morning?

Sam shifted, and with her next breath, she inhaled the

familiar scent of the soap that Mrs. Sundberg used to wash clothes. Like the deep of the woods, an earthy and piney blend.

Reverend Smith strolled to the pulpit and began his message. Kristin forced herself to concentrate. She still didn't understand much English, although she could pick out more and more words. But today, any effort to do so seemed in vain. She willed the tension from her shoulders and silently prayed.

How do I behave, Lord? Happy to see Sam, because I am, or angered by his...philandering?

The latter had threatened almost as soon as she'd set eyes on him.

Kristin's thoughts shifted to Uncle Lars and Mr. Sundberg. Two angry men, insulted, offended, and quick to judge and condemn. She didn't want to be like them. Therefore she would accept Sam's presence, be cordial, and when the appropriate time came, she would inquire over this morning's visit.

Unless he announced his impending marriage first. Maybe he wanted to be the one to tell her the news.

At long last, the service came to a close. Kristin couldn't wait to sidle out of the pew. However, several of Sam's friends hailed him in the vestibule, and he blocked her way out the door. Turning in the other direction, Miss Betsy stared up at the ceiling beams. She wasn't going anywhere fast.

Kristin resigned herself to the waiting.

"It is only polite that we wait for Sam," Miss Betsy leaned over and whispered in her ear. "After all, he escorted us here."

"*Ja*, I suppose you are right."

"Of course I am." She patted Kristin's arm.

Several ladies paused to chat with Kristin and Miss Betsy. Soon after their conversations dwindled, Sam's friends also left the church.

Sam turned to Kristin and Miss Betsy. His eyes darkened

with apology. "Sorry to have kept you both waiting. Shall we go eat lunch? My treat."

"Marvelous! We accept." Miss Betsy smiled broadly.

After flicking her employer a glance of mild annoyance, Kristin turned and faced Sam. Her heart raced when her gaze met his. And here she'd taken great pains to avoid this reaction. "Thank you, Sam." She made sure to use English.

"*Bra, bra*—good, good." He looked both pleased and amused. He offered Kristin one arm and Miss Betsy the other. "I am a fortunate man."

"And so sincere," Kristin quipped. Lifting her chin, she tried to hide the laugh that bubbled forth.

"You are as plucky as ever, I see."

"Pluckier," Miss Betsy attested.

Kristin held back further comment, knowing she was outnumbered.

They strode to an establishment near Lake Michigan called The Fish Bone. Kristin had never been there before. She glimpsed the line of what she assumed were sailing men seated at the long bar, and her step faltered.

Sam coaxed her along. "This is a respectable place, trust me."

She did, although she couldn't help casting a quick look at Miss Betsy. Gauging from her expression, Kristin didn't get the sense of any impropriety.

"Mr. Owens makes a tasty lunch from the catch of the day. Pa and I have dined here in the past."

"So have I." Miss Betsy spoke above the din. "I would come more often, but the location is too far from my shop." Her eyes met Kristin's. "The café is closer."

Kristin agreed. And, because she and Miss Betsy didn't have family, Mr. Findley, the proprietor, opened to them on Sundays too, but only for evening repast. Most times she and Miss Betsy were invited to friends' homes after church.

After they were seated, Kristin and Miss Betsy removed their gloves.

"You are looking well, Sam." Miss Betsy tilted her head. "I take it you fared well in Madison."

"I did." He patted his midsection and grinned. "Perhaps too well."

Resentment nipped at Kristin. "*Ja*, Mary came in to the store to tell us about your letter."

"Great. You know about the hearing then."

Before Kristin could say, a barkeep appeared at their table to take their dinner order. Sam ordered the special, whitefish rolled in flour and fried in butter along with boiled potatoes and butternut squash.

The man sauntered off to prepare their meal.

"Oh, and before I forget…" Sam set his forearms on the table. "Ma sends her regards."

A heartsick knot formed in Kristin's throat. In spite of the rejection she felt, she missed Mrs. Sundberg.

"How has your mother been feeling, Sam?" Thank goodness Miss Betsy found her voice.

"Good, for the most part. I only got back late Friday. But Ma has hired a house girl. Her father is Menominee and her mother is white. Her name is *Atāēhemen-kēsoq*, which means Strawberry Moon." Sam grinned sheepishly. "We just call her Attie for short."

"I imagine she's pretty." Kristin could envision the young lady's round, brown face, dark, shining eyes, and a shy smile. She watched Sam's expression closely.

"I guess she's pretty. Personally, I did not notice, but my uncle, Running Deer, seems to be taken with her. She seems to like him too from what I have seen. Ma said she is tired of losing house girls and next time she will hire an old woman."

"If I did not already have a job," Miss Betsy joked, "I would inquire."

The very idea made Kristin smile.

Small talk, benign in nature, continued until their food arrived. Not much was said during the meal, and Kristin thought they all must have been quite hungry. When they finished eating, Sam paid for their dinner while Kristin and Miss Betsy pulled on their gloves. Then they left the eatery but took their time walking back to the shop.

"I think this walk did me good." Miss Betsy smiled up at Sam. "But now I am ready for a nap."

He chuckled.

"Thank you for a most enjoyable meal and your charming company."

Sam gave a slight bow. "You are most welcome, Miss Betsy."

"*Ja*, thank you, Sam."

"My pleasure, Kristin." His gaze followed Miss Betsy to the door before sliding back to hers. "May I speak with you privately?"

She nodded. The moment she'd been dreading all morning had arrived.

"Ma told me about what happened. Any detail she forgot, Jack and Mary supplied." He lowered his gaze. "It is regrettable."

Kristin stared down at her folded gloved hands and pressed her lips together to stave off the urge to weep. She had thought she'd gotten past the sadness of that particular untimely departure.

"I am sorry, Kristin—sorry that my father's actions wounded you."

She attempted a careless shrug. "I am content working and

residing with Miss Betsy." The last thing she wanted was Sam's pity.

"I can tell."

When she finally mustered the nerve to look at Sam, he offered his arm.

"Shall we continue our stroll?"

Kristin didn't think that was wise. "Sam, perhaps you should state what is on your mind and get it over with."

"Get it over with?" His brows drew inward.

"*Ja*, I sense you have something important to tell me."

"Well, I do, but I can think more clearly when I am walking."

Kristin gave in, dreading each step. Dried leaves crunched under their footfalls, and the lagging conversation rattled her nerves. Maybe if she started it off…

She gave Sam a sideways glance, noticing the strong set of his jaw once again, along with his broad shoulders beneath his dark wool jacket. What woman wouldn't be proud to wed such a hardworking and handsome man? "Mary told Miss Betsy and me about your new girl and how her expensive perfume tickles your nose."

"What?" Sam stopped short and gazed at Kristin. "What girl?"

"Samansam." At least that's the name she'd heard.

A grin became a smile, and then Sam's chortles filled the quiet autumn air. "No, no…her perfume gave me a splitting headache. And she's not my girl. Never was."

"So you took her to the symphony and parties for what purpose?" Kristin tugged her hand away. "To impress her rich father? You must have succeeded. I understand you have a new job in Madison. Is this the news you wanted to—"

Sam touched his fingertips to her lips. "No, Kristin, you have it all wrong."

She quieted and he drew back.

"I did escort Miss Evans to the symphony and a couple of parties. But Mr. Evans was there too, and I only agreed because I did not want to be rude." He narrowed his gaze and leaned forward once again. "But you are very pretty when you're jealous."

"I am not jealous." Seconds later she recanted. She never wanted to lie to Sam. "All right, perhaps I am jealous, but only because of the promise you made before you left."

"And I intend to keep it." Sam held her gaze a long moment before walking to his horse. Reaching into his saddlebag, he removed what appeared to be documents. He shoved them in his coat's inner pocket.

Returning to her, he offered his arm once more. Slowly Kristin wound her hand around his elbow.

"Let us sit over there." He pointed into the distance, near the schoolyard.

She followed his lead to a grassy place near a towering oak. Only a few stubborn leaves remained on its barren branches.

Kristin sat down and straightened the skirt of her blue and green plaid dress. Sam lowered himself to the ground and then removed the papers from his coat pocket.

He gazed at her intently. "I have missed you, Kristin."

She dropped her gaze. "I missed you too." But he would never know just how much. Words couldn't describe the way her heart twisted whenever thoughts of Sam in another woman's arms had flitted across her mind.

"Look what I have." He unrolled the papers in his hand and explained the generous gift an Indian chief had bestowed on him. He pointed to a map and showed her where the land was situated in conjunction with Brown County's location. "It's about a half-day's journey from here...maybe more with a team of horses and a wagon."

Sam went on to recount his survey of the property. "There is a stream that borders two sides of the area. The water is so clear, Kristin, that I could see trout, swimming beneath the surface, in between the rocks.

"There's wide open space, and my first night camping out I saw a buck." Sam reclined, propped by one elbow. "He looked majestic with his full rack of antlers, standing against the back-drop of the half-moon."

Kristin didn't utter a word. Why was he telling her all this? To explain why he would be leaving once again?

Sam didn't seem to notice her silence and continued with his description. "And there is a dense wooded area of oak trees, like this one, also maple, birch. And pine trees too, so tall they whisk the clouds. But the woods need thinning—which means there will be plenty of lumber to build our home come spring."

"Our home?" Kristin blinked.

Sam sat straight up. His face reddened to his hairline. "Forgive me. I should not have been so presumptuous."

She gave him a small smile "Of course I forgive you, Sam." However, as he'd been speaking, a sad niggling grew stronger and more persistent until she couldn't ignore it. "But a match between us seems impossible."

"Because of your dreams to be a shop owner one day?"

She shook her head.

"I would never ask you to give up your dreams for me."

"It is not that, Sam. No one can take away my dreams. I will take them with me wherever I go." She made little circles in the grass with her forefinger. "Besides, if given the option, I would much prefer a family to a shop."

"Then what is it, Kristin?"

"Your father. He despises me. He thinks I partnered with my uncle and that I cashed in stolen silver for money."

His gaze softened. "I know. Ma told me."

"And she agrees with him."

"No, she does not."

"She agreed to send me away. Your parents were willing to leave me on the Brunettes' doorstep."

"That is not quite so. Ma knows how stubborn my father can be. His temper flares and he says unconscionable things. Note that I am not defending him, Kristin. I am merely trying to explain. Ma saw how hurt you were and Pa being his unreasonable self. She wanted to spare you more pain. Finding you another home seemed the only solution. All along, however, Ma knew the Brunettes would care for you."

"But I do not want to be cared for. I want to make my own way. I am a hard worker."

"No one is disputing that, least of all me."

She felt discouraged. "I see no point in discussing this further." She moved to stand, but Sam caught her wrist and, with a tug, sat her back down.

He leaned in so his face was close to hers. "Kristin, you will have to trust me—and pray for my father. His judgment has been clouded. He has no biblical basis to object to our courtship. In fact, his prejudice against you, along with his bitterness toward the entire Eikaas family, have taken him out of God's will. Therefore he is hardly in a place to discern God's will for my future." It sounded correct, and Sam seemed so certain...

But she didn't want to come between a son and his father.

"All I am asking for is your permission to court you, Miss Kristin Eikaas." Sam took her hand, enfolding it in both of his. "The rest, all the strife between Pa and me and the feuding with your uncle...let's give it all to God. At least for now."

Kristin glanced at her gloved hand in Sam's then searched his face, gazing into his expressive eyes. She touched the side of his face, and he leaned forward, his lips touching hers. Kristin closed her eyes as their kiss deepened. She'd dreamed of this moment since the day they'd met.

Sam sat back and her eyelids fluttered opened. She glimpsed the intensity of emotion written across his expression and realized it had a name—love. It was then she knew she loved him too. She'd loved him since he'd taken her into his arms during the curtain dance.

Still, there seemed a great divide between them.

"I cannot live with your father's resentment. I cannot and will not."

"But I own a piece of land now, Kristin." Sam reached for the deed. "We will move away."

"No." It pained her to continue, but she knew she must. "You will want your children to know their grandparents. And what of Jack and Mary? If you walk out of their lives in this way, it will have a devastating effect on them. They will feel hurt and abandoned—and I know that feeling only too well."

Sam gazed off in the distance. Moments of awkward silence ticked by.

"Are you telling me you plan to reconcile with your uncle and his family?"

"No. I never enjoyed a close, meaningful relationship with any of them even though I wished it would have been so. But you and your family…there is a tie that binds. I cannot sever that, no matter if I wanted to."

Kristin brushed away a willful tear, wanting desperately to retract her words and agree to a courtship—and so much more. She drew in a ragged breath, and Sam looked her way. Kristin stared at the grass, praying he wouldn't guess her tumultuous feelings.

"We should be going." Pushing to his feet, Sam offered his

hand and helped Kristin to stand. He set his hands on her shoulders. "But I am not giving up so easily."

She pushed out the best smile she could muster. "I certainly hope not."

CHAPTER 20

*P*ULLING BACK THE heavy lace curtain, Kristin peered out onto the walk. She sighed. No sign of Sam. They hadn't spoken in ten days, and she'd been hoping—no, praying!—that she'd see or hear from him today.

"Why don't you walk up the block and see if the Sundbergs came to market today. Perhaps Sam is in town," Miss Betsy suggested.

"No." She blew out a breath laden with disappointment. "What good would it do anyway? Sam has to make peace with his father before we can ever have a life together."

"I am certain that Sam is working on it." Miss Betsy walked to where Kristin stood. "Stop fretting, dearie."

Letting the curtain fall, Kristin walked from the window. "I am sure you are right."

"Well, then, seeing as you do not want to walk to the market," Miss Betsy said, "I will go." She strode off into the back room and returned with her bonnet, gloves, shawl, and a basket, dangling from one arm. "It is one of the last street market days before the snow falls. It will be interesting to see what the farmers have left to sell. Perhaps I will find an apple pie."

Kristin's mouth watered. "*Ja*, pie would taste good." Since there wasn't a kitchen in either the shop or the upstairs quarters, they didn't keep much food on hand.

Miss Betsy left the shop. As Kristin watched her go, she hoped she'd find out news about Sam. Meanwhile, she busied herself with tasks around the store. A new shipment had arrived, and the garments needed to be ironed before they could be put on racks or on display.

Walking into the back room, Kristin decided she felt contented to work in Miss Betsy's shop. It almost felt like her very own. Kristin touched the necklace she freely wore outside her blouse now since there was no reason to hide it any longer. *Mor* would have been so proud to know her daughter worked in America knitting accessories like dress collars and shawls. Miss Betsy was impressed with her handiwork. *Mor* would have been too. The idea brought a sense of satisfaction to Kristin.

A long while later, Miss Betsy returned with a full basket. "I found apples, but no pie." She clucked her tongue. "And would you believe I could not get more than a grumble out of Karl Sundberg?"

"*Ja*, I believe it."

"Well, it is hard for me to see him this way, like a dam about to burst. Years ago, when Green Bay was a settlement, folks looked up to Karl. They sought him out for advice." She removed her bonnet. "Now he is so stubborn...just like that Lars Eikaas."

"I will have you know that my father was nothing like *Onkel*."

"Of course he was not, and the fact is evident by the way in which you conduct yourself, my dear."

Kristin had grown increasingly aware of and grateful for the gifts of love and integrity that her parents had bestowed on her in the too-short years they'd lived together. She had never understood that blessing until she lived with Uncle Lars and his family.

Miss Betsy put away her bonnet, gloves, and shawl. Minutes later she strolled up front again. "I did find out a little something about Sam."

Kristin felt hungry to hear the news. "Do tell."

"He will begin working at Kalb's Smithy Shop, alongside Oskar Frantzen—his future cousin." Miss Betsy cackled softly. "Imagine that. Mr. Frantzen is marrying Inga, and Sam is marrying—"

"We are far from that point, Miss Betsy."

She sent a glance upward. "It is nothing that our Lord cannot fix."

"True, and may He not tarry." Kristin thought over what she'd heard. "A blacksmith, eh?" Surprise enveloped her as she straightened a rack of petticoats. "I had no idea that Sam knew the trade."

"That boy can do anything he puts his mind to."

Kristin smiled, thankful that Miss Betsy held Sam in such high regard.

"The way I understand it from Mrs. Kalb, whose husband is the proprietor, is that Luke Smith, who works there too, got Sam the job. Apparently Sam had been hunting for winter work."

Kristin knew it was common for farmers to seek work in town over the winter months.

"Evidently, Mr. Kalb, Mr. Smith, and Mr. Frantzen will continue their smithing and forging, and Sam will take care of the details, ledgers, customers, and such."

Kristin could tell Miss Betsy enjoyed hearing all the tidbits.

"As Green Bay grows, so does Kalb's Smithy Shop."

"It seems so."

"Sam will begin working over there the first of the month."

Miss Betsy cleared her throat. "I imagine you'll see a lot more of him after that."

Kristin wondered.

<hr />

Sam trudged in the direction of the house, hurrying to get out of the frosty, late afternoon air. He admired the way the lighted lanterns inside the home shone through the glass windows. The place looked cozy, inviting—but lately home had been anything *but* that. He and Pa weren't on speaking terms, although they said what they needed to in order to get the last of the crops harvested. Ma was having one of her episodes and took to her bed. Attie was distracted by Running Deer, who'd been making a pest of himself like nothing Sam ever remembered. Jack and Mary had to pitch in and do more chores along with their schoolwork, so they were given over to complaint. The only thing keeping up Sam's spirits was the thought of seeing Kristin on Sunday. He sensed her feelings for him went almost as deep as his did for her. But the hurt she'd experienced plunged to far greater depths than he could fathom. He purposely didn't call on her for nearly two weeks in hopes she'd take the time to rethink his offer. He could only pray she had.

A rider approached, and Sam squinted into the encroaching darkness to see his identity. Making strides in the direction of the barn, he met Oskar Frantzen just as he reined in.

"Greetings." Sam watched as Oskar dismounted and tethered his animal. "What brings you out here at this hour?"

"I need to speak with you." Oskar's words came out in frozen puffs. "Can you spare some time?"

Sam hid his surprise. He and Oskar weren't close, although they were friendly enough and would soon be fellow workers at Kalb's Smithy Shop. But to come out on such a cold evening signaled urgency.

"I'm a dirty mess at the moment. Won't you come in and have a cup of coffee?"

"*Ja*, thank you, Sam. That would be good."

They entered the house, and Sam found Attie. She set to making a pot of coffee while Sam washed up and changed clothes. Jack and Mary were still out in the barn with Pa.

Some minutes later he met Oskar in the sitting room.

Sam offered a handshake. "I apologize for my delay."

"I'm familiar with the need to change clothes at the end of the workday, as you will soon see when you start your job at Mr. Kalb's."

"Is that what you wanted to speak with me about? My new job?"

"No, it's another matter." Oskar hesitated. "Are you aware that I am not attending the Norwegian church?"

Sam shook his head. He hadn't heard.

"I have been accused of...*improprieties* where Inga Eikaas is concerned. Her father demands I marry her." Oskar tipped his head. "The thought is not displeasing to me, but I'm innocent of any wrongdoing. I never touched her, Sam. I swear!"

"I believe you." He did too. "Go on."

"Inga is awfully young, and since I deny the charges, Reverend Wollums suggested I create some distance between myself and the Eikaas family."

"Sounds like a wise plan. But if you are telling me this because I hope to court Kristin, I can assure you she has no contact with her uncle and his family."

"*Ja*, well, I was not sure."

Sam sensed the man's sudden disappointment. "But you may confide in me if you think I can help."

Oskar raked his thick fingers through his russet-colored hair as he weighed his options. "Inga came to see me today at the shop."

"Did she?" Sam drew his chin back.

"*Ja*, she was supposed to be in school but skipped." Oskar rubbed his hands over his knees. "She had a lot of money with her, Sam. About thirty dollars. She asked me to marry her—to run away with her, to Milwaukee or maybe Chicago."

Sam's eyes widened at the news.

"I didn't know what to do because she begged and pleaded with me. I finally turned her away, but then I wondered if she was in some kind of trouble at home."

"Are you thinking she is being beaten by her father?" Sam clearly recalled Mr. Eikaas threatening to horsewhip Kristin.

"*Ja*, and I also wondered where she got that money."

Sam couldn't guess. He only hoped to earn as much each month at Kalb's—and that at a ten- to twelve-hour day.

"Lars Eikaas doesn't have that kind of money."

Sam stood and walked to the window. Staring out at the now dark lawn, he placed his hands on his hips as he thought of a solution.

"I want to ride over and make sure Inga is all right," Oskar said. "But I cannot be sure what Mr. Eikaas will do. Could be that I will find myself looking down the barrel of his gun."

"You might." Sam had the very experience, the day he and Pa went to fetch Kristin.

He thought some more, and then slowly a few pieces came together. Ma had told him that Pa believed Kristin was in cahoots with her uncle because a pawnbroker reported that a "blonde-haired, blue-eyed" Norwegian young lady had brought in the coin silver, asking for cash. Inga too fit that description. And it would explain why she possessed extra funds today...

"Oskar, I believe we need to contact the sheriff." He turned from the window. "Tell him what you told me. We will let Sheriff Brunette decide what the next move should be."

⁓❦⁓

The following Sunday morning a persistent *rap-tap-tap* on the side door sent Miss Betsy scurrying to answer it. Kristin wondered at the urgency, although a cold rain fell outside this morning. Perhaps the caller didn't want to stand outside too long and get wet. Moving to the window, she glanced up and saw the gray skies and prayed the precipitation would let up before they walked to church.

Miss Betsy came rushing up the stairs as quickly as she'd descended them. "Quick and get ready to leave. We have a ride to church!"

A mad scramble ensued. Kristin hurried to pull on her black ankle boots and knot their laces. She tied her bonnet, grabbed her gloves and shawl, then met Miss Betsy at the doorway.

Downstairs a sleek black covered buggy awaited. Kristin blinked when Sam set aside the reins and jumped down to help them board.

"Sam!" She thought he looked fine in his coal-black dress coat and black hat.

"*God morgen*, ladies." His gaze lingered on Kristin until just before he helped Miss Betsy into the buggy.

"Where did you ever find this vehicle, Sam?"

"It belongs to the Brunettes. They allowed me to use it for this very special day."

"And what special day might it be?" Kristin placed her hand in his, and emotions renewed assailed her. She'd missed him these past two weeks.

Sam smiled into her face. "I am taking you both to the

Norwegian church today, and afterward, we are invited to the Wollumses' home for noon dinner."

"How delightful!" Miss Betsy clapped her gloved hands together.

But before Kristin could reply, Sam assisted her into the buggy's front seat. He climbed in next and stepped over Kristin's legs before taking up the reins. He steered the team down the road and made a left turn at the street on which the market had been held each Wednesday. Then, with a flick of the reins, the animals quickened their strides as Sam drove the buggy out of town.

"It will be an enjoyable day."

"Well..." Kristin had her reservations. She pulled on her gloves and nodded. "I have not seen the Wollumses in more than a month." She donned her bonnet next, hoping Sam didn't notice her state of unreadiness when he arrived.

It appeared he hadn't. "You look lovely today, Kristin."

She felt pleased by the compliment, but still her cheeks pinked—as usual. "Why, thank you, Sam." Her reply was in perfect English, and from behind them in the black leather backseat Kristin heard Miss Betsy's amused cackle.

"Well, now..." Sam looked impressed. "Your English is coming right along."

Kristin smiled and glanced at him. Her gaze caught his, and a swell of emotion rose inside of her. How she loved this man!

She glanced down at her lap. "I had not expected to see you today, although I hoped I would." She brought her gaze up and glimpsed the smile working its way across his face.

"I wanted to call on you several times in the past two weeks, but I figured you needed a chance to think things through and pray."

"And pray she has," Miss Betsy interjected. "We have been

asking the Father to heal these many wounds between the Eikaas and Sundberg families. And specifically for you, Sam, because Kristin loves you so much."

She froze. How could Miss Betsy divulge something so personal? She dared not turn around and glare at her friend, although she desired to do exactly that!

"Is that right, Kristin?"

And, of course, Sam thought to make a sport of the blunder— or whatever it had been!

Collecting herself, Kristin raised her chin and trained her gaze on the rain-soaked road ahead. "*Ja*, it's true. Miss Betsy and I pray together as we knit and sew in the evenings."

"Is that one of the dresses you sewed?"

She smoothed the skirt of the blue material. "*Ja*." Soft black velvet cuffs accentuated her tiny wrists and the matching collar added depth, Kristin thought, to the light blue color of the fitted bodice and flaring skirt. "I drew the pattern from a dress I saw displayed in a shop window in New York City."

"A flattering creation."

"*Takk*." There were still those times when Kristin forgot herself. "I mean...thank you."

"The blue brings out the color of your eyes."

"You are very kind." Again perfect English. Giving him a sidelong glance, she watched his smile broaden. The fact that she'd impressed him caused her to feel a grand sense of pleasure.

They arrived at the church, and Sam helped both ladies alight. They hurried through the rain and entered the church while he parked the buggy. As they shook off, Miss Betsy's eyes roamed around the small vestibule.

"Goodness, I haven't been here since..."

"Since when?"

She wagged her head. "Oh, never mind. It's not important."

Frowning, Kristin stepped closer. "Do we keep secrets from each other?"

"No, of course not." She let out a sigh, and her features relaxed in resignation. "I loved a man who used to attend this church."

"Oh?" Kristin tipped her head.

"John Jorde was his name. He came from Illinois and his business was in lumbering." A faraway look entered Miss Betsy's gaze. "I would have married him if he had asked. I think he intended to. But when he told me he had to return to Illinois for a month, I was angry. I thought he should stay with me. Before he left, he wanted to talk to me, kiss me good-bye, but I was too stubborn and walked away without a single parting remark. When he never came back, I felt the need to inquire." Miss Betsy's eyes grew misty. "I learned John was killed when about one hundred Indians, a mix of Potawatomis and Sauk, attacked the settlement in which he'd been staying. That was more than sixteen years ago."

Kristin ached for her friend and linked her arm around hers. "Tragic."

"Oh, *ja*. Women and children were also killed. It is referred to as the Indian Creek Massacre nowadays."

Kristin hugged her arm.

Several more people entered the small country church. They greeted Kristin and Miss Betsy. Although Kristin had seen them before, their names escaped her. She bid them a *god morgen* just the same.

Miss Betsy turned and stared hard at Kristin. "But do you see why peace is so important among God's children? I let John go without saying good-bye and telling him I loved him. Who knows if things might have been different if I had put aside my foolish pride." She shook herself. "God's plans are not my plans, and I do not mean to sound like I feel guilty. But tomorrow is not promised to any of us."

"I understand the point you are making." And Kristin did too. "I will be sure to tell Sam how I feel about him before we part for the day."

"Good. You are very wise."

Movement outside the front door caught her eye. Kristin turned to see Sam running through the rain. She smiled. "You are quite the wise old owl yourself, Miss Betsy."

Sam reached them and removed his wet overcoat, which he must have donned after they disembarked. He walked to a line of wooden pegs and hung it up. Next he removed his hat and finger-combed his hair.

"Shall we find a seat, ladies?" He offered each of them an arm.

His overdisplay of formality amused Kristin. However, nearing the front pews, her smile vanished when Uncle Lars saw her and sneered. But even that didn't trouble her as much as Mr. Sundberg's glare.

And suddenly Kristin wondered why she had allowed Sam to bring her here.

CHAPTER 21

*K*RISTIN FELT SAM's hold on her upper arm and realized there was no turning back.

"Pay them no mind, Kristin." Sam whispered close to Kristin's ear while escorting her and Miss Betsy to the front pew where Mrs. Wollums and the Brunettes sat.

The reverend's wife smiled broadly and gave Kristin's hand a pat. "So good to see you again."

"*Takk.*"

From one pew back, she could feel Mr. Sundberg's hateful stare boring straight through to her heart.

A tap on her shoulder made Kristin jump. She turned to see Mary. Her dark eyes shimmered as her smile grew.

"Hello, Kristin." She draped herself over the top of the pew. "I am happy you came today."

The words were English, and she recognized a few, but she figured out what Mary said. "I am happy too."

She snagged Sam's glance then saw his discreet and silent applause. His antics made her smile. But when she looked back at Mary, she caught sight of Mrs. Sundberg's disapproving expression aimed at Mary's most unladylike manner. "You had better sit down. I will see you after church."

The girl nodded and took her seat.

Reverend Wollums strode to the pulpit and led the congregation in a hymn. Afterward, he opened his Bible and read from the Book of Judges.

"'And when the Lord raised them up judges, then the Lord was with the judge, and delivered them out of the hand of their enemies all the days of the judge: for it repented the Lord because of their groanings by reason of them that oppressed them and vexed them.'"

Reverend Wollums shifted his stance at the pulpit. In the time since Kristin had last seen him, the good pastor had grown a beard. But, of course, many men did in the fall. The hunting season was in full swing.

"Our God is a good and mighty God. He has delivered all of us here today out of a land that oppressed us. I recall as a boy in Norway, going hungry at night because my father, a fisherman, couldn't afford the taxes imposed on his catch that day. So he brought home nothing to his family even though his net had been full." The reverend's gaze wandered about his flock. "This morning I caught four brook trout, and my wife fried them up for breakfast along with eggs that our chickens laid. I did not pay a single cent for any of it.

"And so it was with Israel. They were an oppressed people, and God delivered them and set judges over them so they would keep God's laws. We have a judge too. He is here with us today. Judge Jensen has been the territorial judge in Wisconsin for nearly a decade. His position will soon change now, for with our statehood, we will have local and state government."

Sam leaned over and whispered to Kristin. "Is it good to be able to understand the message from the pulpit for a change?"

"*Ja.* Very good."

"But even living here in America we are not free from oppression. In fact, Christians oppress each other rather than love one another as God's Word instructs. We see that God resists the proud—because that is where oppression begins, with one man thinking he is better than another. God resists that man, but promises refuge for the meek and the oppressed."

As Kristin digested the reverend's sermon, she couldn't help thinking of *Onkel.* How proud he was to be the king of nothing. Little wonder why his crops withered and house and barn fell down on top of his head. There were no spells involved. But no blessings either. Just God's hand of resistance.

All at once, Kristin pitied her aunt and cousins. They had no choice but to live under such...*oppression.* Now, with winter just around the corner, what would happen to them?

When the message ended, Kristin stood. Sheriff Brunette immediately approached her.

"Miss Eikaas, I need for you to stay a few minutes." He looked at Sam and inclined his head. "You too."

"Certainly."

Sam reached for her hand. "Do not worry." He sat back down and Kristin did also.

Within minutes only Mr. and Mrs. Sundberg remained in the pew behind her and Sam. Across the aisle sat *Onkel, Tante,* and Inga. The children had gone. Miss Betsy left too. However, farther back Kristin spied Mr. Frantzen seated beside a man whom she didn't recognize.

"What is this, Sam? What is going on?"

He leaned over and whispered, "It is not about you, Kristin. Be patient."

Relief flooded her, and she sat back.

Finally the reverend came to the front, accompanied by Sheriff Brunette.

"We have a little family business to discuss," Reverend Wollums said. "I will now turn the matter over to Brother Brunette."

"Before we begin," the sheriff said, stroking his full, dark beard, "I want to warn you, Karl and Lars, that I am a lawman too. Any outbursts from either of you will land your hides in jail. Got it?"

Mutters came from both men, and Kristin shifted, growing uncomfortable once more.

"Now, then..." He held his arm out. "Inga has something to tell us."

The thick fingers on the sheriff's large hand beckoned the girl from her place next to *Tante*. When she finally stood beside him, Inga's blue eyes darted around the sanctuary.

"Whenever you are ready, Inga."

Saucer-round blue eyes looked up at him as if pleading for mercy. Obviously this was not something she wished to do. The sheriff only gave her a single nod.

"I have lied, and I need forgiveness." Inga's voice shook with each word. "Mr. Frantzen has always been a gentleman where I am concerned, and I lied about him."

Uncle Lars stood. "What? You shameful girl!"

His booming voice made Kristin wince.

"Lars, need I remind you that I have a jail cell with your name on it?"

"I have the right to question my daughter!"

Kristin noted her uncle's appearance hadn't changed, from his platinum curls to his worn woolen jacket.

"If you stay quiet long enough, I believe Inga will answer your questions."

Kristin saw her cousin shudder.

"Inga," the sheriff softly coaxed, "please go on."

With first a glance at the reverend, Inga looked ahead at Mr. Frantzen. "I have wronged you, Oskar, and I hope you find it in your heart to"—she wiped the moisture from her cheek—"forgive me."

Mr. Frantzen pushed to his feet. "It is already done, Inga. I forgive."

Kristen's own gaze clouded with happy tears.

"Now there is a separate matter." Sheriff Brunette dipped his head.

Inga nodded back. "*Ja.*" Her gaze went just beyond Sam, to the Sundbergs. "I was the one who stole your silver spoons."

"You?"

Kristin turned to see Mr. Sundberg push to his feet.

"Why, Inga?" His voice was filled with surprise. "What did my family and I ever do to you to make you want to steal from us?"

"It is not what you did, Mr. Sundberg. It is what I did not have." Inga lowered her head in shame. "No money for food. No nice things..."

"I will not hear this anymore!" Uncle Lars stood also and shook his meaty fist in the air.

"Oh, you will hear it, Lars." Sheriff Brunette's features narrowed while his bushy dark eyebrows slanted inward. "Here or at the jailhouse."

Uncle Lars sat down with a *thud.*

Mr. Sundberg slowly lowered himself into the pew.

The sheriff set his hand lightly on back Inga's shoulders. "Please continue, Inga."

"All right, but it is not easy to confess." She continued to stare at the tips of her scuffed leather boots.

"I understand," the reverend said empathetically. "But your confession will clear the air and free your soul."

Inga smoothed the skirt of her faded plaid dress but kept her gaze averted. "It happened when we first moved to Brown County. The Sundbergs invited my family and me to have supper, and afterward, I helped with the dishes. I was in the dining room and pulled out the wrong drawer. I saw the pretty red velvet pouch tucked away in the corner and looked inside and found the silver spoons. I knew they were valuable and could be melted down into coins. So I...I put the pouch in the deep pocket of my skirt."

"Such an embarrassment! Why? Why did you do such a thing?" Uncle Lars remained seating, but his voice still thundered through the sanctuary.

Inga began to shake uncontrollably, and Reverend Wollums put his hand on her shoulder. "Finish your story," he said gently.

"I wanted my family to have all the fine things that the Sundbergs had. I was so tired of being poor and feeling hungry." She gulped a breath of air. "That night when I got home, I buried the silver so no one would find it. I was not familiar with Green Bay and did not know where I should go to exchange the spoons for money. But, days later, the men came to build the barn for *Far*. I thought for sure they would find the tin coffee can in which I had placed the pouch of silver spoons. But, no, instead they built a wall right on top of it! I could not get at it no matter how I tried. So I put it out of my mind and kept quiet." She swallowed hard. "Then the sheriff came to ask *Far* about the stolen silver. He searched for it, but I knew he would not find it. *Far* was so angry. I did not dare tell the truth."

Kristin hated to think of what *Onkel's* method of punishment would have been, had he learned of Inga's thievery.

"I did not care that Mr. Sundberg hated *Far* and blamed him."

Inga wetted her lips and stared at the polished wood floor. "I hated *Far* too." She spoke the words with forcefulness.

"What is this, girl?" Uncle Lars slowly got to his feet again, and Kristin saw the furious glint in his eyes.

On impulse she slipped her hand around Sam's elbow. He gently flexed his bicep in a silent but reassuring reply.

Inga's frightened gaze flew to the sheriff.

"You are safe here, Inga. Continue, please."

She collected her wits. "I have hated *Far*, and I ask God to forgive me for it." Sudden tears filled her blue eyes. She sniffed and the reverend offered his handkerchief. "And *Far*, too, I ask forgiveness." She peeked at him for a moment, then lowered her gaze again. "Ever since I was young I watched how, time and again, God bestowed my father with the means to meet our basic needs. Each time he has squandered them, like buying rounds of drinks for his friends at the tavern—or allowing good lumber to rot in the yard."

"She lies!"

"Lars, this is your last warning." The sheriff pointed his forefinger at him. "Next outburst, I will summon my deputy."

"But she defames my character—and in front of Reverend Wollums, no less!"

The reverend spoke up. "News of your visits to Tommy's Tavern on Main Street have already reached my ears."

To his credit Kristin found no traces of condemnation on his face.

"And, do not forget," Sheriff Brunette added, "I have broken up many fights at that place, and I have seen you there with my own eyes as recently as last month, the night Peder Olstad got himself into trouble."

"Lars," Aunt Esther breathed, "you did not spend the money

from your brother's pocket watch on drinking at the tavern, did you?"

"*Ja*, he did, Momma," Inga insisted. "Peder Olstad told me right before he went into the barn to pack his belongings. The sheriff was waiting for him and Mr. Olstad."

"It was my brother's watch, and I could do what I pleased with the money." Gazing at *Tante*, he arched a brow as if daring her to speak further.

She didn't. Folding her gloved hands, she stared at them in her lap.

"Inga, tell us how you retrieved the silver spoons."

"The next day, after the Olstads left, a terrible storm destroyed our cabin and damaged the wall of the barn, covering the silver. I was able to dig it up, and instead of going to school on Monday, I went to the pawnbroker. I knew where his shop was because I was in the wagon when *Far* stopped one day and took in Momma's wedding ring for money."

Kristin saw her uncle's face redden.

"When I sold the silver, I gave Momma some of the money."

Which explains how Tante afforded her trip to Miss Betsy's. Kristin put the pieces together.

"Then last week, I could not stand it at home a moment longer. I tried to convince Oskar to marry me and move away." What little resolve Inga had suddenly cracked. "I so desperately wanted to run away and begin a new life. No more living in squalor. No more feeling ashamed that I am an Eikaas because of…of *Far*."

"Now, see here, girl…" Uncle Lars's voice was as taut as a thread about to snap.

"I just wanted to be loved," Inga became distraught. "I–I wanted someone t–to take care of m–me."

Mrs. Brunette ran to Inga, put her arms around her shoulders, and then led her out the doorway, leading to the parsonage.

Kristin's hand flew to her throat. Tears welled in her eyes. She felt her cousin's pain.

The sheriff handed the velvet pouch to Mr. Sundberg. "Here is your silver. It is all there."

If there was a reply, Kristin didn't hear it.

"Now, the way I see it, Karl, you owe Lars an apology." The sheriff moved toward the Sundbergs. "All these years you have accused and blamed him when, unbeknownst to him, his daughter stole the silver."

Kristin held her breath. She couldn't imagine a man like Mr. Sundberg apologizing to anyone.

But to her surprise, Mr. Sundberg spoke. "I guess you are right, Sheriff. Eikaas might be a lot of things, but he's not a thief—at least as far as my coin silver goes."

"Apology accepted," Uncle Lars declared.

What apology? Kristin turned in the wooden pew and peered at each man. Uncle Lars sat back, appearing quite self-assured.

"See, Esther, I am not a thief."

Tante looked away.

"Is that all, Sheriff?" Mr. Sundberg asked.

"Not quite. There's the matter of repaying Mr. Errens." Sheriff Brunette looked from Mr. Sundberg to Uncle Lars. "He paid out good money for those spoons. But I think Judge Jensen and I have worked out a solution."

"Fine. But before we discuss it," Mr. Sundberg replied, "I need to say something else."

To Kristin's immense discomfort, Sam's father came around the pew and hunkered in front of her.

She looked at Sam with wide eyes, but his attention was on his father.

"Miss Eikaas, I have been a fool, not to mention a regular bully. It took my twelve-year-old to point that out to me weeks ago. I am ashamed to admit that I disliked you, then despised you because I thought you not only stole my silver, but...you stole the heart of my son."

Her lips moved to explain that she didn't steal Sam's heart, but the words stuck in her throat.

"Please..." He sent a glance to Sam before refocusing on Kristin. "Sam is a fine man, Miss Eikaas. He did me proud while he was in Madison. And here at home he has shone me through his respectful words and diligent work how crooked my own heart had become." Flicking a glance at the floor and then back at Kristin, he added, "I am sorry for the way I mistreated you. I had no right and no just cause."

Was he sincere? Kristin looked at Sam askance. What did she do?

Sliding his arm along the back of the pew, Sam leaned close to her ear and whispered, "This is the part where you forgive him."

Half of her wanted to refuse. She'd already been wounded and Mr. Sundberg only added to it. Yet she knew it was her Christian duty to forgive him. If she obeyed, perhaps God would mend her broken heart once and for all.

"*Ja*, I forgive you, Mr. Sundberg."

"And Kristin?" Mrs. Sundberg stood beside her husband when he got to his feet. "I never meant to cause you more pain. I had hoped to spare you from it."

"I know that now." She stood and hugged Mrs. Sundberg. With her chin gently pressed against the Indian woman's shoulder, Kristin realized how terribly she'd missed her.

"Bah!" Uncle Lars snorted. "Get on with this meeting, already!"

Mrs. Sundberg gave Kristin a final squeeze then followed her husband back to their pew.

Kristin sat down.

The sheriff cleared his throat. "None of us want to see Inga incarcerated."

Tante gasped.

"So I have a suggestion, which I have discussed in great length with Reverend Wollums. We feel that Inga is truly repentant. Therefore, my advice is that, for the time being, Mrs. Eikaas and her children, including Inga, move in with my wife and me. Mr. Errens has agreed to allow Inga to work for him after school, sweeping floors and such. She will pay off her debt in two years. In the meantime, Lars, you can make the necessary repairs to your house and barn, not to mention your heart and soul."

"We will all help you, Lars." The promise came from the reverend's mouth. "But we will not do it for you. Not again. Not anymore."

"Ah, who needs you?" Uncle Lars folded his arms stubbornly.

Kristin gaped at him.

"Perhaps," the reverend continued, "after your family moves in with the Brunettes, you will have time to ponder that question...alone."

Tante stood, looking more confident than Kristin had ever seen her. "I accept the offer. Thank you, Sheriff." She scurried around Uncle Lars. "I will go and pack our things."

~❦~

The rain cleared, and when the sun broke through the clouds, it made for an unseasonably mild afternoon. The air smelled fresh and clean to Kristin as she and Sam strolled down the wet gravelly road near the Wollumses' brick home. She had enjoyed a nice meal with all the people she held dear sitting around the dining room table. Miss Betsy, the Sundbergs, the Wollumses...and Sam.

"You have been awfully quiet this afternoon." Sam sent her a sideways glance. "You must have a lot on your mind."

"Not really." She walked across a thatch of brown grass. Reaching the planked fence that kept the cows penned, Kristin rested her forearms on the top rail.

As she hoped, Sam followed her. "What are you thinking about, Kristin? Was it the meeting after church? I thought I explained that I knew about it only because Oskar—"

"Shh..." Twisting slightly, she touched her fingertips to Sam's lips. "I do not want to discuss that meeting anymore."

Sam's palm encircled her wrist and pulled her hand away. "What do you want to talk about?"

"Maybe I do not wish to talk." Since amends had been made, Kristin actually felt...playful.

Sam leaned against the fence with a frown stitched upon his brow.

"We are always so serious, Sam, forging through one situation after another."

He pursed his lips in a way that made Kristin want to...

So she did. She wrapped her arms about his neck and pressed her lips against Sam's. After a moment of initial shock, his arms encircled her waist, and he responded with a kiss of his own.

"I love you, Sam," she murmured against his mouth. Then she gazed up into his face.

"I love you too. With all my heart." He pulled her against him, and Kristin's feet left the ground.

She laughed and he released her.

Sam squared his broad shoulders. "You, young lady, are much too forward."

"*Ja*, I guess I am." She couldn't hide her smile. "Especially after such an emotional morning as today's."

"All right. You are granted this once."

"Only once?" With a hand on his shoulder, she stood on tip-toes and pressed a kiss to his cheek.

"Kristin, you know what this means?"

She lolled her head to one side and arched her brows.

"You will just have to marry me."

Happy, she slipped her arms around his waist and tipped her head back. "Yes, I will marry you, Sam Sundberg." She laughed at his surprised expression.

Her English had never been more perfect!

EPILOGUE

August 13, 1850

*T*HE STEEP, JAGGED cliffs bordering Lake Michigan jutted in and out of Manitowoc, Wisconsin's, shoreline. Beyond them Kristin saw magnificent sailing vessels with billowing white sails.

Pangs of anticipation surged up inside of her. "Do you think the ship has arrived yet, Sam?"

"Should have." He pulled their wagon to a halt. "Luggage should have been unloaded by now too." He crossed over her and hopped down.

Kristin turned into his strong, outstretched arms.

"Careful now."

Her feet touched the ground, and she straightened the material covering her protruding midsection. "I feel as huge as one of those tall-masted ships out there, full sail and all!"

Sam grinned.

Kristin noticed he didn't argue. But, then again, any sighted person could see she was great with child. Their first.

She and Sam married the first week in April last year. But God didn't bless them with a child until now, nearly a year and a half later. But if there was one thing Kristin knew for certain, it was that God's ways were not her ways. She would have liked a baby immediately. However, as it happened, Sam had time to build them a fine home and a barn, and acquire cows, pigs, and sheep. He purchased the necessary farming equipment and, this year, brought in an abundance of crops.

Kristin too enjoyed the harvest. She'd spun the wool from their sheep on the spinning wheel, which once belonged to Sam's mother. She knitted and crocheted for shops here in Manitowoc, and whenever they traveled to Green Bay, they dropped off various creations for Miss Betsy's shop. Kristin also knit her babe wool blankets and sweaters to keep him warm this winter. God knew that now they were ready to welcome their firstborn, and Kristin had an inkling that he would be a boy. His name would be Daniel, after Poppa.

Sam took her arm and helped her waddle to the baggage area. He guarded her from being bumped and jostled by passersby. Manitowoc had become home to a busy port.

"Do you see them, Sam?"

He blew out a breath. "I see a lot of people who would fit the description you gave me." He hugged her to him. "Remember, my *kjære*, things might have changed in the two years since you saw your friend—"

"Sylvia!" Kristin spotted her all at once. She would have known her anywhere. Moments later she and her childhood friend held each other in a fierce embrace—as fierce as possible with eight months of an unborn child between them.

"Oh, let me look at you, dear friend." Sylvia held her by the shoulders and ran her light-green gaze up and down. Light-brown curls waved on the lake breezes. "You do not look tired for one who keeps so busy. I feel exhausted after just reading your letters."

"I am not so busy."

Mrs. Olstad held out her long, thin arms and hugged Kristin next. "Why, you are glowing, Kristin."

Her eyes misted up, but Sam was ready with a handkerchief. She caught his helpless shrug, making her smile. "Please meet my husband, Sam Sundberg."

"Welcome." With calloused fingers, he lifted each lady's hand and gave a courteous half-bow. "My pleasure to meet you both. Kristin speaks highly of you." His gaze fell to the wooden sea chests nearby. "I will find porters to transport your belongings to our wagon. Meanwhile, Kristin will lead you to it."

As they made their way from the docks, Kristin decided to ask about Peder. Mr. Olstad had returned to Wisconsin and found a job splitting ties and laying track for the new railroads, which would soon take passengers from Lake Michigan all the way to the Mississippi River. Uncle Lars took a job with the railroad too, and the men relocated to the central part of the state. Uncle Lars made amends with Aunt Esther, and she, Anna, and Erik moved in with him again—and into a fine home. But Inga remained in Green Bay and married Oskar Frantzen. They appeared very happy. And soon, after a brief visit here, Sylvia and her mother would travel the distance to be with Mr. Olstad at long last.

"I am afraid Peder succumbed to gambling."

Kristin's heart sank at the sad news.

"He struck gold and has since lost his fortune. But first he paid for *Mor* and me to sail to America. We are grateful to him for that." A look of sorrow crept into Sylvia's bright blue eyes. "*Mor* and I tried, but we could never save the funds."

Kristin understood.

Sylvia stopped short and grabbed hold of Kristin's elbow. She leaned in close. "Is America everything we always talked about and dreamed about as girls?"

"America is even more, Sylvia." She glimpsed Sam, making his way toward them. Her handsome husband in his freshly laundered brown trousers and tan shirt. His broad shoulders had developed all the more in the last two years, but it was the abundance of love and patience that he carried in his heart that made him so dear and special.

He caught her gaze, and his entire countenance lit up. He loved her without question. And the love she felt for him rivaled the vast Wisconsin sky!

"Are you happy, Kristin?"

"Oh, *ja*." She turned to her friend and saw hope, doubt, and even fear glimmering in her friend's eyes. "*Ja*, Sylvia." Her hands glided down her bulging belly of the precious burden she carried. "My life is so full, and I have never been happier."

COMING IN OCTOBER 2012
THREADS OF FAITH

Now faith is the substance of things hoped for, the evidence of things not seen.

—Hebrews 11:1

CHAPTER 1

June 1877

*R*UN, IF YE know what's good for ye, dearie. Run far and run fast!"

Julianna Wayland needed no further warning from the aging, plump cook, waving her floured rolling pin. She bolted from the tiled kitchen, making her way through the servants' doorway at the side of the brick manse. Her heels clicked against the cobbled pavement in quick succession as she ran down the bustling, cart-lined lane in which hawkers sold their wares. But where could she go? Certainly not home.

Thinking of the cramped room with a single cot above the Mariner's Pub that she shared with her sister, dread sank like a stone inside of her. After her sister's treachery, Julianna might not even have that miserable place to call home. How could Flora have done such a cruel thing?

Julianna hastened past shoppers until she turned onto another street. Perspiration trickled down the side of her face, and the joggling threatened every pin in her thick hair, tucked beneath the white, floppy cap. With one hand holding it in place, she managed to glance over her shoulder and spied two men. Panic weakened her limbs. Were two of Mr. Tolbert's hired men chasing after her? She'd seen the duo, clad in fancy, dark suits, about the manor, and snoopy beasts they were too! Would they really track her down like a couple of hounds?

Apparently so.

Oh, Flora, what have you done this time?

Julianna zigzagged her way down one street and up another until she reached London's wharf. A row of warehouses lined the Thames, and, thankfully, the wind had shifted so the stench of dead fish and human waste wasn't as sickening as in days past.

Rounding the corner of a warehouse, she paused and leaned against the wall, fighting to catch her breath. Dear God, had she outsmarted her would-be captors? If those men caught her, there'd be no convincing them to let her go. Julianna knew from being in Olson Tolbert's employ for the past eighteen months, ever since she turned sixteen, that whatever he wanted, he got.

And for some terrible, horrible reason he wanted her!

Memories of his dark, soulless eyes, watching her every move as she served dinner last night, and then his icy touch upon her hand and forearm when she'd set down his plate of food, were all enough to propel her onward. The man was old enough to be her father—even though Julianna hadn't ever known hers. Perhaps her real father was twice Mr. Tolbert's age. Flora said he'd been a sailor, and their mum, a woman who welcomed every man's advance.

And Flora...well, she'd turned out like Mum.

The rapid approach of footfalls brought Julianna from her musing. Her gaze darted around. What should she do? No longer could she run, lest she meet up with some scoundrels and ne'er-do-wells, a fate that might prove worse than marrying Olson Tolbert.

She eyed the various sized crates stacked against the brick wall of the warehouse. Hiding was her only hope.

She moved toward the stockpile, when all at once she spied a box in which she'd likely fit. Hurrying, she scrambled onto a nearby apple crate and peered inside the tall-standing container.

Empty.

Julianna vaulted over the side. Once within its narrow-slatted confines, she gathered her skirts and tucked her black dress around her ankles. Then she hunkered down, praying she wouldn't be found.

Seconds later, men's voices came upon her, and, suddenly, her hiding place jerked from side to side. Julianna's head whacked against a wooden side slat and pain shot down her neck, but she dared not make a peep. Instead, she slid her hand up through the tight space and massaged the growing knot just above her ear.

"It's full, all right, Mr. Bentley."

"Fine. Fine. Now load 'er up and ye can have the job."

The men were not Mr. Tolbert's thugs, and relief coursed through her. But before she could cry out and make her presence known, a lid clamped down over the top of the tall crate and was hammered into place.

<hr />

Captain Daniel Sundberg squinted into the sun and scrutinized the unshaven faces of his newly acquired crewmen. A motley assortment of fellows, some wearing bedraggled clothing, they stood broad shoulder to broad shoulder, chests puffed out, and whiskered chins held high.

"Well, sir, what do you think?"

"I think, *Mr. Bentley*," Daniel said with emphasis, "that you must have scrounged up these men after the pubs closed this morning."

His first mate chuckled, and Daniel's annoyance mounted. Selecting a crew took careful consideration. After all, he was responsible for both the ship and its cargo, which consisted of several some four thousand bales of wool, several tons of tallow, and sundries. But the most precious of it all were several master paintings going to the Metropolitan Museum of Art. Daniel had personally overseen to their safekeeping.

"Need I remind you, Bent," he stated in controlled frustration albeit using his nickname for the first mate, "we've got almost a three-week voyage ahead of us, and it'll seem like a lifetime with the wrong seamen aboard."

A hint of a smile still curved Al Bentley's thin lips. "No reminding required, Cap'n. I've been your first officer for a long while now, and I know what you expect." Bent counted on his fingers. "Isaac Cravens has been your second and Billy Lawler your third."

"I know who my officers are, Bent!" Daniel fought to quell his impatience.

"And Dr. Morrison is, of course, sailing with us too. Mr. Ramsey wouldn't have it any other way."

Daniel dipped his head in reply, knowing good and well the requirements George Ramsey put in place for his fleet.

"So how 'bout these able-bodied fellows? I've a hunch they'll serve us well, and the faster we get to New York, the faster they'll get paid and return to London."

Again, Daniel nodded. "I suppose they'll do."

"I interviewed 'em like ye tol' me, and each seaman proved

himself while loading up the *Allegiance*. We're ready to set sail anytime you give the word."

Daniel kneaded his chin. "I presume there is a cook on board." He arched a brow before glancing back at his brawny crewmen. Two voyages ago Bent had overlooked that *small detail*.

"Hired the cook yesterday, sir." This time chagrin edged the lanky man's reply. "He's been in your employ b'fore. Jeremy Kidwell's his name, and he's presently down below, arranging the galley to his liking."

"Kidwell, eh?" Daniel recalled the young red-haired man. "If my memory serves me correctly, Kidwell serves up a hearty meal."

"Aye, sir, he's both skillful and resourceful." A hopeful glimmer entered Bent's sea-green eyes.

"Good work." Daniel rarely dolled out compliments, but he made a point to do so when they were warranted. He gave Bent a friendly clap on the back.

"Thank you, Cap'n." A smile stretched across the first mate's leathery face, revealing a dark space where a front tooth had once been rooted. "Although I was sorry to learn this'll be our last voyage together for a while. Maybe even for good, if you take over for Mr. Ramsey on dry land instead of the high seas."

"Yes, well, that's always been the plan." Daniel clasped his hands behind his back and widened his stance on the deck. "But before I step into the role of executor and chief of Ramsey Shipping, I need a knot in that *proverbial tie that binds*." A private man, he didn't want to reveal too much, although he had confided—to a degree—in his first mate before. He felt an inexplicable urge to return to his family's farm and see his father.

Poppa has taken ill, his mother, Kristin Sundberg, wrote. *Please come home soon.*

Daniel's heart twisted painfully at the thought of losing his father forever, even though he'd hardly given the man a single thought over the past decade—or longer. But now, after hearing that Poppa lay dying on the other side of the world, Daniel knew he had to see him one last time—that is, if he wasn't already too late.

But what would George have to say about his visit to Wisconsin?

"Cap'n?" Bent's voice broke through the reverie. "It's possible, ye know, that your father'll recover." Bent leaned in close. "My own mother suffered a debilitatin' illness. But now she's back on her feet an' spittin' nails like always."

Daniel wrestled with a grin. "I'll take encouragement from that bit of information." The warm summer wind brushed over his face, bringing along with it the stench from the Thames. Thank God he wouldn't be docked on this crowded, stinking river for weeks, such as had happened several voyages ago. With his crew now in place and the cargo stowed, he would soon skillfully glide the *Allegiance* out of London's port.

Arms falling to his side, Daniel turned toward his cabin to finish the paperwork awaiting him on his desk. "We'll set sail in one hour's time," he called over his left shoulder.

"Aye, Cap'n!"

Darkness shrouded Julianna so that she couldn't even see her hand in front of her face. Beneath her, the sea roiled. Waves crashed rhythmically beyond the walls of her tomblike confines.

A ship. She'd been loaded into the bowels of a ship, for pity's sake!

Julianna swallowed back tears of fear and frustration. How could this have happened? She'd tried to cry out. However, her voice hadn't been heard above the din of sliding crates and sailors' shouts. And the language—it had been blue enough to burn the ears of any delicate female. But, of course, Julianna had heard the same foul words, or worse, coming from the pub beneath the chamber she shared with Flora. How her sister could abide serving ale every night, Julianna would never know. Of course Flora didn't have much choice, thanks to Mr. Tolbert. But, sadly, more often than not, a drunken sailor assisted Flora upstairs. When he didn't, Julianna fetched her. And that's as close as she cared to be to the reviling place.

But who would tend to Flora tonight—or tomorrow morning when the aftereffects of the alcohol wore off?

A kind of heaviness crept over Julianna. She had cared for Flora for as long as she could remember. She loved her sister and would do anything for her—

Well, almost anything.

Julianna wondered what Flora would say when she discovered her disappearance. She'd surely committed two great sins by running from both her job and Olson Tolbert. Flora drank away her pay, so they relied on Julianna's income for food and shelter. And now the marriage...Flora had apparently been counting on that too. She was sure to have one fine fit, that's for sure!

Blades of betrayal pierced Julianna's being. Earlier the old cook said Flora had quite a tidy sum riding on Julianna's impending nuptials—well, Cook hadn't said it quite that way. She'd referred to the union as "a deal."

Julianna bristled. So when had Flora made her pact with the devil? Julianna would have never agreed to such a thing!

Over the past year and a half that Julianna had been in Mr. Tolbert's employ, she'd managed to sidestep his advances. At the same time, she'd observed his abusive hand come down hard upon several household maids.

Julianna shuddered. Marriage to that cruel, pompous man would be worse than... than...

Than being in the depths of this sailing ship?

The answer remained to be seen.

Struggling within her confines, Julianna tried to move her limbs. Prickles of numbness moved from her feet to her ankles. She wiggled, but there wasn't space enough to shift positions. Worse, she needed to use the loo!

"Help!" Julianna's voice drowned beneath the noise of the sea and the myriad of cargo. "Help me, please!" When she thought that she might never be found, a sense of panic began to rise. Suddenly she needed out of here—and now! "Anyone! Please, help!"

Experience the *inspirational* sagas
of the McCabe family in the

SEASONS OF REDEMPTION

SERIES

The War Between the States has Valerie Fontaine
frightened about her future. Will it keep her from
her newfound love?

978-1-59979-985-8 / $10.99

Sarah McCabe knows exactly what she wants—a
life of luxury, culture, and social privilege. But
what does God want for her?

978-1-61638-023-6 / $12.99

Nurse Fields is drawn to a blind patient searching for his past. But will his recovery reveal the
secret she is trying to keep?

978-1-61638-192-9 / $12.99

Evil threatens the lives of the women the McCabe
brothers love and leads them into the fight of
their lives.

978-1-61638-205-6 / $12.99